# Whiskey Wednesdays

## Palm Springs Poolside Book 3

### J. L. Brannick

SMART MOUTH
PUBLISHING LLC

*Whiskey Wednesdays* Copyright © 2024 by J. L. Brannick

www.jlbrannick.com

Published by Smart Mouth Publishing LLC



Paperback ISBN: 979-8-9879188-8-3
Ebook ISBN: 979-8-9879188-7-6

# Chapter 1

I'd never met my dad's employer before. But the tall, overpowering man standing in front of me firing off instructions matched his description.

Connor McCoy was more intimidating and arresting in person than in his online photos. He had a broken nose and a scar across his sharp cheekbone, and his dark hair and eyes enhanced his harsh magnetism.

I stood in my bare feet, watering my dad's flowerpots when he spotted me from his oversized garage and strode up. My dad lived in the caretaker cottage on Connor's estate, and worked as his landscaper and property manager. I was here visiting him for the weekend.

Connor stared down at his phone while he talked to me. "There's a to-do list hanging on the fridge in the main house. When I get back from the arena, we can exchange contact information. Sherrill, my admin in Canada, will go over your responsibilities."

I held up my free hand. "My name is–"

"I prefer texting. Have her send me your contact information."

He obviously thought I was one of his new employees. "I'm not–"

He cut me off again. "We'll talk later, but make sure you get my daughter's birthday presents sent out. She's turning five and likes anything girlish and pink."

I paused at that. My dad hadn't mentioned Mr. McCoy had a child.

"I don't want your daughter to be disappointed. Listen–"

He talked over me for the *third time*.

"She won't be. Just pick out a few nice things and get them sent today." He paused for a split second to look me up and down, then went back to his phone.

I tried again. "Sir, my name is Isabella Cruz. My father works for you, but I–"

"Good to know. I need to take off, but we'll talk later." He turned and started walking away.

"Hey, you!" I dropped the watering can and let out a shrill whistle in case yelling didn't get his attention. So much for keeping my temper in check.

He stopped dead and turned around slowly. His eyebrow winged up and his mouth tightened. But he wasn't talking over me.

I put my hands on my hips. "First, please stop interrupting. It's rude and annoying. Second, I'm *not* the person you think I am. Javier Cruz is my father, and I'm here visiting him."

Dad mentioned he'd only talked to his employer twice since he started working for him almost two years ago. I doubted this guy even knew my dad's name.

It was obvious from the immaculate estate and lush desert landscaping that Dad worked hard and knew what he was doing. Even if this jerk didn't appreciate it. I was already annoyed at the man for making my dad feel inconsequential, and his dismissive manner didn't help.

Connor McCoy was a retired professional hockey player, also known as The Hammer. He had hot, rich, entitled asshole written all over him.

I held up my hand, trying to waylay more instructions. "Mr. McCoy, I don't work for you."

Connor studied my small but curvy frame. I'd been doing schoolwork all afternoon, my hair was pulled back in a ponytail, and I had on an old black tank top and white board shorts. It was still hot during the day here in October.

"Then who the hell are you?"

Geez, really? I was standing in front of my dad's little caretaker house watering his plants. And I'd just *told* him who I was.

"Not your assistant. Obviously."

He stepped toward me. "How'd you get on the property?"

My temper flared and I leaned into him. "My dad picked me up from the airport this morning. He's your on-site property manager and landscaper here. In case you didn't know."

"Huh." His eyes swept me again.

"I'm visiting him this weekend over my fall break." I worked to keep the sarcasm out of my voice. And failed. "Like I just told you."

He thought for a second. "The man with the large hat who trims the hedges?"

"Yes," I ground out. "And his name is Javier Cruz. He's been working here for *two years*." He'd called my dad "the man with the large hat." My throat hurt from wanting to yell at him.

His phone vibrated and he looked down at it. "You don't know what I'm talking about then, eh?" I could hear his Canadian accent a little.

"No." My voice sounded strangled.

"Okay then." He strode away without another word.

Hadn't I heard somewhere that Canadians were usually friendly? That one certainly wasn't. I picked up the watering can and continued watering the plants while trying to rein in my temper.

Dad lived in the small caretaker home on the sprawling estate. Potted herbs and a red geranium dotted his kitchen windowsill, and his eclectic book collection overflowed the shelves lining the wall.

A stunted black and white shorthair cat named Marshawnda kept him company. We called her Shawnda for short. She'd been half dead and had a terrible eye infection when Dad found her, and the vet hadn't been able to save her eye.

"How do shrimp wraps with homemade kimchi sound for dinner?" he asked.

Dad was lean and weathered from working outside all day. He'd given me his tan skin tone and dark hair, which now had streaks of gray in it. His eyes were his most startling feature. They were a light golden brown, and my brother Liam and I had inherited them.

"It sounds great. And we can play *Ticket to Ride, Europe* while we eat. You ready to lose again?"

He smirked. "I thought memory loss usually came with old age."

Before my mom died, my family would play games together at least three or four times a week. It took Dad a couple of years before he could play with us again after she died. But when Liam gave him the popular German-style board game for his birthday, there was no going back.

Dad sniffed. "Are you going to play dirty again, and block my train routes instead of trying to build your own?"

I smiled and laid out the board that showed train tracks snaking through Europe, then started dealing out the cards. "If I've told you once, I've told you a million times, old man. You need to abandon your flawed strategy of focusing on your long train route."

Shawnda wound her way around my feet, then jumped up into my lap, and I absently scratched behind her ears.

"Oh really? Who won last time?" He held his hand up to his ear. "What's that? I can't hear you."

I laughed and smacked his arm. As we played, we talked about my schooling and upcoming schedule. I'd be finishing my clinical hours during winter semester to complete my physician's assistant master's degree.

In December, I planned to move to a little apartment nearby in Palm Springs to finish up the last of my hours and be near my dad.

He grinned. "I can't believe you're so close to graduating."

I used a wildcard to block one of his routes, and he frowned down at the board.

"It feels like I've been going to school forever. I'm glad the university worked with me so I could finish here."

"It'll be nice to have you around." He patted my hand.

"I met your new boss today. Well, kind of." Drawing a card, I studied the board. "He started spewing a to-do list at me, and wouldn't let me get a word in edgewise before he tried to walk away." I left out the part where I'd lost my temper.

"Did you tell him who you are?"

"Yeah, finally. He thought I was his new assistant. When I told him he said, 'okay then' and walked away."

Dad shrugged. "That sounds about right. Did you see his brother, Noah?"

"No. He was alone."

He put his cards down. "I can't remember if I mentioned last night that Connor's younger brother, Noah, sometimes comes and stays at the main house."

"I don't remember you mentioning him."

Dad's eye twitched. "Isa, stay away from Noah if you can. I don't want to speak ill of Connor's family, but Noah is..."

"He's what?"

"I don't trust him. Connor's last assistant quit without giving a two-week notice, and I'm sure it had something to do with Noah."

I shrugged and took another bite of my wrap. "Okay, I'll stay away from both of them." I paused and chewed. "It shouldn't be hard. Connor made it clear he can't be bothered, and I'm sure his brother is the same way."

Dad rubbed the back of his neck. "Don't be too hard on Connor. He was one of the best hockey players in the league until he retired. A lot of people want something from him."

"You work for him. Even if he's not your best friend, he should at least know who you are." He seemed like one of those rich, self-centered athletes to me. "Did you know he has a five-year-old daughter?"

My dad's head snapped up. "No. How do you know that?"

"He told me. He asked me to send her some 'pink girlish' presents for her birthday."

Dad frowned. "Huh."

We played for a few more minutes until my conscience got the better of me. "Do you know Connor's assistant in Canada?"

"Yes. She's the one who hired me. Why?" Dad asked.

I sighed and set my cards down. "Because I want to make sure his daughter gets a few birthday gifts from her dad for her fifth birthday."

He smiled and patted my hand. "Let me call his assistant." He pulled out his phone.

While he made the call, I texted one of my best friends from Seattle. Abigail was a single parent with a three-year-old daughter, so I asked her for some ideas.

Less than a minute later, she started bombarding me with texts.

"Hi Sherrill," I heard my dad say. "This is Javier Cruz, Connor's property manager in Palm Desert." He paused. "Everything is fine. Did Connor get ahold of you to send a few birthday gifts to his daughter?"

He shook his head at me. "No? Okay. Can you order a few items and send them to her for Connor?" He paused again and looked at me with a panicked expression. "I'm not sure..."

"I have some ideas," I whispered.

"Sherrill, I'll send you a list in the next few minutes. Would that be okay? All right, I'll send them to you soon. No, I haven't seen his new assistant. You have a nice evening too."

He hung up and looked over at me. "I know you don't like Connor, but you did a good thing. Now let's pick out some pink birthday gifts."

For the next hour, Dad and I read through my friend's list and googled ideas online. Then we came up with a few items for Connor's nameless daughter.

We decided on bath bombs that turned into sponge animals, a fairy garden with plants and seeds, and a soft green and purple handmade blanket I found on Etsy that any five-year-old girl would love. A pink tutu also caught my eye, and I added it to the list on a whim. Then Dad sent the order with instructions to Sherrill.

When we finished, we continued our game. As we played, I stewed over Connor and what I knew about him.

To be fair, he didn't treat my dad one way or the other, and I had no idea if he was a good father or not. I still didn't like him.

Dad nonchalantly put down tracks and completed one of his short rails. He was now officially winning.

"Well, shoot." I pushed thoughts of Connor aside and concentrated on the game.

# Chapter 2

When Dad moved to the Coachella Valley to work for Connor, I'd put in a request to finish my clinical hours in Palm Springs. That way I could be close to him for a few months until I started working full-time as a PA.

My two rotations would be at a pediatric office and a sports medicine clinic. The sports clinic had a contract with the Coachella Valley Thunderbird ice hockey team, which was the farm team for the new national team, the Seattle Hydras.

And Connor McCoy held a significant stake in both teams. I hadn't cared when I signed up for the clinical rotation. Now I wondered if we'd run into each other sometimes and whether I'd have to be nice to him.

Connor and some of his business colleagues started the team not long after he'd retired. From what I'd read in the news the cost had been staggering, and I knew Dad wasn't exaggerating about how much money Connor made over the years if he could afford an ownership percentage.

The next morning, I sat out on Dad's back patio enjoying my morning coffee. A few minutes later, he walked around the corner in his big sun hat with his electric trimmers.

I gestured to my coffee cup. "I made coffee, and breakfast is in the oven if you're hungry."

"Sounds good. Let me wash up." He set his trimmer down and pulled off his gloves and hat.

We ate out on the back patio. It was a great little spot, and he'd added comfortable patio furniture and colorful planters out here. It felt like a tiny oasis. I propped my bare feet on his coffee table, and sniffed the pungent rosemary and basil in the orange pot next to me.

Dad grinned. "It's so nice having you here, even if you're eating me out of house and home. I'll be done in an hour or so, then we can go."

We planned to go to the Moorten Botanical Garden in Palm Springs, and then maybe the zoo. My dad and I shared a love of plants and animals.

I ate the last bite of my English muffin. "I'll help. It'll go faster."

"Just like old times, huh?"

"Yeah, and you won't be breaking any child labor laws this time."

He shook his head. "It was good for you. It built character."

I laughed. "You go ahead and believe whatever makes it so you can sleep at night."

I scrounged around and found a pair of old sneakers, a hat, and work gloves. Then we trimmed up the hedges around the north end of the property.

Dad worked as a landscaper for years until Paul Curtis, one of his wealthy clients in Seattle, persuaded him to move onto Paul's large estate and take care of the home and sprawling grounds full-time.

It had changed our lives in many ways. Paul made it possible for my dad to be home for us after Mom died. And they had become good friends.

I thought we'd made Paul's life a little better too. Not long after we moved in, Paul became a regular at our dinner table and taught my dad how to play golf. He also loved our game nights. When Paul got sick and died of colon cancer a few years ago, we'd all been grief-stricken.

When we finished trimming the hedges, we stood in the driveway. I glanced around the estate and looked over at the enormous main house. It was a beautiful modern design, and the house wrapped around a giant courtyard area with a luxurious pool and spa.

But my favorite part of the property was the desert landscaping and the overflowing flowerpots.

"Dad, there's still some sandwich meat and sourdough bread. We can eat here before we go, so we don't have to buy lunch."

He shook his head. "There are a few fun lunch spots close to the cactus garden in Palm Springs. It'll be my treat."

"You sure? The best way to double your money is to keep it in your wallet."

"Yes, I'm sure, Ms. Tightwad Penny Pincher."

Because of my mom's lengthy illness and medical bills, money had always been tight in our family. She'd died of pulmonary fibrosis, and the fatal disease had eaten away her energy, her strength, and eventually her ability to breathe.

Being frugal and helping my parents stretch what little money we had was one of the few ways I could help. But Dad was in a better financial place now, and he liked to take us out at least one time when we came to visit him, so I grabbed my purse and a hoodie and didn't argue.

"Sounds great, thank you. Where's your favorite place to eat around here?"

We were discussing lunch spots as we walked to Dad's car. I glanced up and noticed a man who looked a lot like Connor, only shorter and less handsome, walking toward us.

He didn't say hello or smile, but pointed a finger at my dad. "I need you to wash and vacuum my car this afternoon."

Dad stopped next to me and put his hand on my arm. "Hello, Noah. I'm spending time with my daughter today."

Noah's mouth tightened. "Javier, I need the car cleaned."

My hackles rose at the man's tone. I stepped forward and stuck out my hand. "Hello. My name is Isabella. And you are?"

Sometimes forcing manners on people was a good way to throw them off. He automatically took my hand, then seemed to regret it. His handshake felt limp and weak, and he pulled back quickly.

"I'm Noah McCoy, Connor's brother." He sounded like I should know this already. "It won't take that long. I also need it gassed up."

I folded my arms. "Today's Saturday. It's my dad's day off."

Noah sneered. "So?"

For Dad's sake, I tried to be civil. "I also wasn't aware he's responsible for maintaining vehicles."

Noah's eyes were glassy and flat. "He's the maintenance man. He does whatever we ask him to do."

"We? I didn't know you were also his employer. I thought it was just Connor. And Dad already worked half the day, even though today's one of his days off."

My dad gently took my arm and pulled me back. "Isa, I've got this."

He turned to Noah. "There's a car wash in Rancho Mirage with a gas station next to it. That's your best bet. Have a good day, Noah." He guided me over to the passenger seat, then walked around and got in.

Noah scowled back at us, and I saw his left eye twitch. I couldn't help myself. I gave him my best resting bitch face.

The botanical cactus garden in Palm Springs was one of my happy places, I decided. It also helped me shake off some of my anger at the McCoy brothers. The variety of cacti was astounding, and the specimens were some of the biggest I'd ever seen. Two large desert turtles also lived there.

Dad and I wandered slowly around the pathways, then through the greenhouse with the smaller specimens. Some of them looked like long hairy snakes and others were almost florescent in color. I had no idea there were so many kinds.

As we strolled around, we talked about what he did and didn't miss about Seattle.

"I don't miss the rain and dampness that sinks into my bones in the winter," he admitted. "But I miss being able to grow almost anything."

I sighed. "Yeah, it's only October and the rainy season is already in full swing. But fall is spectacular."

He smiled nostalgically and glanced at me. "Are you seeing anyone?"

"I see lots of people every day."

He shook his head. "You know what I mean, smart mouth."

"No. I don't have time."

"If you found someone interesting enough, you'd make time."

At least once a month, Dad dutifully asked me the same questions. And every month I gave him a variation of the same answers.

He knew me well. My mom used to say Dad gave her tingles and made her heart flutter, and I hadn't found anyone who did that for me. Mom had suffered for so long before she died, and I'd seen the light in my dad's eyes dim and fade over time.

We ate lunch at a little tiki bar located in the Caliente Tropics, one of Palm Springs' iconic lodges not far from the cactus gardens. I wanted to soak up the sunshine and warmth before I had to head back to Seattle the next day, so we sat out on the patio by the pool.

Dad nudged my knee under the table. "It seems like Liam and I just went to your college graduation."

"Yeah, I only have six months to go. Now I just need to figure out where I'm going to work after graduation."

Sunday morning, before I flew back to Seattle in the afternoon, I got up early and hiked the Bump and Grind Trail to watch the sunrise. Dad decided to sleep in.

When I got back to the estate later that morning, Noah was coming out of the large garage behind the main house. When he saw me drive in, he turned and started walking toward me. I winced inwardly and slowly got out of Dad's car.

Noah walked right up to me and stepped into my personal space. "Are you planning to move in, or what?"

I instinctively backed up against the car door and put a hand up to keep him from getting closer. He tilted his head and looked me up and down.

My heart started racing. "Back up."

He smirked, then glanced down at my dusty legs and running shoes. "Does being sweaty and dirty all the time run in your family?"

What a fucking asshole. My dad did maintenance and yard care, so of course he was dusty and dirty sometimes.

I straightened and put my hand down. "Did you want something?"

He nodded. "Yeah. I want to know if you plan to move in with your dad here. Because Connor's gonna have to charge rent if you do."

I cocked my head and stared at him. "Why is my dad, or me, any of your concern? You don't live here, you're not his employer, and your name isn't on the paychecks."

"You better watch your mouth, bitch. I could get your dad fired in about two seconds."

I stepped forward and he instinctively backed up. Then he glared at me.

"I don't care," I said slowly. "And my dad wouldn't either."

Noah looked at me as if assessing for weaknesses, then his eyes lowered and he blatantly stared down at my breasts. I had on a plain blue racerback tank top and a sports bra. The fucker was still trying to intimidate me.

I snapped my fingers in his face. "Hey. Eyes up here."

He jerked his head up as if he hadn't expected me to call him out on his atrocious behavior.

I shook my head in disgust. Then I stepped to the side and started walking around the car to get my backpack out of the passenger seat.

"I'm not done talking to you," he said loudly. He followed me and grabbed my arm, wrenching me around to face him.

The estate was deserted, and I didn't know if my dad was awake yet. Noah scared me, but I didn't want him to know it.

"But I'm done talking to you. Now let go of my arm." My voice was loud and steady, even though my heart raced.

He squeezed my arm hard, then let go. I grabbed my backpack and walked to the front door.

"Listen, you little cunt–"

I beeped the lock on the car, walked inside, and shut and locked the door. I was so mad, my hands shook a little. Taking a deep breath in and out, I toed off my shoes and socks in the foyer and unpacked my backpack with unsteady hands.

My dad would be able to tell something was wrong if he saw me right then, so I tried to get my emotions under control. I debated whether to tell him what had happened. But in the end, I let pride win out. I didn't want to give Noah the satisfaction of knowing he'd scared me.

# Chapter 3

F all semester finally ended, thank God. It was mid-December, and I'd spent the past couple of days driving from Seattle to Palm Springs to move into the tiny one-bedroom apartment I'd rented.

The place came right out of the 1970s, with dingy gold linoleum and a popcorn ceiling. But it sat between the pediatric office and the hockey arena where I'd be completing the rest of my clinical hours, and the rent was cheap.

It was also one of the few places that would take a six-month lease. When I walked into it for the first time, I understood why. But I'd lived in some crappy places over the past five years. I'd be fine.

There was a two-week break before my clinical hours started again, and I was giddy to have so much time off. Dad had invited me to dinner that night, and while I unpacked I called my brother, Liam, to catch up.

Liam sighed. "I wish I were there with you guys." The three of us loved our dinner and game nights.

"How are things with you?" I could hear restaurant noise in the background, and figured he was probably eating a late dinner somewhere in Washington, D. C where he lived.

"The same. Did you get done with your hours in Seattle then?"

I grinned. "Yes, thank God. Just one semester to go."

"I bet Dad's proud of you."

Hefting a box onto my little kitchen counter, I started unpacking my secondhand dishes. "Thanks. Not as proud as he is of you, but I'll take it."

Liam was three years older than me, and he worked as an engineer for a tech company of some kind. I didn't fully understand what he did.

"How's Dad doing?" he asked.

"He seems a little lonely."

"What makes you think so?"

I put my mismatched plates and bowls into the cupboard. "I haven't heard him talk about any friends here. And Connor Mc-Coy isn't like Paul. I'd be surprised if Connor could recognize Dad if he saw him on the street."

Liam hummed. "You might be judging him too harshly. Doesn't McCoy have three or four houses?"

"Probably. But his younger brother is a complete asshole. And he seems to let Noah do and say whatever he wants."

"Is it that bad?" Liam sounded skeptical.

I told him about Noah trying to make Dad wash and gas up his car on Dad's day off. I didn't tell him about Noah cornering me against Dad's car and manhandling me.

"Dad also told me that Noah screamed at Connor's new assistant a few days before she quit, and he wrecked one of Connor's motorcycles. He also leaves beer cans and trash around the estate when he's there."

"Does Connor know about all this?" Liam asked.

"I have no idea. But if he doesn't, he should. And it puts everyone in an impossible position since it's his brother doing it."

"You're right. I definitely want to come visit him now."

"You should, and not just to check in with Dad. I miss you too, Waldo." When Liam started working, it seemed like he was always out of the country somewhere. I couldn't keep track of where he was half the time, so I'd started calling him Waldo.

He chuckled. "Love you too."

Early that evening, I punched my dad's code into the front security gate and drove into Connor's estate. I'd texted to let him know I was almost there.

I hadn't been back since October, and I worried about running into Noah again. As I pulled up to Dad's little place on the estate, I regretted not talking him into coming over to my apartment for dinner instead.

Dad walked out when I pulled up. "Hey, you made it." He waited until I got out of my car, then gave me a big hug and pulled me off my feet.

I laughed and hugged him back. "Dad, I'm not five anymore."

"You still weigh about the same though."

It was so good to see him, I hugged him again. "I have a couple of weeks off before my clinical hours start. It's more time than I've had in years."

Dad nodded. "I know. I had to spend the holidays with just Liam last year."

They'd ended up going to a little place in Mexico to fish and watch the whales migrate. I didn't feel sorry for him at all.

I felt a prickle between my shoulder blades, and looked over to see Noah standing in Connor's driveway, watching us. He gave me the creeps.

Dad patted my arm. "Let's eat. I made butter chicken and blueberry cobbler."

I loved it when Dad baked, and he didn't skimp on the best ingredients.

While we ate, I reviewed my winter schedule with him. "The pediatric clinic takes Fridays off. I'll be working over the weekend during a few of the home games with the hockey team, but my schedule is completely manageable." I clapped my hands together in happiness.

While we talked, I absently wiped the sauce off a few choice pieces of chicken and cut them up into small pieces. Dad's little cat, Shawnda, waited patiently under my chair. I was a sucker, but I didn't care. I loved that little furball.

After dinner, I fed her my chicken scraps and we cleaned up. Neither of us felt like playing a game, so we took drinks out to his back patio and talked and enjoyed the quiet evening. Around eleven I decided to go home so I could get up early and finish unpacking.

On Sunday morning, I ran over to Town Bagel Bakery to get a fresh bagel with jalapeño cream cheese. I didn't have any groceries yet, so I decided my splurge of the week would be breakfast. The little bagel shop was packed, but I got in and out quickly. I made coffee and ate my breakfast at home while I unpacked.

Around lunchtime, I needed a break so I grabbed my longboard and headed out for a ride on a nice wide asphalt trail outside the apartment complex. I found a good playlist, and just asphalt surfed and listened to music.

Later that afternoon as I wondered where to put the last few miscellaneous odds and ends, Dad called.

He didn't say anything for a few seconds, then sighed. "Isabella, I'm at the main house with Connor McCoy and his brother, Noah."

The mention of their names made my hackles rise.

"Are you all right? Do you need me to come get you?"

"No sweetheart, but thanks for offering." I could hear a smile in his voice. He used to say the same thing to me when I was young and I'd call him.

"Mr. McCoy's house was robbed early this morning."

"Oh no! Is everyone all right?"

My dad paused again. "Everyone's fine. It wasn't a forced entry. Isa, Noah is accusing you. I'm sorry. I never would have had you come here if I'd known this would happen."

I knew in my gut Noah was trying to set me up.

"Dad, are you in the same room with them?" I asked.

"Yes."

I sat on the couch. "Okay. What do they want?"

"Connor asked that you come to the house."

"Do you want me to come?"

He sighed. "No, but I think it would be better to address this head-on."

I laid my head on the back of the couch and looked up at my water-stained, popcorn ceiling. "Later today when you're alone, call me so we can talk freely. I'm not coming today. Tell them they'll have to wait until tomorrow evening."

"Alright. I'll let them know."

"I have a meeting with my supervising pediatrician tomorrow at the clinic. But if Mr. McCoy *still* hasn't pulled his head out of his ass by then, I'll come by."

"Okay, Isa." I could hear a little humor in his voice. He knew I had a fierce temper and could be stubborn.

"You can also tell your stupid boss if he calls the police, feel free to give the officers my phone number."

"If it comes up, I'll tell him," he replied. He probably didn't want to give Connor any ideas.

"Dad, I want you to quit," I blurted out.

He sounded tired. "Right now, I do too."

"You don't need the job, and I bet my landlord would work with me." I hoped I was right, but I'd pay rent on two apartments for the next six months if I had to.

When he didn't respond, I kept going. "We could rent a bigger place together, and you could golf and just enjoy the nice weather. Be retired."

He puffed out a breath. "I don't know why, but I feel like I need to stay for some reason."

I rubbed my forehead and held in my objections. "Call me when you can talk. I love you. Don't worry." I hung up, and had the sudden violent urge to throw my phone against the wall.

Early Monday evening, I drove into the estate and parked in the driveway of the main house. If I was being summoned for this meeting, then I'd park in Connor's driveway and walk through that asshole's front door with my head high.

My dad and I had talked on the phone yesterday evening for over an hour. The conversation was mostly me trying to talk him into quitting. He finally promised he would think about it. Probably to shut me up.

When I reached the tall front door, I noticed a festive holiday wreath hanging on it. Through the glass, I could also see an enormous Christmas tree with hundreds of expensive white ornaments and lights. The thing was probably worth more than my car, and I hated it on principle.

When I rang the doorbell, Dad answered.

"Dad. I love you. But I'm giving you fair warning. I probably won't be able to hold my temper tonight."

He grimaced but nodded. "Just try your best. Come in and I'll officially introduce you."

As we walked into the living room, I saw Connor standing in front of the wall-to-ceiling bifold doors that ran the length of the huge space. I could see the long pool and courtyard area the house was built around behind him.

I stopped next to my father and folded my arms. Noah lounged back on the couch, and I didn't bother looking at him.

Dad put his hand on my shoulder. "This is my daughter, Isabella Cruz. Isa, this is Connor McCoy." He didn't introduce Noah.

I stared at Connor and didn't say anything.

Connor finally unfolded his arms. "Hello, Isa."

"Friends and family call me Isa. You can call me Ms. Cruz."

Dad shifted next to me.

Connor raised his eyebrow and studied me. "Okay then, Ms. Cruz. Damien Andreasen, one of the owners of the security company I use, wants to be at this meeting. He should be here shortly."

I glanced at the large clock above the mantel. "I'll wait for ten minutes. Then I'm leaving." I didn't have anywhere I needed to be, but I wasn't going to sit here longer than that.

Turning my back on him, I walked over to the other side of the couch and sat down. I didn't say a word. Noah glanced over at me several times, but I ignored everyone. Connor finally turned his back to the room and gazed out at the pool with his arms folded. Just over eight minutes later, the doorbell rang.

Dad answered the door again, and I could hear voices in the entryway. A handsome, competent-looking man with a laptop case walked in, and a tall, gorgeous woman came in behind him.

Dad introduced me to Damien and his partner, Harley.

Connor nodded at Damien. "You said you wanted to come by and discuss the break-in. Noah said Javier's daughter was the only one who came to the estate over the weekend."

Dad straightened. "Isabella has a right to come see me." He turned to Noah. "And you're wrong about her being the only one who was here this weekend. I was here. And so were you."

Noah took his foot off the coffee table. "Are you saying it could have been me, Javier? Are you accusing me of stealing from my brother?"

Javier leaned forward. "You're strongly insinuating it was Isa, just because she visited me this weekend. But she didn't sleep over, and I'm pointing out you were here too. All weekend."

I touched Dad's arm. "They're not worth getting upset over. Your boss is too stupid to see what's staring him in the face."

Connor frowned and studied me. Then he turned to Damien. "Which code was used to turn off the cameras and security program?"

"Your personal code," Damien said.

Noah waved at us. "You gave Javier your personal code when you hired him. I was there. You said he could use it until they created a new one for him." He glanced at me with a sad expression. "He probably gave it to his daughter or wrote it down where she could find it."

"That means you heard Connor's code too since you were there," Javier pointed out.

Noah shook his head. "Why would I steal from my brother? It's obvious neither of you has a lot of money. Connor's a decent guy; I'm sure he'll let you work something out."

Damien ignored Noah. "This'll be easy to clear up. There are two backup security cameras in place in case the main system goes down."

Everyone in the room went still. I smiled and patted Dad's hand.

Noah shifted nervously. "What are you talking about?" He didn't sound condescending and self-righteous now. He sounded panicked.

"What kind of backup security cameras?" Connor asked at the same time.

"A couple of hidden motion sensor cameras by the exterior doors. The footage is only retrieved if the main system goes down. My business partner is a cynical bastard and doesn't trust one system."

Connor nodded grimly. Noah started sputtering and protesting as Damien pulled out his laptop.

Dad's shoulders slumped a little as he gazed at Connor. "You have enough on your plate right now, but tomorrow morning I'll be putting in my official notice." He turned to Damien. "Tell Zeke thank you for being a cynical bastard.'"

Thank God for whomever Damien's partner was. If I ever met the man, I'd give him a big hug.

Standing up, I turned to my dad. "Let's go. We don't need to be here for this."

Connor looked over in surprise. "You're not going to watch the video?"

"We already know what's on it."

I took hold of Dad's arm and we walked out. When we reached the front stoop, Connor came striding out.

"Javier, I don't want you to quit. I'm missing something important here."

Letting go of my dad's arm, I turned on him. "You know what's going on, you just don't want to admit it." Then my temper broke loose and I stuck my finger in his chest. "You're too stupid and self-absorbed. It must have been all the concussions you suffered from playing hockey."

"What exactly do I know?" Connor asked carefully.

"That Noah is a mean, dangerous asshole, he's the one who stole from you, and he's probably been doing it for years."

Connor's face went still. "Really? And how would you know that?"

"Because unlike you, I'm *not* stupid or clueless. When you aren't here, he treats everyone like trash. He harasses your staff and abuses your property."

Dad touched my arm. "Isa, let's go. You don't want to get involved in this."

I didn't take my eyes off Connor. "I already am. Noah tried to frame me because I stood up to him and called him out on his bullshit."

Connor tilted his head and studied me. "What bullshit?"

I ignored his question. "And you know what? You're more culpable than he is."

"In what way?"

"You subject the people you hire to his poison and toxicity, then you ignore it or pretend it doesn't happen. And you don't care." I shook my head and turned around. "You're not worth it. Come on, Dad. Let's go."

Connor's calm demeanor slipped, and he suddenly looked angry and overwhelmed.

He turned to my dad. "Javier, please come back tomorrow morning so we can talk."

Dad nodded. "Alright."

"I need to go back inside, but I want you to stay on." Connor ran both hands through his hair and rubbed his face. "From how all this went, I probably have a mess I need to clean up."

I leaned forward. "You can't pretend you didn't already know–"

Dad put his hand on my shoulder. "Isa, you had your say. Now it's his turn."

I looked at my father and bit the inside of my cheek. "Okay, I'll listen. For you. But he doesn't deserve your kindness."

Connor studied us for a moment as if we were a puzzle. "My daughter is coming to live with me full-time, and she's coming this week. It's better for us not to be in Vancouver right now."

My stomach bottomed out. Dad would never leave now; he was a bleeding heart for small children and injured animals.

"Your daughter?" Dad asked. "Isa said you'd mentioned you have a five-year-old." He made it sound like Connor had told me this in polite conversation, not while he'd been spewing orders at me.

"Will you stay?" Connor asked again. "Even for a few months? I want people around her I can trust while I figure out what the hell I'm doing."

"I'll stay. Until you get settled."

I put my hand on Dad's arm and squeezed. "He'll stay on one condition." They both turned to me.

"What condition?" Connor asked cautiously.

"Noah doesn't come around here anymore."

"He's my brother, Ms. Cruz."

"He's not someone you want around your five-year-old daughter."

Connor went still. "Is there something else I need to know?"

"I doubt you'd believe me since you think I'm a criminal. Call your last assistant and ask her about your brother."

"I will. You and I are not done talking."

I disagreed but didn't argue. I just wanted to get out of here.

Connor turned to Dad. "I'll find you tomorrow." Then he walked back inside.

# Chapter 4

The following week, I stayed away from Connor's estate and got ready for my clinical rotations. Dad came over for dinner and to check out my new apartment.

"The location is convenient, I guess," he said diplomatically as he looked around.

I pushed his shoulder. "It's cheap and centrally located. What more could I ask for?"

He scratched his cheek. "A kitchen that's been updated in the last fifty years, a ceiling that doesn't have water stains, and flooring that isn't dingy gold linoleum?"

I shrugged. "I thought the linoleum was dark tan. It's only for a few months anyway."

We discussed the situation at Connor's house while we ate dinner, and Dad gave me an update.

"It's been a lot better without Noah there and with Connor taking an interest. I think Noah believed that when he turned off the security system he wouldn't get caught, but the backup footage showed him nonchalantly taking Connor's valuables out of the house."

"How did the conversation with Damien and Harley go?" I asked.

"Harley advised Connor to press charges and call the police. I heard Connor also filed a no-contact order. That's about all I know."

I ground my teeth. "That bastard tried to set me up. And Connor believed him."

"Connor didn't say much. I couldn't tell what he really believed."

"Hmm." I didn't agree, so I didn't say anything. But my conscience was pricking me. "Dad, I need to tell you something. You have to promise not to be mad."

He looked at me cautiously. "What is it?"

I put my fork down. "I had another run-in with Noah in October while I was there visiting you. When I came back from hiking the Bump and Grind Trail, he cornered me by your car."

Dad was quiet as I explained what had happened, but his lips pinched together.

"Isabella, why didn't you tell me?" He only used my full name when he was angry or disappointed.

"Because I didn't want to cause problems." I sighed and admitted the full truth. "And I didn't want to give Noah the satisfaction of knowing he scared me."

He shook his head. "I need to tell Connor. Something similar probably happened with Connor's last assistant."

"That's why I asked Connor to talk to her. Let me think about it, okay? He's not my favorite person. How are things going with his daughter?"

Dad sighed. "Not well. Connor doesn't know what to do, and Elodie seems bewildered and lost. She follows me around outside while I work."

"Why would she do that? I used to try anything to get out of hanging out with you."

He smiled. "I remember. But I put *you* to work. I give Elodie Skittles and cookies."

"Her name is Elodie? Huh. That's different. Cute, but different."

"We need to have an intervention with Connor. He needs help."

I sighed, long and loud. "How about we see what we can do when I come over tomorrow for Christmas?" I didn't like Connor, but I wouldn't take it out on his little girl.

"Okay. Now, what do you want for Christmas dinner? And pizza isn't an option."

After Dad left that evening I texted my best friend, Abigail. She lived with her parents in Seattle. I didn't like her parents, and I worried about her and Stella, her daughter. Abby called me back two minutes later, and we talked for over an hour. I could hear her giving Stella a bath.

"How're you doing?" I asked her.

"Okay. Mom and Dad are still as disapproving and judgmental as ever. It's hard living with them."

Her parents were some of the most self-righteous, rigid people I knew, and they were angry at Abby for getting pregnant and not being married.

"Let me know if you need a break this winter. You can come visit me. The weather is perfect here right now."

I could hear the smile in her voice. "Thanks, Isa. I might take you up on that. Now tell me about Connor McCoy and his little girl."

I told Abby what had happened, and about Connor's daughter coming to live with him. "He needs help with her."

"Geez. Your life is never boring, I'll give you that. The main thing Connor needs is support," she said. "Does he have family around?"

"He has a worthless brother who I wouldn't leave a pet rock with, let alone a five-year-old. But Connor is rich and can hire help."

"It doesn't matter if he's richer than Midas. Being a single parent is hard on so many levels. He needs people he can trust, who love his daughter and can pick up the slack and help out. That's hard to find. Hell, I live with my parents and they don't give me that kind of support."

"That sucks, Abs. You and Stella are always welcome. You know that, right?"

She was quiet for a moment. "Thanks, Isa. That means a lot. You know you're going to have to work with Connor, right?"

"But I hate that man," I whined.

Abby laughed. "Hey, you asked. Now tell me what else is going on." We talked for a few minutes until she had to go.

When we said goodbye, I had a new respect for Abby. And along with my intense dislike, I also started feeling a little sorry for Connor.

On Christmas Day, Dad and I slept in. We'd both stayed up way too late talking with Liam in D.C., and playing Settlers of Catan with most of the extension packs.

Before I went to bed, I'd made the rookie mistake of not closing my bedroom door. So after the third time Shawnda crawled across my face and meowed in my ear for her breakfast, I finally rolled out of bed to feed her. Then I got ready for the day and started coffee.

When I glanced out the kitchen window, I noticed a nice white truck in Connor's driveway. A few minutes later as I was pulling eggs and cheese out of the fridge to make a breakfast casserole, I looked up and saw Connor and Damien Andreasen coming out of the main house. They walked toward the front gates of the estate. I wondered what was going on, and had a suspicion Noah was somehow involved.

Fifteen minutes later, there was a knock on the front door. Harley and a beautiful little girl with dark brown, messy hair and mismatched clothes stood in the doorway. Harley held a few Christmas treats.

The girl had on red Christmas leggings and what looked like an orange Halloween t-shirt. I was also sure she'd done her hair herself. Probably without a mirror.

Harley raised her hand. "Hi, Isa. I don't know if you remember me–"

"Of course I do. It's nice to see you again." I looked down at Elodie. "You must be Connor's mother."

The little girl's eyes went wide. "No."

"His grandmother?" I tried again.

"No. They're dead. And I'm little."

"Oh. Then who are you?"

"Elodie. He's my dad." She shyly swayed back and forth.

"Aw, that was my next guess. Come in."

Harley handed me what looked like a tin of shortbread cookies and Christmas chocolates.

"We're regifted-ing," Elodie informed me. Harley slapped her forehead.

I laughed. "Thank you! I think you already know *my* dad. He's the one who gives you Skittles."

She smiled for the first time. "Yeah, and you know what?"

"No. What?"

"Sometimes he gives me cookies too. And you know what? He said I could pet his cat. Can I?" She looked around.

"Sure. If you can find her."

Harley turned to me as Elodie wandered around the living room, looking under the furniture for Shawnda.

"I'm sorry to come over on Christmas, but she needs help."

"We know. My dad and I were already planning an intervention with Mr. McCoy."

Elodie stood up. "Where is the kitty?"

"She's a little scared of strangers. Let's see if we can coax her out with treats."

"What's her name?" Elodie asked.

"Marshawnda, but we call her Shawnda for short."

Harley raised her eyebrow. "Marshawnda?"

I grinned and shrugged. "Yeah. My dad thought 'she' was a 'he' at first and named her after his favorite football player, Marshawn Lynch. But then he had to improvise."

Harley grinned. "The football player who kept answering interview questions with 'I'm just here so I won't get fined'? That guy?"

"Oh, he's so much more than that. I grew up in Seattle, and I love football. He's a freaking legend." I turned to Elodie. "Let's draw her out with some turkey."

We spent the next few minutes coaxing Shawnda out of her hiding spot.

When the cat finally came out, Elodie looked at Shawnda's face and gasped. "Belly, your cat is hurted!"

Shawnda sat next to Elodie, eating tiny bits of sliced turkey.

"No one's ever called me Belly before. Can I call you Ellie then?" I asked.

She pointed frantically at Shawnda's eye. "Your cat!"

"Honey, don't worry. It happened a long time ago. When she was a baby she was really sick. My dad found her and made her better, but her eye was already too damaged. It doesn't hurt anymore."

She looked dubious. "Oh. Can she see?"

"Yes. Her other eye is fine and sometimes she gets the zoomies, and she'll race around the room and jump off the furniture. She's doing great now."

"Okay. That's good." Elodie settled down.

She kept petting and feeding Shawnda, and my heart melted a little.

"Belly, are you my friend now?" she asked.

It was an abrupt change of topic, but I rolled with it. "Of course."

"Good, 'cause you know what? Your dad is my bestest friend. And now I have three friends." She smiled at Harley and continued petting the cat.

"Aw hell," I muttered.

Harley glanced over at me. "What's wrong?"

"I'm going to have to help Connor, aren't I? And actually be nice to him."

Harley chuckled. "It's going to be painful after last week, isn't it?"

I sighed. "It's not just going to be painful. It's going to be excruciating."

"Well, look who's here?" Dad said as he walked in.

Elodie waved. "I came to see your kitty."

Dad smiled. "Hi, sweetie. I see you've met Shawnda."

"Belly told me her eye doesn't hurt anymore."

Dad grinned at my new nickname, then promptly invited Harley and Elodie to eat Christmas brunch with us.

"We'd love to," Harley said. "But Connor might worry when he gets back and we're not at the main house."

Dad nodded. "We can take it over there then. I don't think he'll mind."

"What about the kitty? She'll be lonely," Elodie said sadly. "Can we bring her?"

Dad squatted down next to her. "Shawnda likes being alone sometimes so she can take her cat naps in peace."

"Okay." Elodie looked down at her shoes.

"You can visit her sometimes if your dad says it's okay though."

She smiled. "Okay."

When the breakfast casserole was done, I wrapped it up and grabbed a fruit and cheese tray. Dad also brought the orange rolls he'd baked yesterday, and we took it all over to the main house. We ate while the casserole was still warm, and sat around Connor's large modern dining table talking and laughing.

I turned to Elodie. "Who's your new teacher?"

She shrugged. "I don't know."

"What's your new school called?" Harley asked.

Elodie shrugged again, but I could see she was getting a little worried.

Harley patted her shoulder. "We got you signed up for soccer if your dad says it's okay, and I think we found a dance class."

This woman was efficient. I knew Damien's truck hadn't been here that long.

Elodie piped up. "Yeah, and I can wear my pink tutu."

I glanced at my dad and grinned. "See? I knew she'd like it. Ellie, we can ask your dad. He may have already signed you up."

"Signed her up for what?" Connor asked from the kitchen doorway.

I jumped a little. Damien walked in behind him and went over to Harley.

She smiled up at him. "Are you guys hungry? We went over to see if Isabella and Javier were around, and they ended up feeding us Christmas brunch."

Damien looked down at the orange rolls. "These look homemade."

I pointed to my dad. "He's the pastry chef. I'm responsible for the breakfast casserole."

"It all looks good, thanks." Damien grabbed a plate, dished up some food, then sat down next to Harley.

Connor looked at us all sitting around his dining table, then studied Elodie. She sat next to me, eating and chattering away.

Ellie leaned over and whispered, "Belly, will you ask Daddy about school? And dancing?"

"Sure." I turned to Connor. "Mr. McCoy, Elodie wants me to ask you to get her signed up for school. She also wants to get into a dance class." I held up my hand. "Don't worry, Harley found one that might work for her."

Connor stared at me. "Call me Connor." Then he turned to Elodie. "The school is closed for the holidays, but I'll enroll you the first day they reopen."

Dad nodded. "That makes sense."

Connor glanced at Dad gratefully. "And we'll find a dance class if that one doesn't work. Maybe we can call Mémé and ask her what type of dance class you were in before."

Elodie got up and ran over to hug Connor's leg.

He knelt down and hugged her back. "Is there anything else you want to ask me?"

Elodie gave a shy shrug, then glanced over her shoulder at Harley and me.

Harley nudged me under the table. "Soccer," she whispered.

I rolled my eyes. I guess Harley was passing the baton to me.

Clearing my throat, I shifted a little. "Harley also got her signed up for soccer if you approve. Ellie wants to play on Lennie and Willie's soccer team. I don't know who they are, but she considers them her friends already."

Connor stared at Elodie. "Have you met Willie and Lennie?"

"No."

He pointed to me. "You call her Belly."

Elodie nodded. "Yeah. And you know what? She calls me Ellie. Belly and Ellie. It rhymes. And she's my friend now too."

Connor raised his eyebrows and turned to me. "What happened while I was outside?"

I shrugged and used my fork to push around crumbs on my plate. "You said you needed help. So we're helping."

Connor studied me over Elodie's head. Narrowing my eyes, I set my fork down and folded my arms. "This doesn't change the way I feel about you," I muttered.

He grinned. "Not yet." I didn't like his grin one bit.

# Chapter 5

The day after Christmas, my dad called. "Good morning, Belly."

"You're so funny." I smiled because he couldn't see me. "Are we still on for dinner tonight?"

"Yes." He cleared his throat, and my radar went off. Whenever Dad said something he knew Liam and I wouldn't like, he fidgeted and cleared his throat first.

"I need to tell you something."

"What? Just spill it," I prodded.

"Connor wants your phone number."

I looked at my phone, then put it back to my ear. "Sorry, will you repeat that?"

"He wants your number."

"What am I missing? There's no way in hell he's interested in me, and I'd rather eat roadkill than be in the same room with him."

"Oh. I can see your confusion." He cleared his throat again. "He wants to talk to you about Elodie and asked me for your phone number. He, uh, wants me to–" His next comment was muffled and unintelligible.

My shoulders tightened. "Dad, what does Connor want you to do?"

He sighed. "He wants me to help take care of Elodie."

"How, *exactly*, does he want you to help take care of her?"

"He asked me to be her nanny."

My mind went blank.

"Isa? Are you still there?"

"Yeah." My shoulders loosened. He had to be kidding. "You're joking with me, right?"

"No, I'm not." He sounded a little offended.

My shoulders tensed again. "Okay, I had to ask. And I'm not implying you wouldn't be the best nanny in the world. Because you would be. I just... didn't give Connor enough credit to realize it."

Dad chuckled. "He didn't. It was Elodie's idea."

"Elodie? How did that happen?"

"She was following me around again yesterday afternoon, and Connor came out and told her he planned to find her a nanny. But in the meantime, she needed to leave me alone and let me work."

My heart hurt for her. "That probably made her feel sad. She told Harley and me the other day you are her best friend."

"Well." Dad sniffed a little. "Anyway, she took hold of my hand, looked up at Connor with big sad eyes, and asked if *I* could be her nanny."

I could tell he was touched, but I was annoyed and confused. Why would Dad even consider it after being invisible to Connor for almost two years?

"Has he found her a school yet? Or any friends?"

"He's working on it, and she'll make friends. I told Connor I needed to talk to you first after what happened." He cleared his throat again.

He wanted to say yes, and he wanted me to get over my anger. But Connor and I needed to come to an understanding first.

"Okay, Javy. Give him my number. But you can't be mad if I offend him. He's on my shit list."

"I know, and for good reason. I haven't said yes yet," he reminded me. "And if you're really opposed to it, I'll tell them no."

I ground my teeth. I wouldn't lose a wink of sleep over telling Connor where to shove it. But Elodie was another matter, and Dad knew it.

About fifteen minutes later, an unknown call came in. I picked up, thinking it was probably Connor.

"Hello," I clipped out.

"Isa, this is Connor McCoy. Javier said you'd be expecting my call." He had a deep, resonant voice.

"It's Ms. Cruz to you. Hello, Mr. McCoy."

He didn't mince words. "Stop calling me Mr. McCoy just to get under my skin. I want your dad to help me with Elodie, but he said we needed to talk first."

My back went up, but I stayed silent.

He waited for an answer. When I didn't say anything, he kept going. "My daughter likes him and feels comfortable around him. He seems like a good man."

"He is. He's also trusting and forgiving, which is why I don't want him around you or your family."

"My daughter is—"

I interrupted. "I'm not talking about your daughter. She's sweet and lovely, and I wonder how you can be her father. It's you and Noah I'm worried about."

He was silent for a moment, then sighed. "I understand you're angry about what happened with Noah, but he won't be coming around. There shouldn't be any more problems."

"Then what was Damien doing at your house on Christmas Day?"

He didn't say anything.

"And what happened to the keypad on your front gate? It looks like someone took a hammer to it," I continued.

"I'm taking care of it."

"Uh-huh."

He growled. "Will you talk to your dad or not?"

I laid my head back on the couch and looked up at my stained ceiling. "We need to reach an understanding first, face to face."

"Fine. When can you come to the house?"

My eyebrows furrowed. "I haven't had the best experience being summoned to your house, McCoy. I'll meet you at the Rancho Mirage park by the fire engine playground. Either tomorrow or Wednesday. You can bring Elodie."

He let out a long, irritated breath. "All right. The park tomorrow."

We set up a time to meet the next day. Connor could be annoyed all he wanted, but my dad's well-being came first.

When I got to the park the next day, Connor was already there waiting for me, and Elodie played on the fire engine jungle gym. She waved at me.

Connor had on sunglasses and a baseball cap. I walked up to the table and sat across from him.

"Hello, Mr. McCoy."

His jaw clenched. "It's Connor, especially since Javier is going to help with Elodie."

I folded my arms. "He told me he hasn't said yes yet."

Connor glanced at me, then turned back to watch Elodie. "He wants your approval. If you're going to cause problems or hold it over us, I'll find someone else."

Anger rose, but I tamped it down. "You want him to help you take care of your daughter after you accused *his* daughter of stealing from you."

His eyes narrowed. "I never accused you. And where are you going with this?"

I narrowed my eyes back. "I don't like you very much, Mr. McCoy."

"I'm well aware of that, Ms. Cruz."

"Are you going to have lunch with us?" Elodie called from the fire engine.

I turned to her. "No. But I'll come over this week to my dad's house and we can play with Shawnda if you want."

Her face lit up. "Okay! Can we have lunch then?"

"If your dad says it's all right. I'm going to talk with him for a few minutes, then I'll push you on the swing. Okay?"

"Okay." She waved and went over to the slide where a couple of little boys were playing.

I watched her for a minute, then reluctantly turned back to Connor. "You can call me Isabella, and I'll call you Connor." I said his name like I was chewing glass.

He nodded and studied me carefully. "So?"

I crossed my arms. "Have you apologized to my dad yet?"

"No. And I didn't accuse you of stealing."

"You're splitting hairs. If my dad is going to nanny for you, then you need to find someone to help with the maintenance and landscaping. And a caregiver for Elodie on the weekends and evenings if you aren't around. He needs some time off."

He nodded. "It's already arranged. And I hired a remote personal assistant as well."

"Good. Maybe this one won't quit on you as quickly as the last one if they don't have to talk to you face to face. One more thing. Pretend you give a shit."

He took off his sunglasses and glared. "What do you mean?"

"Your employees. Call them by their names, and show some appreciation once in a while.'"

His jaw flexed but he kept silent.

"And don't allow other people to mistreat them. I know they get paid, but my dad is a kind, hardworking person. You've never thanked him, and you called him 'the guy with the big hat' who trims your hedges. Your yard looks immaculate, and your flowerpots and gardens are stunning."

He nodded stiffly. "I'll apologize. This isn't an excuse, but there's been shit going on in my life..."

I stared at him flatly.

Connor sighed and watched Elodie play with troubled eyes. "I won't take him for granted again. This isn't about me."

Elodie was talking animatedly with the two little boys at the bottom of the slide.

My shoulders slumped. "This isn't about me, either. I'll tell my dad we're okay."

Just then Elodie waved at me excitedly. "Belly, I have two new friends!"

"See? I knew you could make friends here," I called back.

"I'd like to hire you to help too."

I sat back, surprised. "No way."

"Why?"

"Because I'm not available."

"Uh-huh." He didn't believe me. "I'll pay you triple whatever you're getting paid right now."

My irritation returned. "I'm not getting paid for what I do, and I already plan to help with Elodie. Soon my schedule will change significantly. Until then, I'll be spending a lot of time with her and my dad. And you don't have to pay me."

Elodie ran over to us. "Belly, can you swing me now?"

"Yeah, sweetheart. Let's go."

She ran ahead of me and I looked back at Connor. "You *would* have to pay me to spend time with you, though."

He leaned back and put his sunglasses back on. "We'll just have to change your mind then, won't we?"

# Chapter 6

Over the next week, I hung out quite a bit with Dad and Elodie. She seemed a little happier and more settled, and she talked a lot about Connor and her Mémé. It was easy to tell she loved them both. She never mentioned her mother though.

"Mémé got broken, so I had to come live here," Elodie told me one day when we were feeding Shawnda.

"Oh? What got broken?"

She pushed her scraggly hair out of her eyes. "Her leg I think. My mom said she's old as dirt."

"Huh. I hope she gets better." Her mom didn't sound very nice.

"Me too. Mom can't take care of me without Mémé."

I stilled at her comment. Dad and I had both wondered about Elodie's mother.

She looked up at me. "My mom is broken too."

"I'm sorry, Ellie. What's wrong with her?"

"She's sad and mad all the time."

Kneeling down, I touched her shoulder. "I understand how you feel. My mom was broken too while I was growing up."

"Was she sad too?"

I pointed to my ribcage. "She was sick here, in her lungs. It was hard not being able to fix it."

She nodded, then gave me a big hug. "I'm sorry, Belly."

I hugged her back, holding her tight for a minute. "I'm sorry too, Ellie."

"Where's your mom now?" she asked innocently.

I tried to smile. "I like to think she's in heaven. She died a long time ago. I miss her, but I'm grateful I still have my dad and brother."

She patted my cheek. "And now you have me. And Daddy."

I didn't think having Connor was all that great, but I grinned at her enthusiasm. "That's right. I do have you."

This little girl was burrowing her way into my heart, and I had no defense against it.

The next afternoon, Dad and Elodie were making cookies together when I walked in. While we waited for them to bake, Dad reviewed the alphabet with her. He glanced at me while Elodie struggled to recognize the letters in her name.

"This is boring, Javy," she whined.

"That's too bad. I wanted to show you their magic."

Elodie perked up a little. "What magic?"

"The magic of letters that are made into words, then put into books."

She looked dubious. "I've never seen that magic."

"You can't see it, you have to read it, then picture it in your head. You've never been reading a book, and suddenly you're in a huge castle, going to school with other kids and learning magic together?"

Elodie shook her head. "No."

"You've never been transported to a beautiful, secret garden with your two best friends? Or walked through the back of your closet to find a whole other world?" he asked.

Elodie wiggled in her seat. "No, Javy. I can't read yet."

He stared down at her. "We need to work on that then, don't we? But first, you need to learn the alphabet, alright?"

She sighed a little. "Okay. Teach me."

I smiled, watching their two heads bent over the table as they carefully reviewed the alphabet. The smell of baking cookies wafted through the small house; Connor didn't know how lucky he was to have my dad watching over her.

Harley invited me to a party on Monday evening. I was happy to get the invitation since I didn't know many people in Palm Springs yet. She also told me the men who owned the security company Connor used would be there, and I was curious to meet them.

She'd called it a Martini Monday party. I thought it was odd to have a party on a Monday, but she explained it was an old tradition that had been started years ago in Palm Springs. The house where the party was located sat in a well-cared-for, iconic neighborhood called Deepwell Estates, not far from my little apartment.

A blooming bougainvillea hedge ran the length of the front yard, and tall palm trees and barrel cacti dotted the landscaping.

It was a charming house, and the surrounding neighborhood was full of well-kept, striking mid-century modern homes.

The front door of the home was painted a cheery yellow. I loved all the outrageous, bright-colored front doors that dotted the Palm Springs neighborhoods.

Damien greeted me. "Hey, Isabella. Nice to see you under friendlier circumstances."

"Thanks for inviting me. Dad gave me this as a housewarming and thank you gift." I held up a bottle of whiskey. "He told me Connor gave it to him along with his Christmas bonus. Dad's an occasional beer drinker, but that's about it."

"Hey, everyone. This is Isabella," Harley said, introducing me. She pointed to a stunning woman standing next to a hot but surly-looking man behind the kitchen bar. "That's Laurel. She owns the house and is hosting the party this week. And the grumpy butt standing next to her is Sebastian."

Lifting up the bottle of whiskey, I put it on the counter. "I appreciate the invitation. This is a small thank-you gift."

Sebastian glanced down at the bottle and did a doubletake. He picked it up and checked the label. "This is twenty-year-old single malt Canadian whiskey."

I shrugged. "To be honest, I'm regifting it. I have it on good authority it's okay to do that."

Harley laughed. "We regifted stale cookies. Twenty-year-old whiskey might be a little different."

Sebastian shook his head. "That's worth at least five hundred dollars."

"Huh. Who in their right mind would waste that much money on whiskey?"

A tall, middle-aged man with an aloha shirt perked up. "I would." He leaned over and held out his hand. "I'm Jonathan, and this is my husband, Ramone."

He pointed to a shorter, handsome man with nice tan skin and salt-and-pepper hair. "Hello, darling. We're Laurel's family."

I smiled at them. "Nice to meet you. Would you like to try some way over-priced twenty-year-old single whatever-he-called-it Canadian whiskey?"

Jonathan nodded enthusiastically. "It's single malt. And hell, yes."

Another tall, muscular man came in from the living room area. "What's this I hear about twenty-year-old whiskey?"

Harley pointed to him. "Isa, this is Zeke. He's our friend and Damien and Sebastian's business partner."

I looked up at him. "You're Zeke, the cynical bastard who doesn't trust just one system."

He looked down at me quizzically, then froze when I impulsively hugged him. Zeke held out his arms for a few seconds then awkwardly patted my back.

"You don't know me, but thank you." I stepped back. "And I'm sorry for mauling you."

He winked. "I don't know what the hell that was about, but I'll take a good mauling from a beautiful woman any day."

Damien pointed to me. "You gonna tell them the story, or should I?"

I turned to the kitchen bar. "You can tell it while we drink Connor McCoy's whiskey. Which is both ironic and highly fitting."

Harley chuckled. "Yeah, that is pretty ironic."

Everyone looked at us quizzically.

Sebastian picked up the bottle again. "Are you sure your dad is okay with us drinking his expensive-as-fuck whiskey?"

"Yeah. He doesn't like hard liquor, and I hear Connor is loaded." I looked at the bottle and sighed. "Dad probably knew you guys would be here. It's his way of saying thank you."

Laurel pulled out some whiskey tumblers, and Sebastian poured the whiskey.

Zeke leaned against the counter. "I'm curious. How is Connor McCoy, aka The Hammer, and one of the greatest fucking professional hockey forwards in decades, related to me being a cynical bastard and you having a five hundred dollar bottle of whiskey?"

Damien told everyone what happened the weekend Noah robbed Connor and tried to frame me. I took a sip of my whiskey and choked a little. It tasted like turpentine to me. I slid my glass over to Jonathan, who grinned and held up his glass in thanks.

Harley shook her head. "What an asshole. Noah was so self-righteous until Damien told Connor about the secondary cameras."

Damien grinned. "And then Noah looked like he was ready to shit a brick."

Just remembering that night made my stomach tighten.

Laurel slid a prickly pear martini over to me. "Try this. I think you'll like it better." She turned to the group. "I'm getting this third hand, but Connor's former assistant told my roommate, Martina, that Noah hit on her. And when she shot him down he got nasty and manhandled her."

"It doesn't surprise me." I looked at Damien. "He was the one who damaged Connor's front gate on Christmas Eve, wasn't he?"

Damien studied me. "Yeah. I got the impression you had a run-in with him too. What happened?"

"I actually had two run-ins with him."

I told them about Noah demanding my dad wash his car. And for some reason, I also told them about Noah grabbing me after my hike.

Zeke shook his head in disgust. "That fucker. What did Connor say when you told him?"

I shrugged. "I didn't tell him. Connor's not my favorite person either."

I was surprised when Sebastian answered. "Isabella, *eso es estupido.* You need to tell him. He can't help keep you safe if he doesn't know."

Everyone paused. I felt a pregnant weight in the air, and Laurel looked guilt-stricken.

Ramone broke the awkward silence. "Well, if I had to drink whiskey instead of martinis, this is a fabulous one."

Zeke studied me and took a sip. "It's fucking smooth. Mc-Coy does have great taste in whiskey."

A few days later, I spent New Year's Eve with the same group at a bar called The Cockpit in downtown Palm Springs. I let Dad know where I'd be, and pulled out the cute little black dress I'd bought a few years ago and kept for these types of occasions. I also spent some extra time on my hair and makeup.

The Cockpit was just off Palm Canyon Drive and Arenas Road, not far from my apartment. Laurel mentioned it was a gay bar their friends owned.

When I walked in, I spotted Laurel and Sebastian at a large table with several other people I recognized from the Martini Monday party.

"Hey, Isabella." Laurel hugged me and handed me a glass of champagne.

I sat down next to Jonathan and Ramone.

"Hello, darling. How are you settling in?" Ramone asked.

"Well, I haven't been accused of felony burglary this week, so I think it's going well."

Jonathan chuckled. "I'm glad you can joke about it. What're you doing here in Palm Springs?"

I told them about my dad working for Connor, and me doing the last of my clinical rotations here.

Ramone clapped his hands. "I've been wanting to go to a hockey game. All that testosterone and male aggression." He turned to Jonathan. "We should plan it."

Jonathan nodded and studied me. "Have things gotten any better with Connor?"

I shrugged. "No, but I like hanging out with his little girl."

Jonathan smiled. "You have a kind heart. You remind me of Laurel."

"That's probably the sweetest compliment I've gotten from someone who isn't legally obligated to be nice to me." I leaned in and kissed his cheek.

I saw Harley and Damien walk in. They looked like they'd just had fast, dirty sex in the parking lot. His shirt was untucked, her halter dress was tied crooked, and they both had messy hair. Well, I was happy someone got lucky on New Year's Eve.

Laurel had also introduced me to Sebastian's cousin, Martina, who lived with her at her house in the Deepwell Estates. The first thing Martina tried to do was talk me into going to karaoke night with her.

"It's the shit. Even if you don't sing," she coaxed.

"I don't want you to get your hopes up, so I'm just going to be honest. It's never going to happen."

She raised her champagne glass and grinned. "I love it when someone gives me a good challenge."

# Chapter 7

I went by the sports medicine clinic and met the staff and two doctors I'd be working with there. Dr. Rasmussen had a lean, muscular frame and black rim glasses that made me think of Austin Powers.

"Hey, Isabella. Call me Ben." He introduced me to the staff, and we went to Dr. Singhal's office. Ben rapped on the doorframe. "Sumit, our PA intern is here."

Dr. Sumit Singhal swiveled around in his chair and looked up at me with a wide smile. He had laugh lines around his eyes.

"Isabella Cruz. It's nice to meet you. Your former clinical placements gave you glowing reviews." He stood up and shook my hand. "And I think the hockey team will appreciate having you at the clinic."

Ben chuckled, then coughed in his fist. I looked over at him curiously.

We talked about what I'd be doing for them, and they discussed the hockey team's schedule.

"We're contracted to have a staff member or intern at the arena before and after practices," Dr. Singhal said. "You'll spend two days a week at the arena helping out and providing basic medical care after practice, then attending the at-home hockey games with Ben."

I nodded. "That sounds good. It'll be different from what I've done so far."

"If there's an injury during a game, we'd assess and treat it," Ben added. "I'll be there with you at the games, but usually not at the practices."

Dr. Singhal grinned and rubbed his hands together. "Some of the players are a bit cheeky but harmless. It'll be fun."

Ben stood up and pointed down the hall. "Come on, I'll finish showing you around."

That evening after I got home from the clinic, I went over to Dad's house for dinner. He and Elodie had made spaghetti together, and she planned to eat with us. Elodie wore purple and white striped leggings and a red print top. Her outfit clashed horribly and her hair was in a lopsided ponytail.

"Did your dad do your hair this morning?"

"Uh-huh. He said some bad words, but he did it."

I wished I could have seen that.

"How are the letters coming?" I asked while we set the table.

"Good. And do you know what? I can write a big E now."

"That's the first letter in your name. And I bet you can write the next two letters too because one is just a line and the next letter is a circle. That's half your name."

"Ooh. Let me see." She dropped the forks and ran over to the desk to pick up her notepad. She'd just sat at the table and was starting to write when the doorbell rang.

I glanced at my dad. He looked a little sheepish.

"Who's that?"

"I forgot to mention Connor's coming over for dinner too. Will you set an extra place?" He walked to the door.

Shaking my head, I set the extra place.

Elodie brought her paper over. "Like this?"

I sat down next to her. The E looked like a drunk person had written it, but the first three letters of her name were decipherable.

"Nice. Your hard work is paying off. You just spelled half your name."

I gave her a high five, then she threw her arms around me. I patted her back and looked up to see Connor studying us.

My smile dropped a little, but I beckoned him over. "Come look what Ellie did. And her hair looks nice, by the way."

He rolled his eyes, knowing I was being sarcastic.

He looked down at the paper. "Wow. You spelled half your name."

She grinned. "Javy showed me the big E."

Connor smiled, and I did a doubletake. The man did have a nice smile.

Dad started bringing food to the table, and I jumped up to help.

He pointed at Elodie. "She's been working hard on her letters this week. We want to make sure you're ready for school, right El?"

"Right." She sounded more confident today.

I watched Connor glance around my dad's house. There were potted herbs on the windowsill and a homemade apple tart on the counter.

He squeezed Elodie's shoulder and smiled at her again. The man needed to stop smiling like that.

I plunked the salad down on the table. "Okay, let's eat."

While we ate, Connor let Elodie know he'd finally signed her up for school.

"You start next week," he told her. "Are you excited?"

She nodded, but her eyes got wide and her feet started swinging.

I leaned back. "When I was around your age, we moved to a new place. I didn't know anyone, and I was pretty nervous the first day of school."

"Did you have any friends?" she asked.

"Nope. And I didn't make any friends at first. I was sad."

Her face fell. "Oh."

Connor scowled at me.

I ignored him. "But you know what I finally did?"

"What?" she asked.

"I went up and asked a few kids to be my friends. And I gave them each one of these."

Pulling out a small origami crane from my back pocket, I handed it to her. "My great grandma showed my mom how to make little animals and birds out of palm fronds. But we don't have palm trees in Seattle. So my mom taught us how to do it with paper. It's called origami when you use paper."

My brother had branched out even further into what I called "pornigami" and sometimes created little paper breasts, penises, or butts. Mom was not amused.

Elodie took the little orange paper crane out of my palm. "Ooh, that's so cute."

"It's a crane, and it symbolizes a few things, but also friendship."

"Did they like them?"

"Yes. And I still make them for a few of those friends, and send them on their birthday."

She set the crane down. "I don't know how to make these."

"Then I'll teach you. We can make some together, and we'll start with some simple animals."

"Were you scared?" She asked softly.

"Yeah, I was. But after I got my first friend I wasn't that scared anymore." I pushed the crane over to her.

"I guess I can do that."

Connor put his hand on her arm. "One thing did come up. You need a couple of immunization shots, El."

"Shots?" Elodie's voice rose.

"Isa likes to call them injections, not shots." Dad glanced at Connor meaningfully. "Maybe we can get Isa to give them to you."

I nodded. "I can do that."

"When do you start interning at the pediatric clinic?" Dad asked.

"Not until next week, but I'm sure they'll work with me." I turned to Connor. "Have you signed Elodie up with a pediatrician yet? The pediatric clinic where I'll be working is great. They aren't taking new clients right now, but I think I can get her in if you want."

Connor's eyes bounced between Dad and me. "What are you two talking about?"

Dad pointed at me. "She's finishing up her physician assistant master's program this winter. She'll be a full-fledged PA in April."

"How come I didn't know that?"

If Elodie hadn't been there, I would have told him because it was none of his business.

Instead, I shrugged. "I still need to pass the exam. Besides, when would I have told you? When you asked me how I got on your property the first time we met, or when you accused me of stealing from you?"

Connor narrowed his eyes, and Elodie froze in her seat. Damn it, I hadn't meant to say that in front of her.

Dad waved his hand. "We're moving past all that, remember? Isa, you told me the pass rate for the exam is above ninety-five percent. You'll be fine." He turned to Connor. "She's on the dean's list, and most of her clinical placements have offered her a job." His chest puffed out a little.

I swatted my dad's arm to get him to stop talking. "Okay, braggy parent. Enough."

Connor eyed me. "You weren't lying when you said you'd be busy."

"No, I wasn't."

"And you're going to be a PA." He leaned back. "How old are you?"

"Old enough," I retorted.

Dad took a sip of water. "She's twenty-three. She'll be twenty-four in March."

I pointed at him. "Hey, diarrhea of the mouth, he doesn't need to know everything."

Elodie wrinkled her nose. "Ew. Gross, Belly."

Connor chuckled. "Yeah, Belly. That's gross."

They both laughed. Connor's laugh was as nice as his smile. I really needed to stop noticing things like that. And stay the hell away from this man. He looked at me and cocked his eyebrow, like he knew exactly what I was thinking, and he was having none of it.

# Chapter 8

When Connor came by Dad's house to pick Elodie up a few days later, I met him at the door.

"We need to talk."

He leaned against the doorframe. "Okay. About what?"

"Elodie and her hair. She starts school next week, and she'll be the new kid."

He straightened and frowned. "I know."

"You let her pick out her own clothes."

"Yeah, and that's not going to change. It seems important to her."

I nodded and moved back so he could come in. "Good. I think it helps kids develop a healthy sense of self. But her hair needs some love."

"I thought about getting it cut," he admitted, following me into the kitchen.

"How'd she like that idea?"

"She didn't. She yelled at me for the first time."

I snickered. "I wish I would have been there." Rubbing the back of my neck, I looked away. "I can, uh, show you a few cute and easy hairstyles if you want."

His lip twitched. "It's hard for you to be nice to me, isn't it?"

I didn't even try to deny it. "Yep. You're like fingernails on the chalkboard of my soul. But she's worth it."

Connor grinned. "She is. She reminds me of you in some ways."

I didn't get a chance to ask him what he meant. Elodie skipped over and grabbed his hand.

"How're you doing, sweetheart?" he asked her.

"Great! Shawnda only scratched me once."

He looked down at a small scratch on her arm. "I guess that's good?"

"Uh-huh. And I learned some paper folding stuff."

"Origami?" Connor asked.

"Yeah, for my new friends. And do you know what?"

"No, what?" he asked.

"We got some hair stuff." She deflated a little. "But I don't know how to use it."

"Neither do I, but Bella's going to help us. She said she'd give me some lessons."

My eyebrow rose. "Bella?"

He studied my raised eyebrow. "Yes. Definitely."

Elodie grabbed both our hands. "Yay! And we can have lunch together too."

I'd kind of walked into that one, so I forced a smile. "Sure. Hairstyles and lunch. I can hardly wait."

"When?" she asked.

"When?" I echoed.

"Yeah, when?"

Dad piped up from the kitchen. "Why not now?"

I loved that man. It was too bad I was going to have to kill him.

Elodie smiled. "Okay! And you guys can eat dinner with us too."

Dad gave her a thumbs up. "Sounds good to me. It'll be hairstyles and dinner instead of lunch."

"I've got chicken we could grill," Connor added. "Javier, come over when you get back. We'll be at my place."

I wanted to make an excuse and run. The thought of hanging out with Connor and eating dinner with them at his house made me nervous and twitchy. But Elodie looked at me expectantly, so I plastered on a big, fake smile.

"Okay. Let's go teach your dad a few hair things."

The first lesson was interesting. Connor watched me pull out bobby pins, hairbands, ribbons, and a few other items. But his brow furrowed when he saw the small spray bottle and hair gel.

"She also needs a good shampoo, hair conditioner, and hair product."

His eyebrow twitched. "What kind of hair product?"

It was annoying the man had such great hair, but didn't seem to know a thing about hair products. "Detangler, maybe a leave-in conditioner. We can look online, and I'll show you."

After trying to teach him how to braid hair, I quickly realized he knew how to brush Elodie's hair, and that was about it.

"All right. Let's start at the beginning. We're going to do ponytails today."

An hour later, I'd covered basic hair care and Connor could do a decent ponytail. Both Elodie and I were ready to quit, but he wanted to keep going.

We'd set up our workstation in Elodie's bathroom.

I stepped back and studied his work. "Not half bad."

Elodie patted his leg. "I like ponytails, Daddy."

"Thanks, sweetheart." He looked at me in the mirror. "You have your work cut out for you. It's harder than it looks."

His frank admission thawed my annoyance a little. He hadn't gotten frustrated, and we'd even joked about some of his failed attempts. His large hands and battered fingers looked so out of place doing Elodie's hair. It was a compelling sight.

"*Is* it harder than it looks?" I joked. Then my eyes widened. "I can't believe I just said that. I'm sorry."

He grinned wickedly. "I'm not."

Looking down at Elodie, I tried to change the subject. "I can, uh, teach you how to do a fast messy bun since you've mastered the ponytail. Then you'll know two hairstyles."

Grabbing Elodie's long ponytail, I started twisting it. "It's three easy steps. You twist, bend, then stick."

After twisting her hair, I bent it around her ponytail, then stuck a few bobby pins in to keep it secure. I fluffed it a little and stepped back.

"See?" Quickly pulling the pins back out, I untwisted her hair. "Now you try. Twist, bend, and stick."

His mouth twitched. "Twist, bend, and stick, huh? I've got a great mental image to help me remember."

My lip twitched, and I shook my head. "Oh, God. I walked right into that one."

He studied me, and his gaze drifted down to my mouth. He finally turned to Elodie, gathered up her ponytail, and started twisting.

"Twist, bend, then stick." I could hear the grin in his voice.

Elodie hummed and played with the little paper flower I'd given her. When he finished, she decided she'd had enough and went out to the kitchen to find a snack.

Connor leaned against the counter, watching me straighten up nervously.

"I also like to twist, bend, and tie sometimes. Or twist, bend, and tease."

My eyelids lowered, and my breath sped up. "You need to stop." Heat spread across my chest and face.

His pupils dilated and he looked down at my lips. "For now."

We'd somehow turned Elodie's hair tutorial into foreplay, and the man hadn't touched me. Later that night I was so restless, I used the showerhead on myself. It barely took the edge off. Connor was way out of my comfort zone, but he now starred in my shower and vibrator fantasies.

He maneuvered me into giving him another hair lesson not long after I promised myself I'd stay away from him. We went over braids and ribbons.

I held Elodie's ponytail in three separate strands. "You place one strand over the other, rotating evenly as you go." Going slowly, I showed him how to braid.

He looked down at me. "Put your hands on mine and guide me through it."

Swallowing, I nodded. It wasn't a bad idea, except he had to plaster himself behind me. His large muscular body dwarfed mine, and his heat and scent surrounded me. My breathing and heart rate sped up.

"Okay, I think you have it." I stepped away a few moments later and handed Connor an elastic and one of the ribbons.

He finished the braid, and Elodie ran out of the bathroom to get something from her room.

Connor picked up a long ribbon. "I need a little more practice. Put your hands together."

When I held up my hands, he silently and expertly tied my wrists.

"I'm not sure what this style is," I murmured.

He studied me carefully. My pulse pounded in my throat and my lips parted as I struggled to process the lust tightening my core.

"That style is my favorite one." He leaned in and slowly unwound the ribbon.

A few days later, Connor and Elodie knocked on my apartment door. When I let them in, Connor stepped inside, looked around, and frowned.

Elodie ran over and grabbed my hand. "Daddy did my hair." She patted one of her side buns. "Are you going to eat lunch with us today?"

Smiling, I patted her hair too. "Your buns look awesome. And I haven't planned that far ahead. I just got done with breakfast."

Connor watched us, then glanced around again. "This place is depressing."

Elodie looked up at me. "You could move in with us 'cause we have lots of rooms. Or you could stay in Daddy's room."

Connor's mouth twitched. "That's not a bad idea, El."

It would've been funny if the thought hadn't sent my blood pressure skyrocketing. I knew my apartment wasn't great, but I'd tried to make it a little cheerier with second-hand throw pillows and a bright rug. But the rug contrasted depressingly against the dingy linoleum.

I looked down at her and tried to smile. "Thanks for the offer, and that's so nice. But I need a place of my own." I glared at Connor. "And the first time I was inside *your* house, I thought it was depressing too."

"What does depressing mean?" Elodie asked.

"It means sad or gloomy. That kind of thing."

"Why do you think our house is sad?"

I might have hurt her feelings, so I squatted down. "I'm sorry. Your house is wonderful, especially now that you live in it. But the first time I was there..."

I gazed up at Connor helplessly, not knowing how to explain.

He studied me somberly. "Noah was there, El, and he wasn't very nice. Neither was I."

"Ooh. Noah is mean to me too." She patted my cheek in sympathy.

Connor rubbed the back of his neck. "Okay, let's go get your injections and then take Bella to lunch to say thank you."

I hadn't agreed to lunch, but I didn't want to hurt Elodie's feelings twice in one day, so I nodded.

I found myself riding shotgun next to Connor in his Range Rover with Elodie chattering away from her booster seat in the back. I turned around and studied her hair again. Her braids were twisted up in buns on the sides of her head, and she looked like Princess Leia. It was even more adorable because Connor had done it. I was so weak.

When we got to the clinic, Connor filled out the paperwork to get her signed up. I'd set up the appointment earlier, and they were more than happy for me to give her the shots. One of the assistants took us back to an examination room and brought the vaccines in. I washed my hands, put on rubber gloves, then pulled up Elodie's sleeve and swiped her arm with an alcohol swab.

"Where's your favorite lunch place around here? You'll feel a little pinch." I gave her the first shot.

She scrunched up her nose but didn't complain. "Maybe Mc-Donald's?"

"McDonald's? Don't get me wrong, I like their strawberry shakes. But we can do better than that."

I glanced at Connor as I swabbed her other arm. He leaned against the wall and watched us.

"What do you think?" Elodie asked me.

"Hmm. We could go to Cheeky's or Tyler's Burgers. Those are the only places I know. You'll feel another pinch."

I gave her the second shot, put a bandage on it, and then rubbed her little arm. The second vaccine was a little more painful.

"Owie," she whimpered.

"Sorry. That last one stings a little, but you were a superstar."

Connor walked over and kissed the top of her head. "You were great, sweetheart. What do you guys think about going to the arena for a bit, then Cheeky's?"

Elodie perked up. "Can I see Jack?"

"I don't know. We'll see if he's there." He looked over at me. "Should I drop you off at your depressing apartment, or do you want to come?"

I rolled my eyes but grinned a little. "I'll come."

As Connor drove, I turned to him. "I've never been to the arena before. It'll be nice to check it out before I start my hours there."

His brow furrowed. "What hours? I thought you were working at the pediatric office."

"I'm doing the other part of my rotation with the sports medicine clinic that provides medical care to the team."

Connor's jaw clenched and he sat up straighter but didn't say anything.

"What's wrong?"

He glanced at the rearview mirror to see if Elodie was paying attention. She stared out the window humming.

"You know I used to be a professional hockey player."

"I do now. I had to google you when my dad told me he'd be working for you." I turned to him. "Most of the online photos are of you with women. Lots and lots of women. You don't really have a type, do you?"

He shifted in his seat. "I was young and stupid. You had to google me? Don't you like hockey?"

"Until recently, Seattle didn't have a professional hockey team. I like hockey more now."

"Vancouver isn't that far from Seattle."

I knew the team he used to play for was in Vancouver. "Huh. Thanks for the geography lesson."

He shook his head. "So you're a sports fan if the team is in Seattle."

"Absolutely. A friend of ours used to give us tickets sometimes, and we got hooked."

"Paul Curtis?"

I turned to him, surprised. "How did you know?"

"I did a background check on your dad before I asked him to be Elodie's nanny, and there's a glowing reference in his employment file from Curtis."

I couldn't be annoyed since I would have done the same thing. "That was smart."

He glanced at me. "You weren't exaggerating. Your dad has been fucking fantastic so far."

"I know. Elodie was smart to ask for him."

"You owe me five bucks," Elodie said absently from the back seat. "And Mémé says fuck is a bad word."

"Damn it," Connor muttered. "You shouldn't say fuck, Els."

"That's two more bucks," she chirped.

"You need to stop dropping the f-bomb in front of her. Can I play this game?" I asked.

Elodie's ability to keep track of the cost of each swear word was impressive.

Connor shook his head. "Absolutely not. She's killing me. She could probably pay for her own college education by now."

"That bad, huh?" I turned around and gave Elodie a thumbs up. She smiled happily.

Connor rolled his shoulders. "As I was saying. Hockey players aren't known for clean language and wholesome living. You sure you want to work there?"

"You're not my dad, although you might be old enough. It'll be fine."

"I'm not old enough to be your fucking dad." He sounded annoyed.

"Another five bucks," Elodie giggled.

"Shit," Connor mumbled.

I smiled. "You might want to be quiet for a while."

He slid me a frustrated look but kept his mouth shut.

The arena was bigger than I expected for a feeder team, and the new facilities were state-of-the-art. When Connor gave me a tour, I found out he had an office at the arena where he worked as the temporary CEO, until he and his partners found a permanent one.

When we got to the floor of the arena, I spun slowly around taking in the entire area. "How many seats are there?"

He watched me. "It can only hold a little over eleven thousand fans, so it's not that big."

Somehow I'd forgotten he was one of the owners. Elodie started climbing up the stairs, counting the steps.

"Do you miss playing?"

He looked up at the scoreboard. "Yeah, but it was time."

"What do you miss the most?"

"Doing something I was fucking great at and I loved doing. And my teammates."

I started feeling a little sorry for him.

Then Connor smirked. "Also the money and women."

My sympathy died a quick death. "You're a walking cliché."

"I'm teasing. I wanted to see that annoyed, self-righteous look on your face again."

"You're an ass sometimes, you know that right? How many years did you play?"

"I was eighteen when I got drafted. Before that, I played in a junior hockey league in Canada. Most players do. I've played pretty much my whole life."

"Why'd you quit?"

"Injuries." He gazed at me. " And Elodie."

"There are a lot of professional athletes who have kids."

"True. But her mother isn't capable of taking care of her."

My heart lurched a little. "Elodie told me her mom is broken." I held up my hand before he could speak. "I didn't ask her any questions. She said Mémé has a broken leg and is old as dirt, and her mom is sad and mad. That's it."

Connor's lips curved, but his eyes looked bleak. "Her Mémé is her great-grandmother. And she has a broken hip. She's also the only reason Elodie isn't fucked up."

I touched his arm. "I'm asking in case there's something my dad and I need to know."

He ran his hand through his hair. "Her mother's name is Amelia. She's also from Vancouver, and we grew up in the same neighborhood."

Elodie started up the next set of stairs, still counting out loud. I noticed she got to fourteen and started over again. We'd have to work on that.

I glanced at Connor. "How is Amelia broken?"

"She has severe clinical depression, she's bipolar, but the worst of all is she's just plain cruel. Something's broken inside, and she doesn't seem to have a mothering instinct."

"I'm sorry. For Elodie and you." I watched Elodie jump up to the next step and sadness washed through me.

I pointed at her. "Does she know?"

He shook his head.

Someone yelled from the locker room entrance. "Did you bring Els with you?"

Connor turned and smiled at the younger man walking toward us. "That's Jackson, my cousin." He raised his voice. "She's hopping up the steps."

He looked a lot like Connor, with the same lop-sided grin and tall, muscular build. He was probably around my age somewhere, in his early twenties.

"Jack!" Elodie squealed.

She started hopping down the stairs toward him.

"Slow down," Connor called.

We all started moving toward her, but Jackson flew. He took the stairs two at a time and swept her up before she lost her footing. She hugged him and laughed like it had been a game, then kissed both his cheeks.

"Hey, honey bear. You need to slow down."

She smiled and patted his face. "Okay. Jack, I'm starting school on Monday. I'm only a little scared. But guess what?"

"What?" he asked as he set her down.

"Daddy is learning to do my hair."

He looked at her buns and grinned. "Did he do your hair today?"

"Yes, and he only said one bad word."

"That's pretty good for him."

She nodded and pointed at me. "And Belly and Javy have a cat with one eye."

Jackson studied me, and a killer smile spread across his face. Yep, definitely related to Connor. "A pirate cat, huh? Are you Javy or Belly?"

"I'm Belly." I smiled. "Also Bella."

Connor turned to Jackson. "Bella is mine. You can call her Isabella or Isa."

My mouth fell open and I stared at Connor. Why did he keep saying things like that?

Jackson grinned. "How do you know these two?"

"My dad works for Connor."

"Do you live around here?" Jackson asked.

"Yes. And I'm going to be helping Dr. Rasmussen and Dr. Singhal with the team."

He cocked his head. "Doing what?"

"Mandatory rectal temperature checks and colonoscopies."

Jackson's head jerked. Then he started laughing. "A few of the players will be lining up if you're the one administering them."

"Just kidding. I'll be doing whatever a physician assistant intern does. I'm here Mondays and Tuesdays, and the home games."

He turned to Connor and jerked his thumb at me. "The players are gonna love her."

Connor wiped his hand down his face. "That's what I'm fucking afraid of."

"You're the second person who's said that," I grumbled.

"That's another five bucks!" Elodie patted Connor's leg and turned to Jackson. "He's said lots of bad words today. I'm rich!"

Jackson laughed. "I bet he has, El. Women will do that to a guy sometimes." He grinned. "The season just got a lot more interesting."

# Chapter 9

The first week of clinical rotations took some adjustment. I'd never done more than one rotation at a time, but I was able to schedule my hours on Mondays and Tuesdays at the arena, and Wednesdays and Thursdays at the pediatric clinic.

On my first day, I met Dr. Ben in the medical room so he could show me the ropes.

I wore my trusty black spandex stretch pants that looked dressy but were super comfortable, and a light blue sweater. Over that, I had on my white PA jacket.

Ben leaned against the counter. "Let me show you around, and then I'll introduce you when the players come in from practice."

We took a tour of the facilities and discussed what I'd generally be doing every day. He also explained common injuries that occurred in hockey players.

Ben pointed to his forehead. "Head injuries are the most concerning. I think complex shoulder injuries from body checking might be next, then hip and knee injuries."

Just then, the physical therapist walked in. She was a husky woman who reminded me of my middle school gym teacher. She had short, cropped hair and wore khaki pants with a white polo shirt sporting the team logo.

She smiled. "Hey Ben, this your new intern?"

"Hi, Phyllis. Yeah, this is Isabella Cruz." He turned to me. "Isabella, this is Phyllis Padfield, the trainer."

I smiled and shook her outstretched hand. "Nice to meet you."

"Call me Phil."

We talked with her for a few minutes, then went to the team locker room where Ben introduced me to the players and coaches. A few team members were changing, and several looked at me curiously. I felt like I was swimming in testosterone.

"Hey everyone," Ben said in a loud voice.

They eventually quieted down and turned our way. Coach Bailey, a fit middle-aged man with sunken eyes and a stern face, walked over and stood next to me with his arms crossed. He didn't look happy.

Ben pointed to me. "This is Isabella Cruz. She's working as a physician assistant intern with us in the medical office for the next three months. Isabella, introduce yourself."

I always hated this part, and it was even harder with so many muscular, athletic, half dressed guys staring at me. I straightened my shoulders and stepped forward.

"Nice to meet you all. I'll be in the medical office before and after practice on Mondays and Tuesdays if you have injuries or health-related questions. If it's outside my purview, I'll let you know and consult with Dr. Rasmussen or Dr. Singhal. Please call me Isabella."

Coach Bailey stepped forward. "No, they won't."

He was going to make it awkward, damn it. I glanced at him with a small, fake smile.

"They can also call me Isa if Isabella is too hard."

He raised an eyebrow and pursed his lips. "They'll call you Ms. Cruz."

I faced him. "Coach Bailey, I'd prefer Isabella."

He folded his arms and glared down at me. "We all need to keep it professional."

I wanted to roll my eyes, but I didn't. "The players are professional athletes, and I know we'll all behave... professionally."

Okay, that was dumb. But I was flustered and mad. Someone snorted, and a few of the players snickered or nudged each other. Ben watched us carefully. I didn't want him to intervene, and I didn't want the team's first impression of me to be arguing with their stupid, sexist coach.

"Half of them aren't even twenty-one yet, Ms. Cruz." Coach Bailey started turning away.

I glanced over my shoulder. "Ben, what do they call you?"

"Ben. And sometimes Doc."

I turned to Phyllis. "And what do they call you?"

She pursed her lips as if trying not to smile. "Nurse Ratchet behind my back." Several players laughed. She shrugged and glanced at Coach Bailey. "Or Phil."

I turned back to Coach Bailey and raised my eyebrow.

He sighed and held up his hands. "Fine. It's not worth arguing over. But if you have any problems, I want to know about it."

Nodding slightly, I stepped back. My first introduction to the team couldn't have gone much worse.

Ben stepped forward again. "We need to get your annual concussion tests completed. Please sign up so we don't have to hunt you down. That's it from us."

A few of the players groaned, but most just nodded, and they got back to getting showered and dressed.

Jackson came over and patted my shoulder. "Hey, Belly. Don't take it personally. Coach Bailey is an ass sometimes. How're your dad and Elodie getting along?"

I smiled, happy to see a familiar face. "They're great. It's like they've known each other forever. Elodie's learning her letters and numbers right now."

Jackson had gone to lunch with us after my tour of the arena with Connor, and he'd talked and joked around with Elodie and me while Connor mostly sat back and watched us.

Several players came up and introduced themselves after Jackson broke the ice. A tall, redhead with a boyish face pushed his way through and grabbed my hand.

"I'm Rudy Robard. I play right defense." He shook my hand vigorously. "So is it against any rules to date one of us?"

I grinned, thinking he was joking. He looked at me expectantly, and I realized he was serious.

"Oh. I'm sorry, Rudy. I don't think that's a good idea, especially after Coach Bailey doesn't even want you guys to call me by my first name. But thanks though." I slowly pulled my hand out of his grip.

Another player with great facial hair and tattoos wrapping around both biceps smacked Rudy on the shoulder. "Real smooth, Rudster."

The guy turned to me and smiled. He was a little older than Rudy, and kind of slick. He stood a little too close, and I stepped back.

"Isa," he drawled out. "I'm Wyatt. And it's too damn bad you don't think it'd be a good idea to hook up with one of us. I'll have to change your mind." He grabbed my hand and shook it, then rubbed my knuckles with his thumb.

I stared at him, wondering what the hell was going on. Luckily Ben and Coach Bailey were talking with a player in an arm sling on the other side of the room.

Jackson put his hands on his hips. "Fuck off, Wyatt. McCoy wouldn't be happy."

I turned to Jackson with wide eyes.

Wyatt squeezed my hand almost too hard, then he let it go. "McCoy, huh? How do you know him?"

I noticed the players around us had gone still at the mention of Connor's name.

"My dad works for him. And since his daughter came to live with Connor, Dad helps take care of her."

Wyatt grinned and rocked on his heels. "Good to know. Welcome to the team, Isa."

When he stepped back, a few other players introduced themselves and welcomed me. Luckily, everyone else seemed fairly normal. I finally slipped away and walked over to Ben and Coach Bailey, who were listening to Phyllis talk with the injured player.

Coach Bailey turned to me and scowled. "I don't appreciate being contradicted in front of my players, Ms. Cruz."

Ben stilled next to me, and my heart sped up.

"I meant no disrespect."

He pointed at my chest. "Don't do it again."

He was starting to prick my temper, and my face got hot. "I can't guarantee anything, but I'll try. And call me Isabella."

Coach Bailey's eyebrows rose. Ben folded his arms and looked down at his feet, and I thought I heard Phyllis chuckle, but I couldn't be sure.

"Coach, Butler has a question for you," Phyllis broke in.

Coach Bailey turned away, and I decided to go back to the medical office so I wouldn't cause any more trouble. I took off down the hall, feeling a little sick to my stomach.

I'd never had a confrontation during any of my clinical rotations before. A few staff here and there had been dismissive or impatient, but that wasn't out of the ordinary.

When I got to the medical office and flipped on the light, I pulled up short. One of the players was sitting in an ice bath with his eyes closed and his head laid back on the edge.

"I didn't know anyone was in here. Do you want me to turn off the light and leave you in peace, or can I quietly fume while you soak?"

The player seemed huge, even sitting in the metal tub. I could also see an intricate tattoo on his shoulder, and his messy thick blond hair looked like he combed it once a week at the most.

"Don't care," he grunted.

"Okay. Lights on or off?"

"Still don't care." There was a hint of Canadian French in his deep voice.

"On might be better, after what Coach Bailey just insinuated to the team," I muttered under my breath.

The player raised his head up, and I noticed he was older than the other guys on the team. Maybe even in his mid-thirties. He also looked annoyed.

I held up my hand. "Cold water immersion sucks enough without listening to someone complain. I'll be quiet."

Walking over to the counter, I picked up the clipboard with Ben's notes regarding the concussion assessments and a few ongoing injuries we needed to watch.

I got lost in the charts until I heard the player rise out of the bath. I glanced over and noticed he had on compression shorts, thank God. Although the shorts were tight and didn't hide much. He seemed to be looking around for a towel.

A stack of towels sat on the counter next to me, and I grabbed a couple. "Here, catch."

His head came up as I tossed the towels, and he caught them both in one hand.

He grunted. "Thanks."

I nodded absently and went back to the clipboard. Out of my peripheral vision, I saw him methodically strip off his shorts and pat himself dry. He threw a towel on the puddle of water he'd made on the floor and wrapped the second one around his waist.

When his towel was securely wrapped, I looked up and met his stare.

"I'm Isabella Cruz. I'll be with Dr. Rasmussen and Dr. Singhal working as a physician assistant intern for the next three months. Call me Isa."

He rolled his shoulders. "Titus." His voice was low and gravelly.

I pointed to his right kneecap. "MCL injury?"

He nodded shortly.

I pointed to another scar on his left shoulder. "AC separation?"

He nodded again. There were other scars on his face and body, and probably a few in the back I couldn't see.

"Huh. Can I quiz you about your injuries and recovery methods sometime?"

His eyes narrowed. "Why?"

Titus was as tall as Connor, and he had a lot of muscle. He also exuded a "fuck off" vibe. But as an experienced athlete, he'd probably have some good insights.

"I'm going to be a PA, but I'm young and don't have a lot of experience yet. I'd like to work on that."

He studied me and folded his arms. I noticed he had a few scars on his knuckles as well.

I pointed to the scars. "I don't know the hockey injury that would cause those."

His fingers flexed. "They're not from hockey."

"Aw."

He lifted his chin toward the locker room. "What did Coach Bailey do?"

I winced and scratched the back of my neck. "When I introduced myself to the team and told everyone to call me Isabella, he stepped in and told them they had to call me Ms. Cruz, and then insinuated I was going to be a problem."

"Huh. What'd you do?"

"I told the team they could call me Isa if Isabella was too difficult."

His lip twitched. "And that pissed him off."

"Yeah. The team calls everyone else on the staff by their first name except him. He made it weird because I'm a female under forty."

He started gathering up his sweats. "So what did the players call you?"

I smiled. "Isabella, and that Wyatt guy went with Isa."

"Watch out for Wyatt."

I nodded. "I figured. He gives off asshole vibes."

His lip quirked. "I'll talk to you."

"Great."

He picked the towel up off the floor and tossed it in the hamper, then walked out.

I watched him leave and noticed a long thick scar along his lower spine. I'd have to ask him about that injury as well.

# Chapter 10

Over the next couple of weeks, I settled in. The pediatric clinic was similar to other doctor offices, only the patients were younger and funnier. There were a couple of chronically ill patients I saw regularly, and I started dropping in to visit them at the hospital next to the clinic a couple of times a week.

The sports medicine clinic was different from anything I'd done, but I liked it. Most of the players quickly got used to having me in the medical office, and I'd already treated several of them for strained muscles, foot fungus, and one broken pinkie finger.

But Wyatt still came in regularly and hit on me. That Monday, Titus had just gotten into his ice bath when Wyatt walked in and leaned against the counter.

I sighed. "Hello, Wyatt. Do you have a medical issue?"

"Hey, sweetheart. How're you doing?"

I cringed. "Sweetheart? My name is Isabella."

He grinned. "Are you still set against hooking up with a player?"

"Wyatt, do you have a medical issue?"

He straightened up. "Well, darling, I've got this ache in my dick here–"

Titus growled from the ice tub. "Tell me you did not just fucking say that to her."

Wyatt's head jerked to the corner where Titus sat with his eyes closed, submerged up to his shoulders in the tub.

Wyatt folded his arms. "Hey, man. I didn't know you were here."

Titus opened an eye and looked at him. "If you don't need medical treatment then get the fuck out."

Wyatt was either stupid or crazy. Probably both. "You marking her, Tremblay?"

From the team roster, I knew Tremblay was Titus's last name.

Titus sighed, sat up, and opened both eyes. "You make it sound like I'm a dog who's going to piss on her leg."

Wyatt straightened. "You know what I mean."

Setting my laptop on the counter, I folded my arms. "Wyatt, quit being stupid. I'm not interested, and this is my livelihood you're messing with."

He reared back. "You've been flirting with me since you got here. I'm getting mixed signals."

"You're joking me, right? I've told you exactly four times since my first day I won't get involved with any players. And this is the second time I've asked you not to use a term of endearment."

Titus stood up, water cascading down his chest. I had to admit, his body was hard and muscular, and his scars only added to the package. But I considered Titus my friend, and I didn't think we saw each other that way.

Grabbing two towels off the counter, I threw them at Titus, who caught them easily and started drying his chest off. Wyatt watched us with narrowed eyes.

I tried again. "You need to take a hint. You wouldn't be such a bad guy if you weren't so... smarmy sometimes."

Titus chuckled, and it sounded rusty. "Smarmy. That's the perfect fucking word."

Wyatt glared at Titus. "I've heard you called worse than that."

Titus shrugged, completely unaffected. "She's not mine to piss on, but I'd watch yourself if I were you."

"Really? Why's that?" Wyatt asked.

"McCoy would rip your fucking head off if he knew you were saying shit like that to her. It's not my career though."

Wyatt straightened. "I know about McCoy. And you. You're both messed up, deviant fuckers."

I'd had enough. "Oh for the love of–I'm not a fire hydrant, for God's sake. No one's going to piss on me. Or mark me. And we're all messed up in some way." I picked up my laptop. "Now, do you have a medical issue I can help you with? If not, I'm sure you're busy." I couldn't tell him to get the fuck out like Titus had done. But I wanted to.

Titus stripped off his compression shorts. Then he threw the wet towel in the hamper while I carefully studied my laptop.

Wyatt watched us for a few seconds. "Isa, you need to watch yourself with these two. And McCoy's nickname, The Hammer? It isn't just from hockey." He turned and strode out.

If Wyatt thought his warning was going to scare me off, he didn't know me very well. I tried not to think about why Connor's nickname was The Hammer off the ice too, and looked back down at my laptop.

Titus shook his head and gathered up his clothes. "He's young and stupid. I hope he grows out of it."

"Me too." I set my laptop down again. "Why did you bring Connor up? We're not even friends."

Titus studied me. "Jackson told me what happened with Noah. He also said he's seen you and McCoy together. You're not stupid."

I blushed and carefully sat my laptop down. "When I first met him, I thought he was an egotistical, self-centered prick."

He lifted his eyebrow. "I think most professional athletes are self-centered pricks."

"What did he mean about Connor's nickname?" I blushed, but I was curious enough to ask.

"You'll have to ask McCoy about that one, *choux*. And for all his faults, Connor's not a bad guy." Titus grimaced, clearly not happy admitting that.

Folding my arms, I leaned against the counter. "I loathed Connor after what happened with Noah, until I saw him with Elodie. He's out of his comfort zone with her, but he tries hard. Don't get me wrong, I still don't like him."

Titus chuckled. "Are you trying to convince me or yourself?"

"What did Wyatt mean about you and Connor being deviant fuckers?" I tried again.

"Again, you need to ask Connor. And you're right, he does love his little girl. We've both had shit luck with our baby mommas. Although his situation is worse than mine."

My eyebrows rose. "You have a child?"

"Yeah. A little boy." He grinned, but there were shadows in his eyes.

"I just envisioned a miniature Titus growling at everyone, with spiky hair, and a big hockey stick tattoo on his little chest. And still in diapers. Is he like you? Do you see him sometimes?"

"He doesn't have any tattoos since he's only eighteen months old, for fuck's sake. But I fly back to Vancouver at least once a month to see him."

"What's his name?"

Titus's face went a little soft. I didn't even think that was possible. "Max. His name is Max."

"What's his mother's name?"

Titus shook his head. "Back to you and McCoy."

I grimaced. "I like talking about your life more."

"Too bad. Connor's parents are dead, and his little brother is the only immediate family he has left. But Noah has always been a rotten little fucker."

"Connor condoned Noah's behavior, and they both treated my dad like crap." I looked away so he wouldn't see the hurt in my eyes. "Nothing is going on with Connor and me, and there never will be."

He grabbed his bag. "You should never say never, *petite choux*. See you tomorrow."

# Chapter 11

B y the end of the first month, I was extremely disappointed to realize I liked Connor. A lot. We spent most evenings at my dad's house, and we often ate dinner or played games together. Having my dad and Elodie there provided a buffer for me to get to know Connor a little better without having to be alone with him.

He was funny, and self-depreciating at times. He also loved Elodie. And the man was testosterone-laden sex on a stick. We'd done a few more hair lessons. He mostly behaved, but sometimes he brushed by me, grasped my hips, or leaned in and subtly smelled my hair while we worked.

When I went home after those sessions, I was always frustrated and aroused. And he still starred in most of my showerhead fantasies.

We played Princess Yahtzee with Elodie one Friday night. "Who's your favorite princess?" I asked as I picked up the dice.

She scrunched her nose. "Maybe Mulan? Or Moana?"

"Ooh, good choices. I love them both."

Elodie patted Connor's arm. "Who do you like?"

He thought for a minute. "The octopus lady in the mermaid movie?"

Dad and I started laughing.

"She's not a princess, Daddy. She's bad!" Elodie squealed.

Connor grinned and glanced at me. "I like the difficult ones. What can I say?"

I rolled my eyes. "Ellie, you'll have to watch *all* the princess movies with your dad so he can pick a favorite."

"Okay, we can start tomorrow."

Connor winced. "I appreciate you suggesting that."

"You're welcome."

Elodie looked at me hopefully. "We're going swimming tomorrow. Do you guys wanna come?"

Dad shook his head. "I'm going golfing tomorrow, but Isa might go with you. She's sleeping over this weekend and she doesn't have anything else to do."

I squinted at him then turned to Elodie. "I didn't bring my swimsuit. Sorry."

Connor eyed me speculatively. "I have some extra ones in the pool house."

"I'm sure you and Elodie don't want me to intrude on your weekend time."

Elodie nodded vigorously. "Yes we do, don't we?"

"Yep. We do," Connor agreed.

"Come with us, Belly."

Damn it, I couldn't say no to her when she looked at me with those big, brown eyes. "Okay. Thanks for inviting me."

She flashed me a smile. "Will you eat lunch with us too?"

For some reason, she was always inviting me to eat lunch. I glanced at Connor.

He grinned, picking up on my discomfort. "Yes, come eat lunch."

So a little after twelve the next afternoon, I knocked on Connor's front door with a container of lemon cookies my dad had made that morning. There were several citrus trees on the property, and Dad enjoyed harvesting the fruit. The house smelled like lemon and vanilla when I'd gotten up that morning.

Elodie answered the door wearing a little red polka dot swimsuit, blue arm floaties, and oversized swim goggles. Her goggles slid down her face as she grinned up at me.

I tried not to laugh. "Cute swimsuit. Dad sent over some lemon cookies, and he reminded me to make sure you put on sunscreen."

I held up the container as she grabbed my other hand and walked me into the oversized living room. Connor came in from the kitchen. He had on black swim trunks but no shirt. His upper body was sculpted and toned, and he had a few nicks and scars.

He also had a detailed, black and red tattoo across his left pectoral of a skull with red maple leaves as eyes, and crossed hockey sticks behind it. Elodie's name had been added under his left pec. It was a stunning tattoo, and his chest was hard and chiseled. I swallowed and tried to keep my eyes on his face, and failed.

"Hey." He grinned at me as he watched me study his tattoo. Then he looked down at my legs.

I'd thrown on some white shorts and a red pullover. His gaze seemed to heat my skin.

He pointed to us. "You two match."

Elodie looked us over. "We do!" Will you take our picture?"

She was only five, and already wanted photos of everything. I could only imagine what she'd be like as a teenager and she discovered social media.

Connor smiled. "Sure. Stand next to each other over there." He pointed to the bank of windows behind us and took out his phone.

Elodie grabbed my hand and pulled me over. I felt awkward, but let her drag me to stand in front of one of the large windows. There were flowerpots and palm trees behind us. It did make a nice backdrop.

Connor looked at us, then walked over and peeled off my backpack, and took the food container out of my hand. Ellie wrapped her arm around my waist.

I looked down and smoothed her hair back. "Do you want to put your goggles back on for the picture?"

She grinned. "They won't stay on my eyeballs."

Connor cleared his throat. "Okay, look at me." We turned to him and he snapped a few pictures.

When he was done, Elodie ran over to him. "You need to be in a picture too."

I walked over and held my hand out. "I'll take a photo of you two."

"How about we do a selfie?" He flipped his screen around, stood behind us, and wrapped his arm around my upper chest.

I looked at his phone screen. He'd gotten the top of Elodie's head and his chin, with only my face showing in the frame. I hoisted Elodie up and he scrunched down a little. We started laughing as we shifted around. Finally, we got us all in.

I was hyperaware of his body molded along my back, and I silently cursed myself for being attracted to him. Nothing good would come from it.

Connor finally let go and grinned. "Let's eat lunch, then I'll get a swimsuit for you, Belly."

"Do you need your ears cleaned out? Only Ellie gets to call me that. Bella is enough."

Connor cocked his head and studied me. "Okay. I'll call you Smelly Belly then. Or how about Jelly Belly?"

Elodie shook her head. "No. Something nice."

"Like what?" Connor asked her.

"Like sweetheart or honey."

Those were two names he called her sometimes.

He ruffled Elodie's hair. "Honey, huh? I like it." Then he turned to me and grinned. "How about honey buns?" He stared at my lips. "Or better yet, honey lips."

Elodie nodded. "That's a good one."

The tingles started up again, and I stepped back. "All this talk is making me hungry. Let's eat lunch and go swimming."

While we ate, Elodie talked about her new soccer buddies. "Sophie and Willie and Lennie are my new best friends." She'd gone to her first soccer practice that morning in Palm Springs.

Connor picked up his drink. "One of the soccer coaches is Damien's business partner."

I looked up. "Is it Martina's cousin, Sebastian? Or Zeke?"

He stared at me, his drink suspended in midair. "Sebastian. How do you know them?"

"Harley invited me to a couple of their Martini Monday parties, and I spent New Year's Eve with them."

He didn't look happy. "Did you have a date for New Year's?"

I shook my head. "There was a large group of us, and we met up at their friends' bar."

He carefully set his drink down. "They own the security company I use." He winced a little. "But you already know that."

The reminder pricked at my temper. "Yeah, I remember. Sebastian told me the bottle of whiskey you gave my dad was expensive."

Connor's eye twitched. "Why would he know about the bottle of whiskey?"

"Because I brought it with me. Dad gave it to me to take as a thank-you gift, and the guys loved it." I reached over and patted his hand. "Dad doesn't like hard liquor. If you want to give him a thoughtful gift, he likes games and books. And maybe herbs. If you're set on liquor, a decent beer is all he drinks."

He looked up at the ceiling. "So he gave you the expensive, aged, single malt Canadian whiskey to take to the party with those three fuckers. As a thank you."

Elodie piped up. "Five bucks!"

I struggled to keep my face straight. "Jonathan and Ramone were there too." I didn't tell him they were a happily married gay couple.

His left eye twitched again. "Good to know."

"And I gave Zeke a big hug for being a cynical bastard."

"I bet he enjoyed that." His voice had gone soft.

"Yes, I think Zeke did. And they all enjoyed the whiskey."

I glanced at Elodie and shut up. She watched us curiously as she stuffed grapes into her mouth. We finished eating, and Elodie ran to her room to get her swimsuit coverup.

Connor leaned over and circled my wrist with his fingers. "Do you know what corporal punishment is?"

Nodding, I swallowed hard. His light, firm touch made my pulse skyrocket.

He raised my hand to his lips and nipped me lightly. "I can make you like it."

My nipples tightened, and I shivered slightly. "You need to behave."

"Only if you do. And Bella?"

"What?"

"Trying to make me jealous isn't behaving."

Elodie ran back in, wearing her coverup.

I tried to change the subject. "How do you like your dance class?"

She plopped back down and shoved another grape in her mouth. "Good. And you know what?"

I smiled and brushed strands of hair back from her face. "No, what?"

She swallowed her grape. "My teacher likes Daddy."

I cleared my throat. "Yeah? It's good somebody does. How do you know that?"

"She touches him a lot and laughs funny."

My eyebrows shot up and I tried not to smile. "Does she do that with the other dads?"

"Nope."

"You might be right. Do you like her?"

"Yeah, I think so." She didn't sound too sure.

"Does your dad like her?" I tried to sound uninterested.

Elodie looked at me funny. "No, Belly. He likes you."

I shifted a little and avoided Connor's gaze. "That's nice. I like him too." I hoped my face wasn't as red as it felt. "And he can like her as well. You can't have too many friends."

Elodie watched me curiously. "Uh-huh." She stuffed another grape in her mouth.

After lunch, Connor took me out to the small pool house to try on the extra swimsuits he kept there. The pool house was about the size of my apartment, but much nicer.

Connor opened a large closet. "Try any of these."

There were a dozen or more brand-new suits, along with new beach towels and other pool paraphernalia. When he left to check on Elodie, I tried a few on and quickly realized they were all pretty skimpy.

I finally gave up and chose a teal blue polka dot bikini that had just a little more material than the others. Wrapping my towel around me, I walked out to the pool area.

The sun was out, and when I put my foot in the pool, it felt like bathwater.

Elodie jumped up and down in the shallow end, waving me in. "Come on. It's warm."

Connor lounged on the side, watching me. I took a deep breath, then unwrapped the towel, laid it down, and started to get in.

I hadn't made it two steps when Connor pointed to the outdoor dining table several feet away. "Before you get in, will you grab Elodie's towel?"

"Okay." I studied him suspiciously before I reluctantly turned around and grabbed her towel off the table. When I turned back to the pool, Connor's eyes were glued to my ass. The swimsuit was cut high in the back and showed off a good portion of my butt cheeks.

He didn't seem to care that I'd caught him staring. In fact, he studied me carefully and his eyelids lowered. He spread his arms out on the pool ledge, and his shoulders glistened with water droplets. It was hard not to stare at his chest and the intricate tattoo there.

Elodie paddled over to me as I laid her towel by the side of the pool and got in. I bent my knees and submerged myself up to my shoulders so she could wrap her little arms around my neck. I reached around and took hold of her thighs to help her hold on.

We bounced around in the shallow end for a few minutes and chatted about her school and soccer.

Connor watched us, and I finally waded over to him. "Thanks for lending me a swimsuit. What there is of it, anyway."

He grinned. "Rachel did a good job picking them out." I thought Rachel was probably his last assistant.

Elodie unlatched herself from me and got out to get a pool toy.

I bobbed in the water next to Connor. "This feels so nice, especially for early February. It's rainy and cold in Seattle this time of year."

He leaned back and stretched his long legs out. "Vancouver has the same shitty weather in the winter. Are you going back to Seattle after you graduate?"

It was a question I asked myself almost every day. "I don't know. Dad lives here now, and Liam, my brother, is in D.C., so Seattle doesn't have as much appeal to me. But I do have friends there."

Elodie got back in with her toy and latched onto me again. "Your swimsuit is pretty. I want one like it."

I laughed at the look of mock horror on Connor's face. "The Brazilian cut isn't that funny now, is it?"

Elodie slid off my back and waded over to his lap, wrapping her little arms around him.

He cuddled her close and put his chin on her head. The content, happy look on his face melted my heart.

Damn it. Of all the men I knew, *he* had to be the one who gave me tingles.

"You should move here," Connor said. "The high is usually around seventy degrees in the winter. You can't beat that."

"Are you going to move here full-time, now that Elodie's in school?"

He studied me. "I think so. It depends on a few things."

My rabid curiosity was killing me, but I didn't ask him what those few things were. If they had to do with Elodie's mother or another woman, I didn't want to know.

Elodie let him go and started dog paddling toward the deep end.

I watched her. "Do you know how to swim, Ellie?"

"Yeah. I like my floaties though."

Connor waded over and stood beside me. "I made sure she had swimming lessons. She's a good little swimmer."

I was relieved. I'd seen a drowning case last year during a rotation in the emergency room, and it scared me when I thought of Elodie. She swam toward a blowup beach ball bobbing in the deep end.

We watched her until she pushed the ball back into the shallow end and played with it there.

Without thinking, I squeezed his hand. "I'm glad you made sure she can swim. You're a good dad."

He grinned and snaked his arm around my waist. "Huh. You just said something nice to me."

Connor slowly hugged me to him, molding my body to his. I froze for a second, then relaxed against him before I could register what was happening. His hard chest and thighs pressed against me, and I instinctively shifted a little closer. By the time my brain caught up a few seconds later, he'd let go.

I tried to get my heart rate under control. "Don't get used to it. There don't seem to be many opportunities."

He licked his lips, then looked down at mine. "We're just getting started, honey lips." Then he leaned over and whispered in my ear, "And when I call you honey lips, I'm not just thinking about your mouth."

# Chapter 12

I went to the hospital on Friday morning to take Molly, a chronically ill patient I knew from the pediatric clinic, a couple of books from the library. Then I sat with her for an hour to give her mom a little break.

Molly waved tiredly when I walked in. "Did you bring me any *good* books this time?"

She was eight years old, but looked younger. Her short hair had been shaved recently when it started falling out again. She had brain cancer, and she'd just gone through another round of chemo after they found more cancerous cells. Her prognosis wasn't good, and my heart broke a little every time I saw her.

"Yep. And guess why? I found books four and five in the *Wings of Fire* series at the library."

She sat up a little and reached out her hands in a "gimme" gesture.

"Holy guacamole, Molly. That's a great hat." She had on a bright pink beanie with little neon yellow flowers embroidered on the edge. I'd started using silly little rhymes when we first met, and a giggle escaped before she'd rolled her eyes. So I kept doing it.

After visiting Molly, I walked over to Jasper's room. He was the other chronically ill patient from the clinic I'd started visiting regularly. He was getting some oxygen therapy today, but when I looked in, he was asleep. At thirteen, Jasper had a swagger and a look in his eye that was way too old for his age. He also had cystic fibrosis, and he spent a lot of time at the hospital getting treatments.

The first time I met Jasper, he'd looked me up and down with a little smirk. "You're smoking hot. Way hotter than the other nurses around here."

I shook my head and pulled a stethoscope from around my neck. Dr. Kendall, my supervisor, stood behind me. She started coughing suspiciously into her fist.

"I'm not a nurse, I'm a PA intern. And you're young. Way too young to be telling women they're smoking hot."

He was a chronic flirt. But despite that, we'd become friends. I set down the *Percy Jackson* novel on his tray that I'd picked up at the used bookstore, and left a little blue origami whale on top so he'd know where the book came from. I gave most of the kids at the clinic a paper animal or flower when I treated them.

As I drove to Dad's house that afternoon, I thought about all the time Mom spent in hospital beds, and I couldn't imagine how much worse it would be for a kid. She used to light up whenever she'd get a visitor.

Dad's house was empty, and I didn't see him anywhere on the estate. I stashed my bags in his spare bedroom and reluctantly rang

Connor's doorbell. When he answered, I noticed a few small pink dots on his t-shirt.

His thick dark hair was tousled, and his feet were bare. I'd been around a lot of good-looking, fit men lately who didn't affect me. But when Connor smiled, the tingles started again.

He stepped aside. "Hey, honey lips. Why aren't you at the pediatric clinic?"

I scowled at the nickname, but my vagina still clenched. "I have Fridays through Sundays off this semester, except home games."

"I take it that's good."

A reluctant grin escaped. "It's the first time in almost six years I haven't had either school, work, or rotations every weekend."

Connor studied me, then stared down at my mouth for several seconds. I started to squirm a little.

Dropping my gaze, I looked behind him into his house. "Is Dad here? I can't find him."

He motioned me inside. "We're painting a wall in Elodie's room."

The flecks of pink paint on his shirt suddenly made sense. "A light pink, I take it."

"She was leaning toward a Pepto Bismol pink, but Javier talked her down."

Dad stood touching up a few spots in Elodie's room when we walked in. Drop cloths covered the dresser and desk, and plastic was taped down underneath the chosen wall.

"Hey, Isa. I need to go get Elodie from school. Will you help Connor clean up? The paint is dry enough to pull the tape and plastic up, but don't touch the wall yet."

"Sure. This looks great." I walked over and gave him a quick hug, dodging a few paint splotches on his shirt and hands.

"It does, doesn't it? She wants a canopy hung over her bed, and some fairy lights."

I stepped back and looked at the color. "It's wonderful. This is so much better."

"Maybe you can help Connor finish decorating." He wiped his hands on a paper towel. "I'm picking her up, then we plan to stop by the library and check out a few books."

Connor put his hands in his pockets. "Javier, why don't you just buy them online? You don't need to go to the library."

I gasped and unthinkingly flicked his chest. "Bite your tongue. Libraries are one of the few magical places left."

Connor looked down at me with a funny grin. "Yeah? What's so magical about them?"

I wiggled my fingers. "You can touch all the books you pick out. Thumb through them. See all the sizes and covers." I leaned forward and lowered my voice. "Smell them. Have you ever smelled an old library?"

His lip twitched. "Can't say that I have."

I thought back to visiting the Suzzallo library on the UW campus in Seattle, the Elliott Bay Bookstore, and all the other small bookstores and libraries my parents had taken me to over the years. And libraries were *free*, which made them even better.

"I'm pretty sure that's what magic smells like. Books. Old books, new books. All the shapes and sizes, Different topics and colors. My mom said the librarians and bookshop owners are the dragons in disguise who watch over the real treasure."

Dad threw his arm around my shoulder and squeezed. "You remind me of her. She loved taking you and Liam to the library."

Connor smiled. "You're a little bit of a nerd, aren't you?"

"It's nice of you to notice."

Dad let go and patted my arm. "Will one of you preheat the oven if we're not back before dinnertime? I have a chicken casserole and a salad in the fridge. Let's plan to eat dinner around six or so when we get back."

I turned to him, a little alarmed. "Where are you going for the next three hours?"

"We're going to the library until her dance class starts. Then after dance, we'll eat together," he said patiently. Then he kissed my cheek and walked out.

Turning to Connor, I felt a little awkward.

I sidestepped toward the door. "I'll just go wait for them at Dad's house."

"No, I need your help. And you should be here when El comes home and sees the changes."

I studied him, then put my hands in my back pockets. "Look, we got off to a terrible start. I'm not going to pretend everything is fine either. But my dad likes you, Ellie is amazing, and I'd like to be in her life. You, not so much."

He smirked like he knew I was full of shit. "Too bad, honey lips. I like a good challenge."

"So do I. But not with you. This isn't a game or a challenge." I loved games, and if we made this into one, my sense of self-preservation would fly out the window.

Connor studied me. "I want us to get past this. I know Elodie and I need you and Javier more than you need us."

He didn't play fair. I'd do just about anything for Elodie, and he knew it. She was sweet and funny, and a little lost. And Connor intrigued me as much as he irritated me.

Sighing, I walked over and sat down on the bed, rubbing my hand across the blanket. It was as soft as the Etsy seller had advertised.

I smiled a little. "She likes the blanket."

He sat down next to me. "Did you pick it out?"

"Uh-huh. And the pink tutu. Dad called your assistant, Sherrill, when you told me it was her birthday. That day you were firing orders at me."

He took my hand and ran his thumb across the back of it, then sighed. "Yeah, I remember that day."

Goosebumps erupted across my skin, but I didn't pull back. "Sherrill ordered everything and used your credit card, so the presents technically came from you."

He studied me. "Why?"

"Why what?"

"Why would you do that after the way we met, and the thing with Noah?"

"Because she's only five years old. I didn't want her to think her dad had forgotten her, especially on her birthday. And it was before you and Noah accused me of felony burglary." I pulled my hand back.

Connor leaned over and rested his elbows on his knees. "I never accused you."

"But you never said you didn't believe it either. You sat there and let him call me a thief and a liar in front of my dad."

He reached over and squeezed my knee. "I'm sorry. There are a lot of things I'd do differently. Hindsight is a bitch sometimes."

"Yes, it is."

"I sent Elodie a few things for her birthday too. But nothing she likes as much as this blanket." He sounded a little annoyed.

I patted his thigh and tried not to gloat. "I got lucky."

My competitive streak was coming out. Liam and my dad both told me it was one of my worst traits.

Connor smelled like expensive sandalwood body wash and something else I couldn't place. His body heat warmed my side, and I suddenly realized how close we were sitting.

I stood up. "Okay then. Let's get her room straightened out."

We cleaned up the plastic drop cloth and tape, then installed the canopy and twinkling lights over Elodie's bed. As we worked, we talked about his hockey career and Elodie's Mémé. He told me Elodie called her almost every night, and she'd talked to her mother once. He didn't tell me how that had gone, but the fact it'd only been once was telling.

Connor also asked me about my clinical rotations. "Are any of the players giving you trouble?"

I glanced at him. "Why does everyone think they aren't going to behave? They're fine. I get hit on more from one of my thirteen-year-old pediatric patients."

He shook his head. "You're lying."

"Why do you say that?"

"Because you're gorgeous and have a great ass, and most of them are degenerate fucktwits."

I jerked on the stool where I stood placing lights in the canopy, and he grabbed my waist. My shirt had ridden up above my waistband, and his hands landed on my bare skin.

His touch felt like a live wire zinging through me, and I involuntarily shuddered. He felt it and slowly stroked me there.

I sucked in a breath. "I'm good. You can let go. I'd return the compliment, but if your head got any bigger you'd fall over and break something."

He chuckled and slowly pulled his hands away. I pulled my shirt down, and finished placing the lights. Connor stood right behind me, and I brushed against his body as I stepped down.

I leaned down to plug in the lights. "Let's see how they look."

He turned off the overhead light, and the lights twinkled in the gauzy white fabric, letting off a soft glow.

Gazing at her room, I slowly spun around. It already looked so different from the first time I'd seen it. Instead of a generic guest bedroom, it was becoming a little girl's haven.

Connor surveyed the room as well, and his arm brushed against my shoulder. I didn't shiver this time, but my body still reacted to him.

"I think she's going to love it, eh?"

"She will. It's spectacular."

He put his arm around my shoulder and kissed the top of my head. "Thank you."

I slowly relaxed against him. "You did good."

"I want her to be happy here, and you and Javier are a big part of that."

"She is happy here, and you're the biggest part of that." I poked him in the chest. "Although I have no idea why."

Connor smirked. "I have a few other things for her room. I'll go get them."

I put a hand on his chest to stop him. "Wait. Can I make a suggestion?"

Looking down at my hand, he reached up and threaded his fingers through mine. "Yeah."

It took me a minute to remember what I wanted to say. "Let her do it."

"Do what?"

"Let her decorate the rest of it, so she feels like it's hers."

"Do you think she'll care?"

I shrugged. "I don't know. But it seems like she's been trying to piece her life back together after moving here with you."

"What do you mean?"

I slowly stepped back. "She asked Harley to help her find friends, and she asked me to make sure you signed her up for school and got her into a dance class." I walked over and sat on her bed. "She also picked Javier to be her nanny."

Connor put his hands on his hips and smiled. "She's smart, isn't she? I'll have to remember that."

I looked around the room again. "She's only five, so it's pretty amazing what she's orchestrated in her sweet, charming way already."

"I try to let her make her own choices if it's possible. Sometimes I want to pull my hair out though."

He sat next to me, and I patted his thigh. "That probably makes you a good parent. You let her pick out her own clothes too." Looking at her closet, I remembered the first time I'd seen her when she'd been wearing Christmas leggings and a Halloween shirt.

He groaned and laid back on the bed. "God, I'm a retired hockey player and don't give a fuck about clothes, but some of her outfits make even my eyes bleed."

I laughed and patted his hard stomach. "Dad said she wanted to wear her tutu over a pair of pajamas to school on Monday. He had to bribe her with a trip to the Zoo Lights to get her to change."

He glanced at me and tucked a hand behind his head. "Am I supposed to know what Zoo Lights are?" He patted the bed beside him.

I lay on my side and propped my head on my hand. "Maybe. I've never been, but I hear they're awesome."

"I feel off-center and inadequate." He sighed. "I used to be great at what I did. I was a world-class hockey player. Now I don't know what the hell I'm doing most of the time, and worry I'm going to fail her and somehow screw her up."

I studied him. "I think being a good parent isn't so much what you know, it's more about what you do. Being kind, letting her make decisions when you can, and spending time with her."

He glanced at me wryly. "That doesn't make me feel better. I only got to see her a couple of times a month for the first year of her life."

I patted his stomach. I wanted to run my hand over his hard abs, but I refrained. "Yeah, that would suck."

"You're not good at fake sympathy, are you?" He reached out and squeezed my thigh.

"Not really. It sounds like you spent time with her when you could, and you're taking custody of her now. You're doing fine."

"Okay. I'll take that." He took my hand. "Tell me what Zoo Lights are."

I laid back and looked up at the canopy. "The zoo installs thousands of lights and these large hand-painted, animated luminaries. Then people go at night and walk around looking at the displays, and visiting the nocturnal animals."

"Huh. Sounds great," he said flatly.

I reached over and flicked his arm. "Jeez, you don't like libraries or Zoo Lights. You probably don't like kittens or puppies either. What do you like?"

He gave me a leisurely grin. "A lot of things. Mostly 'adult' things."

"What 'adult' things?" As soon as the words were out of my mouth, I regretted asking.

"Hockey. Most other sports. A good whiskey..." He trailed off.

"And sex." I finished for him. "I told you I saw all the pictures online when I looked you up. You seemed to have a flavor of the week. Like ice cream." I sat up.

He scowled and sat up next to me. "I didn't have 'flavors of the week.' And it's been a long time."

My stomach knotted when I thought about him bringing one of them here.

I gave him a fake smile. "I'm not judging or telling you what to do. But I'd be careful about bringing anyone around Elodie if you aren't serious. She loves almost everyone on sight, and it might be confusing for her."

"You said she loves *almost* everyone. Who doesn't she love?"

"She doesn't like Noah. I'm going to start on dinner." I stood up and walked out of the room, trying to get some distance.

But he followed me into the kitchen and pulled out a beer and a bottle of white wine from the fridge. He poured a glass, and slid it over to me.

I looked at it. "Is this a peace offering?"

He shrugged. "Maybe."

I tasted the wine. It was delicious. "Wow. This is way better than what I usually drink."

He shook his head, then started the oven and leaned against it. "How are the players really treating you at the arena?"

"They've been fine. Seriously. You called them degenerates, but you used to be one."

He took a drink. "Not all of them, but enough. And I used to be one, so I know. This team's average age is maybe twenty."

I shrugged. "Not Titus. He's probably in his mid-thirties, and from all the scars on his body I'm sure he's been playing for a while."

Connor carefully set his beer bottle down. "How do you know Titus? And how'd you find out about the scars on his body?"

"Your first question doesn't deserve an answer. And I saw his scars."

"When?"

Picking up my glass, I took another sip. "The last time was on Tuesday."

He ground his teeth. "The last time?"

"Yeah."

"Where?"

"In the medical office. If you keep grinding your teeth, you're going to wear down your molars. And he takes ice baths after practice. Do you know him?"

Connor nodded. "Yeah. I know him well. We used to play together in Vancouver. He suffered a pretty severe injury, and he's playing on the farm team this season so the professional league can assess his recovery. I'm not sure what's going to happen with him."

That's probably where the scar on his back came from. "That's too bad."

Connor narrowed his eyes. "I can be an asshole and I like… certain things. But if I'm an asshole, Titus is the antichrist."

I had a vague idea of what certain things Connor liked, but I didn't dare ask him. I was half afraid he'd tell me in explicit detail.

I studied him. "That's basically what he said about Wyatt."

"Shit," Connor bit out. "And how do you know Wyatt?"

Rolling my eyes, I set my wine down. "I work there, remember? And he introduced himself." Okay, maybe he had a point about Wyatt.

Connor blew out a breath. "Yeah, I bet that fucker did. Titus is right about Wyatt."

"They can't *all* be assholes. So which one is the bigger asshole, Wyatt or Titus?"

"Wyatt. But I'd prefer if you stayed away from both of them."

I threw up my hands. "I work there. And I don't really care what you prefer since I don't plan to be your flavor of the week."

This conversation needed to end. I turned around and started looking through his cupboards. "Where are your plates?"

He came up behind me, caging me against the counter. He set his drink down next to mine, then opened the cupboard above me and pulled down four plates.

I froze and sucked in my breath. His arms came down around my sides as he set the plates on the counter in front of me, his body pressing into my back.

"Here are the plates," he said in my ear. "And I know you're not a flavor of the week. You're more like a fucking five-star, four-course meal. That I plan to thoroughly enjoy when the time is right."

Then he stepped back, and I slowly turned around and stared up at him. My heart was pounding, and I couldn't form a coherent thought.

"Why would you say that to me?" I sounded hoarse. "I shouldn't like you. Or want you."

"But you do, Bella. And you can't deny it." It wasn't a question.

I looked up at him but didn't say anything. Because he was right.

He nodded, as if my reaction confirmed what he already knew.

"I can't... We don't..." I sputtered.

He grinned. "You can, and we will. There's something I have to take care of first. But I'm giving you fair warning."

"Well, you shouldn't," I snapped.

He laughed softly. "I shouldn't give you fair warning?"

"You shouldn't want me. Or give me fair warning." I slipped around him and started pacing. "What am I supposed to do with this?"

He watched me. "Stay away from Titus, for one thing."

"Damn it, Connor. Stop saying things like that!"

"No."

I stopped pacing. "No?"

"Nope. And so you know, I already told your dad."

"Well, fuck," I muttered, picturing that awkward conversation. "I didn't tell him I wanted to do that, but he's a smart man."

I was saved from having to answer Connor when Elodie and my traitor dad walked in.

# Chapter 13

Before the home game that Sunday, the players seemed hyped. Nervous energy crackled in the locker room. I was taping up an ankle when Coach Bailey walked in.

He called for everyone's attention. "Listen up, team. This is our first home game of the new year, and I expect you not to leave anything on the bench."

I sat in the back of the locker room, zoning him out as he continued giving his uninspiring speech. I glanced over and noticed Titus still had his earbuds in.

Jackson stared blankly at the coach, his knee bouncing nervously. Wyatt was putting lotion on his tattoos.

When Coach Bailey paused, I patted Mikael's knee, the Swedish player I'd been taping up. "Does that feel all right? Not too tight?"

He shook his head and smiled. "*Nej*, it's good. Thanks."

Coach Bailey shot me a dirty look from across the room, then he continued droning on. Finally, he finished up and the players continued getting ready.

Wyatt came up after Mikael walked off, his pants only half done up.

He smirked. "Hey, Isa. I'd like you to wrap something for me. I'd like you to wrap your mouth around–" His head snapped forward.

Titus had swatted the back of Wyatt's head, and he growled low. "Shut your mouth, asshole. I've already warned you. You may be a decent left wing, but you're a fucking moron. Quit harassing her."

Wyatt turned around to confront Titus, but I tapped his arm. "Hey."

"What?" Wyatt snapped.

I kept my voice low. "You're a professional. You need to act like one."

He gave me a dirty look. "I'm just teasing. It's not a big deal."

"It *is* a big deal if Coach Bailey decides not to let me finish my rotation, or he decides you're not worth the risk and lets you go."

Wyatt laughed. "Let's me go?"

"You never know. And Titus is right, you're kind of a moron to risk it."

Wyatt glanced back at Titus, then rolled his shoulders. "You might be right. You're not worth it."

I shook my head. If he thought his words offended me, he was in for a sad surprise. "You're right. I'm not. Now, do you want something besides that little thing in your pants wrapped?" I tilted my head toward his crotch.

Wyatt smirked. "I'm good." He bumped Titus's shoulder as he went back to his locker.

Titus gave me a small nod, then finished getting ready. I let out a quiet breath and hoped Connor never heard about this.

Ben and I watched the game from the end of the front row, close to the team. I fidgeted and my leg bounced. Hockey was physical, fast-paced, and a little nerve-wracking. And, I reluctantly admitted, exciting to watch.

The first time Jackson checked an opposing player against the plexiglass, I jumped out of my skin. Ben laughed.

"What? It surprised me, that's all."

He smiled. "Uh-huh. Have you ever been to a hockey game before?"

"No. I grew up in Seattle and we'd sometimes go to sporting events whenever we could scrounge up tickets. But never hockey."

Titus played center and I watched him pass to Wyatt, who shot at the goal but was blocked. Wyatt fought and regained possession but didn't pass the puck back. Instead, he took an awkward shot and missed again.

Ben shook his head. "They don't play like a close-knit team. I don't know what's missing, but my daughter's softball team is more cohesive than these guys, and they're middle schoolers."

"Why do you think they aren't more cohesive?"

"I don't know. But they don't seem to know or trust each other."

"Huh." I glanced at Coach Bailey, who looked annoyed and angry.

Titus finally scored when he kept the puck, shot it around the back of the goal, retrieved it, then fired it in.

His teammates cheered, but no one slapped him on the ass or pounded on his helmet like I'd seen the other team do after one of them scored.

"Do they ever have any activities or team-building exercises together?"

Ben shook his head. "I haven't heard anyone mention it. This is such a new team."

Ben's comments stuck with me throughout the game. They lost by a goal, and the team was subdued afterward.

I met Dad and Elodie outside the locker room afterward. I pointed to her little jersey. "Hey, Ellie. You look awesome. You've got to be the cutest fan here."

Her little red Thunderbirds jersey had a number nine on it, and "Lil McCoy" written across the back.

"My dad and Javy got it for me. And you know what?" She jumped up and down. "They got one for you too. With my dad's number on it."

I stared at my dad above Elodie's head. "That's so... nice."

He grinned and shrugged. I didn't know what had happened over the past month or so, but he'd started to like Connor.

Elodie suddenly squealed and ran off. I looked over and saw Jackson kneeling down to scoop her up. "Hey, El. Love the jersey. But you need my number on it."

He walked over to us, still holding her. "Well, that sucked."

I patted his shoulder as he set Elodie down. "You'll get 'em next time."

"Jack, are you coming to my house for lunch?" Elodie asked.

"I haven't been invited, El. And I think your dad is out of town this week."

Dad mentioned that Connor had gone out of town last minute, and I felt disappointed he hadn't been there for my first hockey game. But I remembered he was part owner of a much bigger professional team, and most of his life was in Vancouver.

Dad smiled at Jackson. "Come over for dinner and family game night on Wednesday, why don't you?"

Jackson grinned. "That sounds great. Connor said your cooking is the shit."

Elodie giggled. "You said a bad word. You owe me a buck."

I grinned at Jackson. "It'll be a nice, quiet evening. As long as you let me win."

"Don't count on it. But I could use some home cooking."

Wednesday evening turned out to be anything but quiet.

On Monday, Coach Bailey was in a foul mood. I tried to steer clear of him, but when Rudy asked me to wrap his wrists before practice, Coach Bailey exploded.

"Rudy, there's nothing wrong with your god dammed wrists," he barked. "And you can wrap them yourself. Ms. Cruz isn't here for any of you to flirt with. You all need to keep your head in the game."

Rudy's face got red, and he ducked his head. I patted him on the arm when he turned back to his locker. It almost sounded like Coach Bailey was blaming me for their loss, and it stung.

I thought about his comment, and the team's issues, a lot that night. On Tuesday I decided to talk with Titus about it. As usual, he was in the ice tub after practice.

"Hey, before you leave today can I talk with you about a couple of things?" I asked.

He cracked one eye open. "Depends."

"On what?"

"It depends on how long it's going to take. I'm fucking starving. And after losing this week, this place is depressing."

I nodded. "Yeah, I know what you mean. How about we talk over a late lunch? My treat, in exchange for your time."

He cocked his head. "You think that's a good idea?"

I stared at him. "What do you mean?"

He studied me, then smirked. "Nothing. How about Elmer's in an hour?"

"Okay. And I also want to go through your injuries and recovery methods if we have time."

Titus pulled himself out of the water. "Might as well."

I absently threw him two towels and turned away so he could strip down in peace, my mind already thinking about our upcoming conversation.

Titus hadn't arrived by the time I got to the restaurant, so I got us a table and ordered a sampler appetizer.

He slid in across from me at the same time the server brought the appetizer. The smell of barbeque wings and garlic hung in the air.

"Thank fuck. I'm famished. So what do you want to talk about?"

"The team seems to play like they barely know each other. How can we fix it?"

He sat back and stared at me. "You asked me to lunch to talk about the team?"

I stared at him. "Yeah." Dipping a celery stick in ranch dressing, I crunched down on it. "Why aren't you guys more in sync, or whatever it's called? Ben said his middle school daughter's softball team has more chemistry than you guys do."

Titus studied me. "Huh. No wonder McCoy..." He trailed off and didn't finish.

"McCoy what?" I asked as I scooped more dip.

"Never mind. The team is brand new, and it's a feeder team." I waited for him to elaborate, but he grabbed another chicken wing instead.

"And?" I asked.

"And what? Any of us could get called up, and we don't know each other. That's why we play that way."

I made a face. "Well, that's dumb. We need to fix it."

"We?" He lifted an eyebrow and licked sauce off his fingers.

"Yeah. You're the oldest and most experienced." I leaned forward. "I think we should have a weekly team-building game night."

He set his wing bone down, sighed, and rubbed his face with his napkin. "Well, fuck. How does this happen? I'm minding my own business, keeping my head down." He glared at me. "I don't like to get involved."

I raised an eyebrow. "How did what happen? Me getting these fantastic ideas, or you whining like a little toddler?"

He smirked. "Both. A toddler?"

"If the shoe fits. I want to have a team-building potluck dinner and game night tomorrow night. You and Jackson need to invite everyone. That way we might get a few guys there."

He looked like he was getting a bad case of heartburn.

I leaned forward. "It's in your best interest for the team to get better, right? I think this would help. You guys don't seem to trust each other."

He leaned back. "That's because we don't."

"Why?"

The server came and deposited our meals. Titus's burger looked way better than my side salad, but this meal was cutting into my weekly food budget, and the sampler appetizer had filled me up already.

He picked up the ketchup bottle. "We don't know each other. And we're a team but we're also competing."

"Wouldn't you all have a better chance if you played well together? And won more games?"

"Yeah." He took a big bite of his burger.

"Okay then. We should do a teambuilding night tomorrow at my dad's house. Jackson is already coming."

"Fine," he growled. "But Jackson sends out the text. Connor and I have a little history."

I took a bite of my salad. "What kind of history?"

"None of your business, *choux*."

"Okay."

He smirked and took another bite. "Now what do you want to know about my recovery methods?"

We spent the next half hour discussing the different injuries he'd suffered over the years, and what worked for him regarding treatment and physical therapy. I took a few notes on my phone and was surprised at how knowledgeable and insightful he was. And he'd had a lot of injuries.

I laid my phone on the table and folded my hands. "What happened to your back?"

Titus tensed. "I don't want to get into it."

"All right. You can tell me when you're ready."

His shoulders relaxed and he leaned forward. "What's going on with you and Connor?"

I'd reached out and picked a fry off his plate, but my hand froze in midair. "What do you mean?"

"Jackson said you spend a lot of time with him and Elodie. He also said Connor considers you his."

"I don't want to get into it." I mimicked his words.

"That's fair. But I think you need to know a couple of things." He looked like the heartburn had come back.

"What?"

"He's at least ten years older than you are. And he likes sex... a certain way. I'm not saying it's bad, and I have a few of the same tastes."

My stomach lurched. "Is it anything illegal or immoral?"

He smiled a little. "No. But sometimes it involves toys, ropes, and mind-fuck games."

"Whew." My shoulders slumped. "Okay, so nothing illegal, immoral, or non-consenting." I picked up another fry off his plate, dipped it in his ketchup, and ate it.

He stared at me, then barked out a laugh. "Goddamn it. Connor's in for a wicked ride."

I leaned forward. "What exactly–"

He cut me off. "I've said more than enough. You'll need to talk to him about any specifics. He also has some baggage he needs to take care of."

"What baggage?"

He ignored my question. "The second thing is his daughter. If you get involved with him, she'll also be a part of your life."

"I hope so. Of the two of them, she's the bigger draw right now."

He smiled and relaxed against the booth. "Just don't get hurt."

My grin faded. "Life is full of hurt and pain, Titus. There are never guarantees."

He nodded solemnly. "I know, *choux*. And I'm sorry you already know it too."

# Chapter 14

On Wednesday afternoon I realized I had a problem. Jackson texted me late that morning and let me know at least eight players planned to come to our game night.

I called him back and started pacing. "Jackson, I thought we'd be lucky to get three or four players to come. My dad's little house can't hold that many people, and I have a tiny one-bedroom apartment." I started brainstorming. "Maybe we can have it at a park, or see if there's a multi-purpose room at the arena we could use."

"Don't worry. I'll call Titus and tell him we're moving it over to his place. He's got a nice house in the Indian Canyons neighborhood in Palm Springs."

I stopped pacing. "He does?"

"Yeah. He's almost as rich as Connor. He plays in the national league, and he's just playing on our feeder team for now because he was injured."

I shouldn't have been surprised. "Okay. Ask him, and if he agrees let everyone know where to meet."

Less than an hour later, Connor called me. And he was furious. "You and Titus are not having a fucking party at his house."

I hadn't heard a word from him since Saturday evening. "Hello to you too. And why is it any of your business?"

"Bella, that's a fucking stupid question," he growled.

"I don't know why you're so angry. And it's not a party. It's a team-building potluck dinner and game night."

He scoffed. "I don't give one holy fuck what you call it. You and Titus are not throwing a goddamned party together." He paused, obviously trying to reign in his anger. "Bella, it'll look like you and Titus are... together."

I knew what he'd almost said. I let out a long breath and tried to control my own temper. "No one's going to think that. We had to move it to his house because we needed more room."

"Honey, don't do this."

The endearment made my insides clench, which made me angrier. "It didn't start out at Titus's house. Dad invited Jackson over for dinner, and we decided to expand." I didn't tell him it was all my idea, and I'd roped them into helping me.

"How did it go from you, your dad, and Jackson having dinner to the whole fucking team, eh?" His accent was showing.

I grimaced. "It's not the *whole* team."

Okay, it sounded like the whole team might show up, but he didn't need to know that.

He cut me off. "If Titus is there, it's one too many."

I tried to reason with him. "They lost again on Sunday, and they haven't been playing well together. They need to get to know each other and maybe become friends. This is a good way to start."

"You're their fucking PA intern, Bella," he snarled. "Not their coach, their agent, or even their girlfriend."

Hurt sliced through me. I was quiet for a moment. "I'm also their friend, I care about them, and I showed up to their last game."

He groaned, long and low. "Bella–"

I interrupted him. "Since I'm just a lowly fucking PA intern I've taken up more than enough of your time. I need to go."

"That's not–" I hung up and turned my phone to mute.

When I found out from Dad that Connor had flown out on Sunday afternoon and planned to be gone for a while, I wondered why he never mentioned he was leaving. He also hadn't asked me to help with Elodie while he was gone.

I'd misjudged his intentions, and I felt stupid and naive. I was just another woman he wanted to screw. And before that, he'd believed I was a felon.

There were enough complications with him being my father's employer, our age difference, and me leaving in a few months. I resolved again to stay away from him. And mean it this time.

Titus called me a few hours before the party. "Are we still on?"

"Yes. Connor called and ripped me a new one, but we're still on."

He was silent for a minute. "You okay?"

"No, but I will be."

"He called me, too. It was a short conversation."

I sighed. "What did you say?"

"He told me we're not having the party. I laughed, told him to fuck off, and then hung up." He sounded almost bored.

I tried to shake off my foul mood. "My dad dropped off four dozen peanut butter bars. He's also loaning us a few games. I hope everyone else knows what 'potluck' means."

Titus grunted. "There'll be a lot of beer and whiskey. And potato chips. I'll pick up some pizza, but don't expect too much tonight."

"Okay." I just wanted to go for a ride on my longboard, curl up in my bed and read, or maybe cry a little. But this had all been my idea, and I was hell-bent on seeing it through now.

Titus's home was located in one of the cul de sacs off Palo Fiero Way in the Indian Canyons neighborhood of Palm Springs. It was smaller than Connor's sprawling estate and didn't sit on two acres, but I liked it right away. The white garden patio house had a mint green door and mature landscaping full of palm trees and flowering bushes. I could smell lemongrass and sage as we walked up to his front door.

Jackson picked me up. "I forgot to tell you, Rudy let me know two other players are coming with him. So we're now up to ten."

"This should be an interesting night."

He squeezed my arm. "Titus told me Connor is pissed."

My face flushed in embarrassment. "You guys gossip like middle schoolers."

"Probably worse. You're doing a good thing, and I think a lot of players are looking forward to tonight. Some of them don't know anyone here, and we're kind of transient."

Titus opened the door in ripped jeans and a thread bare t-shirt. "You're early."

Jackson smirked. "We came to make sure you'd buried all the dead bodies."

"Kitchen's that way." Titus pointed down the hall.

We walked into a bright kitchen with cream quartz countertops and expensive appliances. The kitchen bar looked out onto the pool area and surrounding gardens.

I turned to Titus. "Your home is wonderful. I somehow pictured you living in a cold, sleek, modern condo with a sex dungeon in your spare bedroom."

"You sound surprised." He nodded toward the hallway. "The sex dungeon's down the hall, third door on the left."

"Okay, I won't snoop in that room then."

Two hours later, thirteen players had shown up. Titus was right, most of the players brought either beer, whiskey, or snacks. One player had somehow found ketchup-flavored potato chips, and Jackson told me they were popular in Canada.

Thanks to the mild evening, we spilled out into Titus's backyard area while we ate and chatted. A few players socialized for a bit, then took off. But most stayed.

Six of us were immersed in a competitive game of Settlers of Catan. While we waited for Rudy to take his turn, I picked up a bottle of Crown Royal Whisky someone had brought.

"Why do Canadians spell whiskey without an 'e'?" I asked.

Titus smirked. "The real question is why do you Americans spell it wrong?"

Jackson leaned forward. "My granddad told me whiskey originated from Scotland and Ireland. He said Canadians follow the Scotts' tradition of whiskey-making and the Americans follow the Irish. And they each spelled it differently."

"The Scottish method is better," Titus muttered.

I looked at the bottle. "There's my fun fact for the day. And I wouldn't know which method is better because I think they both taste like paint thinner."

A couple of guys chuckled and Jackson booed.

When Rudy was done with his turn, I picked up the dice. "I heard the Green Bay Packers played this game together as a team for years, and they became obsessed with it."

Mikael, the player from Sweden, nodded. "*Ja*, I heard that too. My family used to play all the time. Especially in the winter."

Mikael also had all the rules memorized. I knew because I'd tried to stretch a few.

Titus gazed behind me as I rolled the dice, then leaned back and smirked. Jackson glanced up and sighed. I finally turned around and saw Connor walking toward us. My heart stuttered, but I turned back around and stared at the board.

He put his hands on my shoulders, and I reluctantly gazed up at him. He looked tired, frustrated, and angry. My heart lurched painfully.

He leaned down and spoke softly in my ear. "You and I are going to finish our talk, Bella."

My throat tightened. I still wanted to yell at him, so I went with ignoring him instead. Conversations died, and most of the players stopped talking and watched us.

His hands squeezed my shoulders again. "A piece of advice? In the future, don't hang up on me and then ghost me when I piss you off. I'll hunt you down, and it won't go well when I find you."

"I'm not worried, because there won't be a next time."

"You don't know me well if you think that. We're leaving."

Titus leaned forward. "Did you get your shit sorted out?" he asked cryptically.

Connor nodded. "I did. It's done."

"What are you two talking about?" I shook my head. "You know what? It doesn't matter. You were a mean asshole, and you called me a fucking PA intern. I think you've said enough." I instantly regretted repeating Connor's words in front of everyone.

Titus narrowed his eyes and folded his arms.

"Dude," a player muttered under his breath.

Connor scowled at the player, then turned my chair to the side and knelt beside me. "It wasn't meant to be rude, and I hear you're a fucking great PA. But I had a shit day, and I didn't like finding out you and Titus were hosting a Goddamn party together." He glanced meaningfully around. "Now please come so I don't beat the shit out of Titus, or someone else, just because I need to let off some steam."

A few players grinned and someone started laughing. What was it with these guys and violence?

Titus gave Connor a nasty smile. "You think you could take me?"

Connor turned to him. "I've been dealing with lawyers and Elodie's bitch of a mother, and now you trying to fuck with me. So yeah, mate. Right now, I think I could take you."

No way. These two weren't going to use me as an excuse to fight.

I pushed my chair back and stood. Connor stood too, and I pointed my finger at him. "I'll go with you because we do need to talk. But you can't be a jerk then expect me to roll over and take it. You hurt me today."

Connor studied me carefully. Then he slowly cupped my face and kissed my forehead. I froze but didn't push him away. He wrapped his arms around me and pulled me into him.

"I'm sorry. I didn't mean to hurt you."

I let out an involuntary sigh and wrapped my arms around him. "I shouldn't have hung up on you."

Mikael raised his hand. "Does this mean we won't be finishing the game? Because I really want to win."

Connor's jaw flexed, but I squeezed him until he grunted.

"This will just take a minute." I sat back down and drew my resource cards based on my roll. Then I laid down a couple of roads, built another settlement, and counted up my points. "I win. We're done."

Jackson groaned. "I fucking hate this game."

Mikael threw down his cards. "I think the term you use in Poker is card shark."

"Don't be a sore loser. It was close." I leaned back in my chair and put my hands behind my head.

Mikael eyed me. "That doesn't make me feel better, *vännen*."

Titus sipped his beer. "Well done, *choux*. You okay to go with Connor?"

Connor pointed at them. "I don't like you fuckers having pet names for her."

They both grinned.

I rolled my eyes and turned to Titus. "I'll come by and pick up the games and the rest of my stuff later. Thank you. This turned out way better than I'd hoped. Except maybe the end." I glanced at Connor. Then I grabbed my backpack and turned to the other players who were blatantly eavesdropping. "That was fun, guys. See you all on Monday."

Several called out farewells. Connor took my backpack and slung it over his shoulder.

I looked at him. "I can carry it."

He put his hand on the small of my back as we walked outside. "I know. I didn't see your car outside. How'd you get here?"

"Jackson picked me up."

"Good." He opened the passenger door of his Range Rover, and I got in. Before shutting it, he leaned over me. "You and I are going to have a long talk. I'm done fucking around."

He slammed the car door and walked around to the driver's side before I could argue.

# Chapter 15

Connor drove to my apartment. He told me he'd just flown in from Vancouver, but we didn't say much else on the drive over.

Butterflies erupted in my stomach when we pulled into my complex. We walked in, and I turned on the living room lamp.

Connor folded his arms and looked around. "This place is just as depressing at night."

My back went up and I started walking toward the kitchen. "If it's so depressing, you don't need to stay. Tell Elodie I'll see her at my dad's house this weekend."

He moved in front of me and put his hands on my shoulders. "Not until we talk."

I poked him in the chest. "You can't tell me one minute you want a relationship, then disappear without a word. Then show up again and be a rude asshole."

He studied me, then slowly pulled me into him. "You're right. It's been a stressful few days, and I took it out on you. But when I heard you and Titus were throwing a party together–"

"It wasn't a party."

He pulled back and smirked. "Excuse me, a team building, potluck, game, whatever-the-fuck night. Not really sure what the difference is, but I'll take your word for it, eh?"

My lips twitched, and I poked him again.

Chuckling, he grabbed both my hands. "You keep poking me and I'll poke you back. But in much more interesting places."

"As fun as that sounds, it's a terrible idea."

"Really? Because your body lights up every time I touch you." He leaned in and ran his lips up my neck.

I stilled as electricity raced through me. "You say you want me. I don't even know what that means. You want me for a week or two? Or until you move back to Vancouver?" I thought about the photos I'd seen online and felt a little sick.

He shifted his hips against me. "You know that's bullshit."

"What about Elodie? What happens when you get tired of me as your flavor of the week? Are you going to introduce her to your next flavor?"

He laid his cheek next to mine and spoke low in my ear. "You need to stop talking about a goddamn flavor of the week. And if I have my way, we're going to be together a lot longer than just a week, or even a fucking year." He closed his eyes and laid his forehead on mine.

This man could break me, I realized, and my breath caught. "Why?"

He pulled back and searched my eyes before answering. "Because you're sweet, and hot as fuck. You already love Elodie, and you come out swinging if someone you care about gets hurt."

My gaze shifted away. "I don't start swinging."

He put his hand on my cheek, and pulled my face back to his. "Yes, you do. And it's usually with your mouth." He grinned and rubbed his thumb across my lips. "I also have fantasies about tying you up and doing things to your sweet, lush little body that are so hot and dirty, they'd probably set your hair on fire."

My mouth gaped, and I stared at his lips. Then I licked my own. "You can't say things like that."

He leaned in and kissed my temple. "Yes, I can. And sometimes I'll be saying those things while we're both naked, sweaty, and I'm planted deep inside you."

Oh God. I was getting wet and I wanted to rub against him and purr like Shawnda. I also wanted to trace the scar on his cheek and run my hands through his thick hair.

But we'd gotten off track. "Tell me about Elodie's mom."

He sighed and let go of me. "Fine, we'll talk." He led me over to the couch and we sat.

"What happened with her?"

"I already told you about her mental health issues. And she's just mean. When she doesn't take her medications consistently, she can also become dangerous."

I was numb and heartsick for all of them. "How did you get together then?"

Connor absently stroked my arm while he talked. "Amelia and I grew up in the same neighborhood. She's a few years younger than me, and I thought I knew her. She was a little wild, but beautiful and different. No one mentioned she has bipolar disorder, or suffered from bouts of depression or rage."

"What happened?"

Connor sighed. "We had sex for a few weeks, then her behavior started becoming strange and erratic. But by then she was pregnant. She'd told me she was on the pill, and I usually wore a condom. But I was a stupid, dumb fuck."

I squeezed his hand. "We all are sometimes. The consequences usually aren't that drastic though."

"I didn't help the situation at first." He looked at me with guilt in his eyes. "I wasn't very understanding, and I didn't want the baby when she first told me. And when Elodie was born, I made Amelia get a paternity test before…" He didn't finish his thought.

"Before what?" I asked.

Connor studied me. "Mémé took care of Elodie when Amelia had custody, but she's old and frail."

"Elodie talks about you and Mémé all the time. But she never mentions Amelia."

He reached over and pulled me into his lap, then tucked my head under his chin. I didn't resist.

Wrapping my arms around him, I squeezed. "What are you going to do?"

"I was recently granted full custody, among other things."

"So that's what you and Elodie have been dealing with the past few years." I cupped his cheek. "I'm sorry."

He raised an eyebrow. "Why are you apologizing?"

"When I first met you, I thought you were a self-centered prick. You're not. You're just a dad who loves his daughter and is trying his best to protect her."

He smiled grimly and picked up a strand of my hair. "I am a self-centered prick. But for the past few years, I've been focused on trying to keep Elodie safe and happy."

"It's working. She seems happier and more settled, and she loves you."

"She loves you and Javier too. On Christmas Day when I walked into my kitchen and everyone was sitting around the table, I thought it was a damned Christmas miracle. She sat cuddled up next to you, smiling and talking your ear off. I'd never seen her so animated and happy."

I patted his chest. "No offense, but I wanted to punch you in the testicles that day."

He laughed and grabbed my hand, then kissed it. "I know. I'm sorry about dragging you into my shit, and about Noah."

I sat up and looked at him. "Titus called Noah a mean, rotten fucker. Have you talked with your last assistant?"

He shook his head. "I got distracted and haven't followed up. What is it with you and Titus? He probably knows more about you than I do."

I couldn't deny it, so I kept my mouth shut.

His eyes narrowed. "What? Don't keep secrets from me."

He had no room to talk. But I should have told him about my confrontation with Noah before now.

Rubbing my lips, I looked up at him. "I need to tell you something, but you have to promise not to be mad."

His face went cold. "Tell me."

"When I was at your estate in October visiting my dad, I ran into Noah a couple of times."

Then I told him about what Noah said to my dad, and how Noah had cornered and then grabbed me. Connor was breathing like a freight train by the time I finished.

He set me back on the couch and stood up. "Why am I just hearing about this now?"

I tried to tamp down my irritation. "Because at the time I didn't think you'd do anything, and I didn't want to give Noah the satisfaction of knowing he'd scared me."

Connor started pacing. "He assaulted you, Goddamn it! And you've had over three months to tell me."

My eyes narrowed. I stood up and faced off in front of him. "The first time we met, you were barking orders at me. The next time I saw you, I was being accused of burglary. And since then, it just hasn't come up."

He glared at me. "You keep throwing that in my face, Bella. Now you're just using it as an excuse to keep me at arms' length."

I glared back. "You asked why I didn't tell you, and I answered. Don't get pissy because you don't like the truth."

He stepped closer, and we were almost nose to nose. "From now on, you talk to *me* instead of Titus."

I glared up at him. "Titus is my friend, and he defended you. Although I don't know why since you're such a moody, bossy asshole sometimes."

His nostrils flared. Before I could step away, he wrapped his hands around my forearms and dragged me to him. His mouth crashed down on mine, and he nipped my lips. I stumbled into his chest and felt his hard, warm body wrap around me. I froze for a second, then fisted his hair and pulled him closer.

When he licked my lips, wanting entrance, I instinctively opened my mouth. He thrust his tongue inside and pulled me into his hard length. The kiss was angry and carnal. When he finally let me up for air, I whimpered at the loss of his mouth.

"Fuck," he bit out, squeezing me tight. "I don't want our first kiss to turn into angry sex. But I'm about two seconds away from throwing you on the floor."

I could feel his hard length against my stomach, and we were both panting.

"I'm not sure what's in this old carpet anyway," I tried to joke.

He pulled back and looked me up and down. I could see him trying to reign in his temper and lust.

"So you can joke about your shitty apartment, but I can't?"

I rolled up on my toes to nip his chin, then quickly stepped back. "Yep."

Studying me carefully, he put his hands on his hips. "Bella, I want you to tell me things like this from now on."

Gritting my teeth, I jerked my head in a reluctant nod. "Okay. Then you need to be honest with me."

He ran his hand through his hair. "Alright, that's fair. When you get off work tomorrow, will you come spend the weekend?"

"I was already planning to, at my dad's house."

"No. I want you at my house. In my bed. With me."

"This is too fast, Connor. I need to talk to my dad, and you need to talk to Elodie."

Connor smirked and leaned in. "You're going too slow, honey. They've known what's been happening between us long before you did. And I don't have to hold back anymore."

My mouth dropped open, and I gaped up at him.

He grabbed my face and kissed both my cheeks, then bit and sucked my bottom lip. "I need to go or I'll be putting more than my tongue into that sweet, wet mouth of yours. See you tomorrow. And don't bother packing pajamas."

# Chapter 16

My shift at the pediatric clinic seemed to crawl by. I thought about calling my dad and yelling at him for not telling me about his conversations with Connor. Then I wanted to call Connor and yell at him for talking with my dad behind my back.

My temper finally simmered down, and I grimaced at the thought of everyone, including Elodie, knowing what was happening. Even Titus had told me to never say never.

During my lunch break, I stopped in to see Molly in the hospital and took her book five in the series she was reading. She was too weak to talk very long, so I left the book and a little green frog on the table by her bed.

After my shift ended, I swung by Titus's house to pick up the games and things I'd left there last night. Titus had just gotten home from practice.

He studied my face and didn't mince words. "You still look frustrated and annoyed. Obviously, you two didn't fuck last night."

I smacked his hard shoulder. "No, we didn't. We yelled at each other, then he kissed the crap out of me and left."

"He's losing his touch."

My eyes slid away from his. "Right before he left, he told me I was sleeping at his house tonight, and don't bother packing pajamas."

He smirked at my embarrassment. "That sounds more like him."

I plopped down on a barstool. "He also told me about Amelia last night."

Titus eyed me carefully and poured a couple of glasses of water, then pushed one in front of me. "Now I know why you were yelling at each other. What exactly did he tell you?"

"He told me about how he got her pregnant, and her diagnoses. He said she can be dangerous if she's not on her meds. Should I be worried about her?"

He cocked his head. "Worried? About your safety?"

"What? No. Worried about Elodie, and whether Amelia's going to try and mess with her to get at Connor."

He stared at me. "I bet he doesn't know what to do with you after years of dealing with Amelia. And countless puck bunnies before that."

I winced. "I think I can guess what that term means. Is that actually a thing?"

"Fuck yes, it's a real thing. Start paying attention to some of the fans at the game and how they dress."

"On Sunday, I saw a woman in red stiletto heels and a modified jersey that showed more skin than most bikini tops."

He nodded. "Classic puck bunny. It's a problem with some of the younger players, but most of us steer clear now."

"Good to know."

He studied me. "Connor and I give each other shit, but he's one of my best friends. And I'll fucking deny it if you repeat that."

"Okay. I kind of figured since you irritate each other so much."

"You're what some men call a unicorn. I'm not going to fuck up his chances with you."

I set my water down. "What do you mean?"

"There are things you and Connor need to discuss." Titus refused to say any more about it.

Driving to Dad's house that evening, I felt jittery and out of sorts. When I walked inside, Connor and Elodie were setting the table for dinner.

Connor saw me first. He set the silverware down, walked over, and wrapped his arms around me. Then he cupped my cheeks and kissed me in front of my dad and Elodie. My eyes were round when he pulled back.

"You're just in time for dinner. Elodie and I grilled a few steaks."

I slowly hugged him back. "This feels weird," I admitted. "Good. But weird."

Dad chuckled behind me, and I turned to see him and Elodie grinning at us.

Stepping back, I pointed at them. "You two troublemakers have been plotting against me."

Elodie came over and patted my leg. "Can you have sleepovers with Daddy now?"

I turned to my dad. "Is that your idea?" I choked.

His lips pressed together and tried not to smile. "Absolutely not."

Connor grinned. "I think it's a great idea."

"Let's eat, I'm starving." I practically yelled.

After dinner, Connor turned to me. "Come over in an hour or so. We'll do another hair lesson, then tuck Elodie in. And you can read with us."

Elodie took both our hands. "This is our very first sleepover. I'm so excited."

"Yeah, me too," Connor grinned.

While we talked, I absently took Connor's other hand. When I realized what I'd done, I quickly dropped it.

He smirked and leaned in to kiss my mouth. "See you in a few."

When they walked out, I stared at the door for a second, then turned to my dad. "You knew. For the past month, you knew what was happening."

"Yeah. Good thing *one* of us did. I like him too. You got off to a bit of a rocky start, but he's a good man."

"A *bit* of a rocky start? That's like calling the black plague a little chest cold."

Dad chuckled and patted my arm. "That's what makes it interesting. I have a new library book I want to start. I'll see you in the morning."

I took a long shower and shaved every nook and cranny, then put on my best matching underwear. Letting out a long exhale, I grabbed my backpack and headed over to Connor's house. I felt a little like Red Riding Hood walking into the forest with a basket of treats.

# Chapter 17

Elodie met me at the door and pulled me into her bathroom. Connor could now do intricate braids and twists, so tonight I showed him how to do a rose braid bun. When he finished, Elodie's hair was done up in a cute half-do, and there was a blooming rose styled from a braid at the base of her crown.

"My work here is done, young Padawan. You're officially better than I am." I stood back and admired it.

Elodie turned and looked at the back of her hair in the angled mirror, and gasped softly. "That's so pretty."

"Thanks, sweetheart."

"It really is," I agreed.

"Daddy, give her one, too."

Connor gestured for me to stand in front of him. Then he styled my hair while Elodie chattered away, giving him encouragement and directions. It felt so good to have his hands in my hair, and the soft, almost erotic tug lulled me. When he finished, he angled the mirror so I could see what he'd created.

"Wow, it's beautiful. You're good." I turned my head and admired the rose he'd fashioned in my hair from the loose braid.

He stared at me. "You are beautiful."

My heart rolled over in my chest, and the butterflies came back.

We piled onto Elodie's bed, and Connor grabbed a few books off her nightstand. I recognized some I used to read as a kid.

"We usually read two," Connor told me. "I choose one and Elodie chooses the other. You can pick for me tonight."

I read a book that had been one of my favorites about a dramatic little piglet named Olivia. Elodie giggled the whole way through.

She started drifting off during the second book, and Connor took out her braid, kissed her forehead, and tucked her in.

His large, scarred hands were gentle as he pulled the blanket up around her. We tiptoed out of the room.

In the hallway, he turned to me. "Do you want anything to drink? A glass of wine maybe?"

"No, I'm good."

"Then let's finish our talk so we can get to the good part."

He took my hand and pulled me down the hall to the entertainment room. There was a large, deep couch that made a U shape around a massive TV mounted to the wall. A popcorn machine stood in the back corner with a strange clown head on top, and a pool table and pop-a-shot sat behind the couch. The room was bigger than my entire apartment.

Connor walked me to the couch and pulled me onto his lap. "Your dad mentioned you're twenty-three. When's your birthday?"

My heart sped up, and I had to concentrate on his question. "In March. Why?"

He watched me carefully. "I'm thirty-four."

I patted his knee. "Good to know, old man."

He grabbed my hand and bit my palm. "I'm also a possessive asshole when it comes to you. I don't want other men looking at you."

Rubbing my forehead against his shoulder, I sighed. "I don't know what to do with that since I'm working with the hockey team, and one-half the population is male. Your past is way more crowded than mine."

"When Elodie was born my life changed drastically. And so did that." He palmed my thigh.

"Okay, if we're being honest with each other, I hate that you've been with so many women. Have you had a girlfriend, or ever been monogamous before?"

"I've had two serious relationships. What else do you want to know?"

I folded my arms and asked the one question that had been haunting me. "Do you like me because Elodie does?"

"Yes."

Nodding, I carefully scooted away from him and stood up. "Okay."

I'd been living with the fear that Connor only wanted me because Elodie and I were close. At least he'd been honest. Connor said it himself. His life irrevocably changed when Elodie was born. He needed someone who would love and care for her, especially with her mother's issues. But I couldn't be with him if he only wanted me for his daughter.

I started for the door. "I need to go. Tell her I'll talk to her tomorrow or Saturday–"

His arms wrapped around my chest, and he pulled my back into his front. I froze.

Leaning in, he kissed my neck. "I also want you because you're sweet and kind when you aren't throwing shade at me. You're also smart."

"Connor–"

His hand slid up my chest, gently circling my neck, and holding me still. "And you're gorgeous, and sexy as fuck. Your face is part innocence, part wet dream. And I want to do dirty, nasty things to you, and make you like it all."

My breath whooshed out and I went limp in his arms. Connor pushed his hard length against my back side.

"You have a naughty mouth, McCoy," I grumbled.

"You have no idea." His nose nudged my earlobe. "You always smell so good. Like coconut and sunshine."

His touch made me shiver, and goosebumps broke out on my arms.

Brushing my hair aside, he let go of my neck and kissed and nibbled my collarbone. "The smell of coconut reminds me of you. It makes me want to bite and lick you."

My breath caught and my nipples hardened. "You smell like sandalwood and sage. I used to hate that I liked your smell."

He chuckled and slowly let go of me, took my hand, and led me back to the couch. Pulling me across his lap again, he tucked me into his side and palmed my stomach.

"I'm ten years older than you, and I'm a selfish bastard. I should stay away, but I'm not going to."

Connor ran his fingers under the hem of my shirt, and my stomach clenched. He skimmed his thumb across the underside of my breast. I started panting and squirming on his lap. His touch ignited me, and I wanted to wrap myself around him and feel his skin on mine.

Palming my breast, he studied my face. "We need to talk, but I can't keep my hands off you. So we'll talk while I touch you."

My body arched into his large, calloused hand and a moan escaped me. I couldn't get my mouth to form words while his hands roamed my body. He slowly raised my shirt up, then pulled my bra down, watching my eyes as he did.

Tracing a thumb across my nipple, he leaned in and licked the other one. "I need to be in control when we fuck, and it'll be a little rough. I also like to use ties and toys sometimes. I'll make sure you like it. Just tell me if there's something that worries you."

My eyelids grew heavy and my breath sped up.

He continued to play with my breasts. "I'll try to go slow, but I saw how you reacted when I tied your wrists up."

He was right, so I didn't deny it. "I... don't have a lot of experience, but I do like sex."

Connor grinned, then slowly reached down and unzipped my pants. "What are your fantasies? What gets you off?"

I blushed so hard, I could feel heat coming off my chest. "I read dark romance and erotica sometimes."

"What kind of erotica?"

I swallowed as he gazed at my flushed chest and exposed breasts. My bra was a basic black one, and I'd probably bought it at Target. But his pupils were dilated and I could feel his long, hard length underneath me.

He leaned in and ran his nose along the swell, then he sucked a nipple and bit down on it. Gasping, I arched into his mouth.

"Tell me."

"Submission. Being tied up. And maybe taken hard."

He buried his lips in my neck and groaned. "Fuuuck."

"I'm not exactly sure what I like since I've only had sex with two people." I shifted restlessly in his lap, then stilled when his hard shaft under my ass seemed to grow.

He pressed his lips to my chest, and I could feel his smile. "We'll explore what you like together. And you'll have to read me a few of your favorite parts."

"No way," I answered without thinking.

"Fuck yes. Are you on birth control?"

I froze.

His head came up. "It's all right, we can use condoms."

My gaze slid away. "Maybe this is too fast."

Connor studied me as I involuntarily arched into his touch when he ran a thumb over my nipple. "It's not too fast. Your semester ends in less than three months, and you might be moving away after that. I want to give you a reason to stay." He bit and licked the side of my neck.

I panted and squirmed as he methodically and expertly played with me. He was so good at making me burn for him. Turning my face to his, he forced me to look at him.

Sighing, I cupped his cheek. "I have an IUD, and I got tested six months ago. I haven't been with anyone since then." Soon I'd be working full-time in the medical profession, but this conversation still embarrassed me for some reason.

He smiled a little. "I went in and got tested a month ago when I knew we'd eventually be here. I'm good."

"How did you know…?" I trailed off. It probably didn't matter how he knew. I wouldn't have believed it.

He ran a finger through my folds, and skimmed his thumb across my clit. I arched into his hand, gasping. My mind went fuzzy, and my vagina pulsed. Then he slid his finger inside me.

"Holy mother," I wheezed as my breath froze up.

Connor reached around and unhooked my bra with his other hand. Then removed it, along with my shirt.

"Are you my sweet girl?" he asked softly.

"If you keep doing that, then God, yes."

I felt him smile as he slid his tongue across my lips and then into my mouth. I loved the feel of his hands skimming my naked torso.

Sliding my hand to his lap, I palmed his thick erection through his jeans as he kissed me.

His head came up. "Fuck me," he groaned. "I haven't made out on a couch since I was maybe eighteen or nineteen. And I came about thirty seconds after she touched me."

I smiled. "Do you want to see if we can beat that record?"

"Hell, no. Tonight I plan to torture you a bit, fuck you hard, and come deep inside you."

"Oh, God." I moaned and rolled my hips as he brushed against my clit again.

Grinning slowly, he reached up and fisted my hair, then deliberately pulled my head back, exposing my neck as he palmed my center. It didn't hurt, but he held me firmly in place and let me feel his control.

My eyelids drooped and my body loosened.

"When I fist your hair or tie up your wrists, your pupils blow and you melt all over me. Nice to know."

"You can't say things like that," I panted.

He smirked. "You keep telling me that, and yet here we are."

My bottom moved against his cock, and he cupped my pussy even harder.

"Open for me," he demanded. When I wasn't fast enough, he gently but firmly shook my head hair.

My vagina spasmed, and I opened my legs. He reached in and slid another finger inside me, watching my face as he pushed in and out. My eyes drifted shut and I whimpered.

"You're dripping wet."

I rolled my hips against his hand. His fingers were big, and they stretched me wide. My vagina stung, but he expertly rubbed his thumb against my clit.

"Open your eyes so you can watch me finger you."

I struggled to open them. When I started rocking against his fingers, he pulled out.

"Don't stop," I moaned.

"Not a chance." He drew me off the couch and started to remove my pants.

"Connor, what are you doing?" I sidestepped him and started coming out of my stupor.

"Taking your pants off, then taking you to my bedroom to fuck you properly."

"I can take my clothes off there. Give me my shirt."

He stood up. "No."

My eyes narrowed, and I bent down to pull my pants back up my legs. He snatched me up and threw me over his shoulder.

"You won't need these." He yanked my pants off, and threw them aside.

Wiggling on his shoulder, I pinched his butt. "What the hell are you doing?" I asked again, laughing and squirming.

I tried to raise my torso up, but he smacked the back of my thigh. "If you want to keep your panties on, at least for a few minutes, you need to behave."

I smacked his ass in retaliation. "*You* need to behave."

"I'm not the one with my ass in the air," he laughed, then smacked my butt cheek.

"Fuck, that stings!" I yelped.

He ripped my panties down and left them in a heap on top of my pants.

"Only good girls get to wear panties." He turned and started walking down the hallway.

He jostled me a little and fondled my bottom. "If you stay quiet, I won't heat up your other ass cheek."

I couldn't help myself. "You can go fuck yours–Ouch, God-damn it! Stop spanking me!" I whisper-hissed when he smacked me again.

He ran his hand up my thigh, then drew his fingers across my wet slit. "No. Your cunt tells me you like getting spanked. And finger fucked. Good to know."

Connor's hand smoothed over my ass cheek, and he reached in and slid his fingers through my slit again, rubbing and stroking me as he walked. His touch was firm and deliberate, and it sent hot pulses shooting through me. I moaned softly.

He stepped inside a door at the end of the hall and shut it. Turning, he put me down and stepped back. When I stood up straight, I realized I was completely naked and he was fully dressed.

I glanced around at Connor's bedroom and started to cross my arms over my chest.

"Don't." His voice was low and gravelly. "When we're in the bedroom alone, you don't need to cover yourself."

My hands slowly dropped. I should have told him to go fuck himself again, but instead my nipples hardened, and my eyes drooped at his command.

His hot gaze slid down my body, and he put his hands on his hips. "You're a sight, sweet girl. With your wild hair, flushed cheeks, and perfect tits and ass, I'm not sure where to begin."

Standing there naked in front of him, I felt vulnerable and turned on all at once. "You need to take your clothes off."

His eyebrow arched. "Do I?" He leaned in and ran his hands down my shoulders, then cupped my breasts.

His hands felt so good. My breath sped up and I leaned into him, grabbing his forearms to steady myself.

"I want to touch you too." I started tugging on his shirt.

Leaning in, he kissed me long and hard, then started walking me backward. "I don't have the patience to play tonight. I need to be inside you."

I felt the backs of my thighs hit his mattress. He let go of me and I pulled his shirt over his head, revealing his sculpted torso and vivid tattoo. I ran my hands up and down his chest, then latched onto his jeans.

"Greedy little thing, aren't you?"

"Uh-huh. Now help me take your pants off. I want to see all of you." I tugged and pulled at his top button, but my hands weren't cooperating.

He took over and stripped the rest of his clothes off. When he pulled me into his arms, the feel of his skin on mine sent lust skittering through me, and I gasped out loud. Melting into him, I pulled his head down for another kiss.

Then Connor stepped back and put his hand on my chest, pushing me back onto his mattress. I tumbled back, letting out a surprised laugh.

Grinning, Connor crawled on top of me and ran his hand up my thigh to grip my hip. "I've had several extremely raunchy fantasies about you sprawled naked across my bed like this."

My legs moved restlessly. "You feel so good."

He sat up on his knees "Lay back and spread your thighs. I want to see your sweet little pussy."

I blinked. Embarrassment and need spread through me. Laying back down, I took my time spreading my thighs. He studied me there, then palmed my vagina.

"You have the prettiest pussy. I bet you taste like honey."

I whined softly. He bent over and kissed my navel, then licked and kissed his way down my hips. When he reached my core, he used his thumbs to pull my folds apart.

Bending his head, he licked me there, long and slow.

"Mmm," he hummed, running his tongue along his bottom lip.

I arched up and cried out. "Aw, God. That feels so good." My mind struggled to process words.

Connor bit me lightly on the inside of my thigh. "Why are you telling God? You need to tell me."

My eyes closed when he burrowed in and licked and sucked me hard. My toes curled to tight points, and my hips arched up to give him a better angle. When I started shifting restlessly and got close to coming, he slowed down and backed off.

"Connor, God. Please."

He grinned and watched me from between my thighs, licking his lips again. Then he slowly pushed two large fingers inside me, his thumb rubbing my clit. I threw my head back and cried out.

He reached up and pinched and pulled on my nipple. "Eyes on me, Bella. I need to see your face when you come for me the first time."

I could barely register his demand. My stomach tightened, and my insides felt swollen and needy. But I opened my eyes and looked at him.

He slowly moved his fingers in and out of my vagina, then pressed in as far as he could go. His thumb rubbed against my swollen, sensitive clit. Then he backed off, drawing out my pleasure and frustration. He was too good at this.

"You're fucking beautiful, with your legs spread wide for me and your breasts flushed and heaving."

"I want to come," I whispered in a needy voice.

"I know you do. Your perfect pink nipples are hard as glass. Play with them for me."

My face flushed even hotter, but I slowly raised my hands and cupped my breasts.

He nodded. "That's it. Now pinch and roll them for me." He started rubbing my clit with his thumb again.

My hips shifted restlessly, and a soft gasp escaped me. I started to close my eyes again, but he leaned in and nipped a tendon in my thigh. "No, Isabella. Eyes open. I've waited too fucking long."

I snapped my eyes open and glared at him, but my hips continued to shift restlessly. He swatted my pussy and I startled, then gasped. Connor leaned in and sucked on my clit again.

He pushed two fingers back inside me. "Hands back on your tits."

My arms had fallen to my sides. His hot eyes drank me in as he watched my hips arch, seeking his mouth and fingers. I tugged on my nipples, and he smiled then went back to licking and sucking me. The pressure intensified, and an orgasm started to build again.

I wanted to lay my head down and close my eyes, but I knew he'd stop. My hips started thrusting against his mouth, and when he flicked his tongue relentlessly against my clit, a blinding orgasm crashed through me.

Trying to hold my head up proved too much, and I let out a long, soft wail as I came. When the last waves crested through me, Connor unlatched his mouth from my clit.

He crawled on top of me, supporting his torso with his arms. "You're so beautiful when you come, sweet girl."

Connor kissed me and slid his tongue into my mouth. I could taste and smell my juices on his lips as he ravaged me. I felt lightheaded and out of breath, and had to finally turn my head to gulp in air.

Pulling back, he knelt between my legs. Spreading my thighs apart, he pushed them up and out. I was completely exposed to him, and I could feel my wet clit throbbing. My mind and body swam with lust and need, and I ached to have him inside me.

He groaned. "I can't wait anymore. We'll play later, but right now I need to fuck you long and hard. Can you take it like a good, sweet girl?"

I spasmed underneath him, and my vagina pulsed. I nodded, but he shook his head.

"Use your words, Bella," he growled.

I glared even as my hips shifted, trying to find his cock. "You want me to use my words? Alright. I want you to fuck me–right now. But I won't be taking it like a good girl."

He leaned in and licked and bit my nipple. "Let's find out."

Pushing hard against my slick opening with his cock, he relentlessly drove himself inside me. It was tight, and he had to work to make it fit. I shifted restlessly underneath him, and my vagina tried to resist the invasion. It was almost too much.

"Fucking hell. Your pussy feels like it's trying to strangle me."

I ran my hands down his shoulders and latched onto his biceps. I didn't know if I wanted to push him away or pull him closer.

"It doesn't fit," I panted. But my hips lifted up to meet his thrusts.

He laughed breathlessly and thrust harder. "Oh, it fucking fits. Like you were made for me. God, I just want to pound inside you and make you scream."

"I... thought you already were," I gasped out as he pulled back, then drilled inside me again.

Connor flexed his hips. "Not even close."

He finally bottomed out, and I could feel his length pressing deep inside me. "Ah, God. It's too much," I gasped. My core ached and pulsed, and my body felt overloaded.

He panted. "Do you want me to pull out?"

"Don't even think about it," I growled and wrapped a leg around him.

Grabbing my hands, Connor pulled them up above my head and planted my palms on his headboard.

He leaned in and kissed my mouth. "Hold on. You're going to need the leverage."

Getting on his knees, he pulled my hips up. And then he let loose.

He hammered inside me, his hips snapping forcefully. I slid back for a split second until I locked my elbows and splayed my palms against his headboard, bracing myself in place.

Pain and lust slammed into me as he shoved himself even deeper, and my head arched back. I'd never been fucked like this before. Not even close. Connor was like a wrecking ball, slamming through me.

He let go of my thighs and used his fingers to rub and press on my clit. "That's it. Take it all." He groaned as he arched back, then dropped his head, staring down at me as he continued to stroke my clit and drive inside me. My body lurched hard with each thrust.

His eyes heated even more as he watched me jerk while he drove into me. "I want to pound you into my bed and make you scream and beg, then tie you up so I can do it all night."

His words sizzled through my brain, and the image of me spread out and tied to his bed while he hammered into me flickered across my mind.

My back arched even more, and my toes curled. My vagina convulsed around him, and a climax rose.

I threw my head back and wailed. "Please, I can't... you're too deep. Aw, god. I'm coming!"

He smiled darkly and gritted his teeth. "Not too deep then."

Connor thrust into me several more times as I convulsed around him. Then he shoved himself against me and found his own release. My arms finally gave way and I slid up the bed a little before he pulled me back, pulsing hot semen into me.

He seemed to climax forever, and by the time he laid my hips back down and fell on top of me, I was semi-conscious and limp. His cock still twitched, and his semen seeped out of me.

I'd never climaxed that hard, and my insides still quivered and pulsed.

He gazed down at me and brushed the sweaty strands of hair clinging to my cheek away, then kissed me gently.

"Are you alright?"

Hazy and disjointed thoughts floated through my mind, and delicious post-orgasmic chemicals slid through my bloodstream. His hard length still lodged inside me.

"I think so." Clearing my throat, I looked at him. "You weren't kidding when you said you like it a little rough."

He seemed to flinch. Slowly, he pulled out and rolled off. Then he turned to get off the bed, but I grabbed his arm.

"I liked it... a lot." I looked away. "I've never orgasmed with a guy before." Of course, I'd only had sex a handful of times, but still.

He studied me silently. If my face got any hotter, it would start on fire. I let go of his arm and tried to turn away.

This time, he grabbed me, laid down, and pulled me across his torso. I was still leaking fluids, and I struggled in his grasp.

I could barely look him in the eye. "I'm dripping all over. I need to get cleaned up."

He kept hold of me and cupped my face. "It's like you were fucking made for me," he murmured. Then he pulled my forehead down and gave me a soft kiss. "Just tell me if I ever do something you don't like. In bed that is. You don't have a problem anywhere else."

I slowly relaxed against him and rested my chin on his chest. "Well, *somebody* needs to keep your fat ego in check."

He slid his hands up and down my sides, then wrapped a leg around me. "You can certainly try."

He grinned and rolled me over, then spread my legs with his knees before I could put up a fight.

Leaning down, he licked and nuzzled my neck. "We're not done yet." Then he started in on round two.

# Chapter 18

The sound of hushed voices outside the bedroom door woke me the next morning. Rolling over, I opened an eye and realized I wasn't in my bedroom or Dad's spare room. And then it all came back to me.

Sitting up quickly, I scanned the rumpled bed and looked around Connor's bedroom. In the light of day, I noticed the soft white bed linens and expensive furniture. His bedstand had a hockey magazine and a couple of novels on it next to his alarm clock.

Across the room from the bed, large French doors faced out onto the expansive pool area Connor's house was built around. The view was partially blocked by gauzy curtains, but I could see the outline of palm trees and flowering bushes outside.

His bed smelled like sandalwood and sex. Traces of us from last night lingered in the air, and I realized some of it came off me.

My sore vagina clenched when I remembered the three times we'd gone at each other last night like rabid animals. I slid out of bed and quickly used the bathroom.

As I cleaned up a little, I thought about what we'd done last night. I should have gone back to my dad's house afterward so I wouldn't be here when Elodie woke up, but I'd fallen into a dreamless sleep minutes after he'd tucked me into his side in the early dawn.

I thought I heard Elodie's giggle and quickly looked around for my clothes. Then I remembered Connor had stripped them off in the entertainment room last night, and my backpack was in the kitchen.

Sighing, I padded over to Connor's dresser and started opening drawers. I found socks, underwear, and what looked like a miscellaneous drawer. Red rope and a little vibrator still in its packaging sat on top. There were other things in the drawer, but I quickly shut it.

My heart slammed in my throat as I cautiously pulled open another drawer and thanked God and Jesus when I saw only t-shirts inside. Grabbing one, I started to close the drawer when the bedroom door opened.

I yelped and spun around, using the t-shirt to shield myself. Connor stepped inside, closing the door behind him. Then he leaned back against it and grinned.

"What're you doing?"

"Looking for something to wear since you stripped me, threw me over your shoulder, and left all my clothes in your huge-ass TV room last night."

He straightened and walked toward me. "Drop the shirt, Bella. I already told you when you're in this bedroom you don't need to cover yourself up."

My eyes narrowed, and I hugged his shirt closer. "And I already told you, you can go fuck yourself. Elodie's out there–"

He smirked. "We'll get to your sassy mouth in a minute. Your dad just picked her up to take her to school. Then he's going golfing with a few of his book club buddies."

"Oh." I didn't know my dad was in a book club, or that he had book club buddies. And then I thought of Dad knowing I'd spent the night here.

"Oh, God." Heat bloomed across my cheeks. "He knows we slept together, and so does Elodie. I meant to go back to my dad's house last night after we..."

"Slept together?" he drawled.

"Oh, shut up. I'm a bad daughter and a bad influence."

Connor chuckled and backed me against his dresser. Then he pulled his shirt out of my hands and stepped between my legs.

"No, Bella. You were very, *very* good." He leaned in and nuzzled my hair.

"I need clothes," I said weakly. "I should have gone back to my dad's house last night."

Palming my cheek, he studied me. "They know we had a 'sleep-over.' And they know when you come here, you'll be staying in my bed from now on."

My face flushed even harder. "Connor, I can't–"

"Bella, you can. If we're going to be together, it's better if we don't try to sneak around. I don't want Elodie or Javier, or anyone else for that matter, to question whether this is serious."

"Well, hell," I muttered. "I like it better when I'm the level-headed, logical one." He felt so good, holding me against him as he stroked my back.

He pulled back and smirked. "Don't worry. When it comes to you, I'm not logical or levelheaded."

We showered together, and he brought me to orgasm with his fingers and mouth, then hoisted me against the shower wall and pounded into me until he came too. I felt loose and zen-like while we made coffee and breakfast afterward.

Connor wanted to go to the arena later that morning to skate with Zeke, so I went over to my dad's house to finish getting ready and get clean clothes.

"You need to bring your things over here," he told me as we got into his vehicle.

"No way, it's too early for that. What's in the bag?"

He'd loaded a black bag into his back seat.

"My skates and shit. I want to get out on the ice this morning before the team starts practicing."

"Do you still skate a lot?"

"It's been a while. I miss it."

On the way to the arena, he called the front desk and asked them to pull a pair of skates for me in my size.

When we got there, we went into the front office first to pick up the skates. I'd met the office secretary before when I got my security pass, but she frowned at me when I walked in with Connor. Valerie was probably in her late twenties, and she didn't have a wedding or engagement ring.

She gave Connor a big smile, and her plum-colored lipstick framed her perfect, white teeth.

"Hello, Mr. McCoy. I have the skates you requested." She stood up and bent over to put them on the end of her desk, giving him a nice view down the front of her blouse.

Then she sat down and turned to me. "Can I help you?"

"You already did. The skates are for me." I smiled and picked them up.

Connor flicked her a glance. "Thanks, Lisa. Have you seen Titus yet today?" He'd barely glanced at her, and he called her by the wrong name.

She pursed her lips. "Yes. I saw him walk by a few minutes ago." Valerie turned to me. "You know how to ice skate?"

I shrugged. "Well enough." Connor was holding the door open for me, obviously ready to leave, so I waved and walked out.

When the door shut behind us, I looked up at Connor. "Her name is Valerie, not Lisa."

"I know." He stopped walking for a minute to type out a text on his phone.

"Why'd you call her the wrong name then?"

He stuck his phone in his back pocket and looked down at me. "She was rude to you."

"It doesn't bother me."

"It bothers me. And she eye fucks me every time I go in there."

I squinted back at the office door. "Okay. You can be mean to her for that."

He smiled and grabbed my free hand. When we got to the rink, we put our things on a bench and Connor started stretching a little.

"You ever skate before?"

Nodding, I did a few cursory stretches myself. "Yeah, but I'm not great. Paul Curtis gave my brother and me an annual pass to the Bellevue ice rink for a few years when we lived on his estate in Seattle. He always did stuff like that. He was a big believer in having experiences instead of things."

Connor's lips twisted cynically. "That's easy for a man with a net worth in the hundreds of millions to say."

His offhand comment bothered me because Paul had been a good man, maybe despite being so rich.

"I don't think he meant basic necessities. My dad believes the same thing, and so do I. My mom's medical expenses were exorbitant, so we never had a lot of things anyway."

His brow furrowed. "Did you ever go hungry?"

"No." I started lacing up the skates. "But my dad did. He'd skip lunch sometimes if there weren't any leftovers or sandwich stuff. Liam and I grew up using the free school lunch program. My dad *hated* it. But he wanted us fed more."

I'd also worn mostly secondhand clothes. Lucky for me, it was considered good practice in Seattle to reuse and recycle, so buying my clothes at thrift stores had been socially acceptable. Connor would probably roll his eyes if he knew I still shopped there.

He sighed and sat down next to me. "I can be an ass sometimes. I'm sorry. My parents died in a car wreck when I was in my early twenties, but they left a large life insurance policy for Noah and me. So we never went without."

Taking Connor's hand, I squeezed it, then ran my thumb across his knuckles. "I'm sorry about your parents. And I'm sorry Noah is the way he is."

He squeezed my hand back. "My parents lived and breathed hockey, so I guess you could say they also believed in experiences over material things. As long as it involved hockey."

He started lacing up his own skates. "My dad drank a lot, and he was an angry drunk. Which was too fucking bad because he was a decent dad when he was sober. And my mom didn't talk much. She was quiet and introverted."

I'd come to realize there wasn't a "one size fits all" to childhood scars and trauma.

Connor finished lacing his skates, then walked to the edge of the ice and took off. He deftly skated around the rink several times, then came back to me and stopped on a dime. My mouth hung open as I watched him.

I cleared my throat. "I want to watch you for a few minutes first."

He quirked his head. "You don't want to skate?"

"I do, but I want to watch you more. It's a nice view." My eyes slid down his front, then back up his length. "I just want to eye fuck you like Lisa-slash-Valerie for a few minutes. Is that okay?"

He grinned and started toward me, but we heard a door bang open in the tunnel.

"Okay you fucking prick, I'm here. You ready to get your ass kicked?"

I turned and saw Titus striding toward us with two hockey sticks and his skates hung over his shoulder.

He smirked when he saw me. "McCoy's the fucking prick, not you *petite choux*. You skating with us today?"

Smiling, I stood up and stepped onto the ice. I was a little shaky, but the muscle memory started coming back. "I'll skate a little, but then I'd like to watch."

Titus glanced at me, then looked at Connor who'd skated up behind me.

Connor's hand splayed across my stomach, pulling me into him. "Hey, asshole."

Titus set the hockey sticks and a puck down. "*Tu as baisé.*" He smirked at Connor. "It took you long enough, dumbass."

I tensed, but Connor chuckled and pulled me closer. "You ready for me to wipe the rink with you, Tremblay?"

"Let's skate with *petite choux* first, then we'll play."

"I fucking hate that you call her little cabbage, asshole," Connor growled.

Titus's smile turned mean. "I know."

I shook my head. "Quit baiting each other."

"But it's so easy, *choux*."

While Titus stretched a little and laced up his skates, Connor took me out on the ice. I'd ice skated a bit, and I was decent. But they made me feel like a one-year-old just learning to walk.

"You're not half bad," Titus said as he zipped around me then turned and skated backward about ten feet in front of me. What a showoff.

Connor circled me a couple of times before skating backward next to Titus. He was an even bigger showoff.

"Did you play any sports in high school?" Connor asked.

I kept my pace slow. "No. We didn't have the money. But I skateboard and longboard."

Titus glanced at Connor and grinned. "You found yourself a brainy, hot little skater girl. It figures."

"I'm not a skater girl."

Titus cocked his head. "Oh yeah? What's your favorite color?"

"Black. Because it doesn't stain easily."

"Uh-huh. Who's Anthony Hawk?"

"It's Tony Hawk." I winced when both Titus and Connor laughed.

"How many pairs of Vans do you own?" Connor asked.

"Three."

"Skater girl," Titus insisted.

"Whatever."

We ice skated around the rink a few times, and I felt more stable with each lap. I finally tried to skate backwards, and about landed on my ass. But I got the hang of it on the fifth try.

Eventually, I skated over to the bench and sat down. "I want to watch you two play."

They grabbed the hockey sticks and a puck, and Connor gave me a hard kiss. Then for an hour or so I watched, mesmerized, as they played what appeared to be a six-shot hockey drill. They were both so fast, I had difficulty following the puck.

They'd obviously played together for years because it seemed they could anticipate each other's moves. I'd never seen Connor play in person, and he and Titus on the ice was something I'd never forget. It was hypnotizing, heart-stopping, and hot as hell.

Someone sat down next to me. I glanced over and saw Jackson in his workout sweats. Mikael came and sat on my other side. I nodded to them and went back to watching the show.

Finally, the rest of the team started filtering in along with Coach Bailey. Everyone stopped to watch them finish up. Even Coach Bailey stared, transfixed.

When the last few players arrived, Connor and Titus headed off the rink. They were both grinning.

Jackson gazed at them. "It never gets old, watching those two play together. I wish they were both ten years younger."

I smiled, but it seemed sad to be at the end of your career in your mid-thirties. Connor squished in between Mikael and me and started unlacing his skates.

Mikael leaned forward and turned to me. "Are we playing Catan again this week, *vännen*?"

Connor scowled. "What the fuck does *vännen* mean?"

Mikael grinned. "Friend in Swedish."

Connor paused, then shrugged. "Alright. Tell everyone Bella's whiskey Wednesday potluck, get-to-know-your-fucking-neighbor thing is at my house this week. And every Wednesday from now on unless you hear otherwise, eh?"

Titus smirked. "That's okay with me. Then I don't have to clean up after these bastards."

Connor leaned over and stared at Jackson on the other side of me. "Make sure everyone knows. Got it?"

Jackson's lip twitched. "Got it." Somehow, I thought Connor wasn't just talking about our Wednesday game nights.

We left the rink and returned my skates. When we got back to his car, Connor turned to me.

"I did this a little backward, but let's go to dinner tonight."

My stomach flipped pleasantly. "As in a date? What about Elodie?"

He smiled and kissed my knuckles. "I love that you think about her. It'll be a late dinner, and we'll go after she's asleep. I have someone on call in the evenings, or your dad may be willing to hang out at my house for a couple of hours."

Connor took me to a popular steakhouse on El Paseo Drive for our first official date together. I wore my go-to black dress and he wore a linen shirt, and shoes that probably cost more than my car.

The host sat us in a semi-private booth, and Connor ordered a bottle of wine. I glanced at the menu, saw the prices, and promptly shut it.

"I'll have a couple of bites of your steak, and the Caesar salad." He was studying me when a couple sitting at a table close by spotted Connor. They got up and came over to talk.

"Connor McCoy, fuck me," the red-faced middle-aged man boomed. "It's good to see you finally out and about." His wife, judging by the huge diamond ring on her wedding finger, was taller and much thinner than the man, and she looked like she wasn't a stranger to Botox. She wore a periwinkle blue sheath that showed off her toned legs, and four-inch gold sandals. They were with another well-dressed couple, and they all looked like they'd been through a few bottles of wine together.

Connor reluctantly stood and shook hands. "Hello, Heath. I got the schedule from your group last week. I'll give you a call so we can discuss some issues."

He turned to me. "This is Isabella Cruz. Bella, this is Heath Perkins. He sometimes rents out the arena for events."

Heath turned to me and eyed me up and down. "Well hello, sweetie. Are you the reason Connor is holed up at his estate every night?"

Ugh. What a shmuck. I hated it when men I didn't know gave me nicknames like sweetie.

"I doubt it." I stood up and held my hand out to his wife. "He didn't introduce you, so we'll have to do it ourselves. I'm Isabella Cruz."

The lady stared at me for a second, then smirked and shook my hand. "I'm Charlene Perkins. And this is Tom and Melodie Watkins." She pointed to the couple behind her.

I smiled at her. "I love your dress. And I have no idea how you can walk in those sandals, but they also look wonderful on you."

Charlene smiled. "Practice. It's actually nice to meet you. I can't say that about everyone I've met through Heath. I'm his third and probably soon to be ex-wife."

"Should I give you my condolences or congratulations?"

Charlene threw her head back and laughed. Her companions laughed too, although I doubted they knew what they were laughing at.

"I'm fairly certain you're new around here. If you ever have any questions, or want to know the best yoga instructors or spas, I'm your gal."

"Thank you, but I'm a poor college student working on a master's degree. I've never paid for a yoga class. That's what YouTube is for, isn't it?"

Charlene grinned, but her face barely moved. "Oh, my God. You are a breath of fresh air." She turned to Connor. "I'll be inviting you over for cocktails one of these evenings. Make sure Isabella comes."

She patted my arm and walked off with her husband, smiling.

We sat down, and Connor leaned back and grinned at me.

"What?" I finally asked.

"You're something else. Sweetie."

"Yuck." I leaned forward and dropped my voice. "I prefer sweet girl, but only from you."

# Chapter 19

That week I found out Connor had no problem touching, hugging, and kissing me in front of other people. It was surprising and unnerving to realize how much I liked it.

Dad patted my shoulder awkwardly as we fixed dinner together. Connor and Elodie were coming over soon, and we planned to eat and watch a movie afterward.

"You two are getting along well. It seems kind of fast though," Dad said, setting a mixing bowl in the sink.

"You and Elodie were the ones plotting against me for the last month or two. And Connor is a force of nature."

He studied me. "Make sure it's what you want too."

"Connor gives me... tingles," I admitted, blushing a little.

Dad smiled softly and patted my shoulder. "Okay." He'd told me once he knew Mom was the one because she gave him tingles.

After dinner, Connor pulled me onto his lap and nuzzled my neck while we watched the movie. We sat on the loveseat, and

Elodie and my dad claimed the couch in front of the TV, with Shawnda curled up in Elodie's lap.

"Your squirming is making me hard," he murmured in my ear. I froze and glanced at Dad and Elodie. They were both watching TV and stuffing popcorn in their mouths.

I stopped fidgeting and slowly relaxed against Connor. Halfway through the movie, my head drooped against his shoulder and I fell asleep.

When the movie ended, Connor gently shook me awake. I was so tired I didn't argue when he walked a sleepy Elodie and me to his house with my bag slung over his shoulder.

Elodie yawned. "Night, Belly. We'll read tomorrow, okay?"

"Sounds good, love. Sweet dreams." I took my bag and shuffled into Connor's room. While he got her tucked in, I changed into one of his t-shirts, cleaned up, and fell into his bed.

Neither one of us had gotten much sleep the night before, and I crashed as soon as my head hit the pillow. Minutes later Connor crawled in beside me.

He gently rolled me over and stripped me before I could protest. Then he opened my legs and expertly brought me to the brink with his hands and mouth.

"You don't need pajamas," he murmured as he licked me.

I was suddenly wide awake. He leaned over me and ran his thigh between my legs, rubbing my core and sending sparks skittering through me. I opened my thighs wider to give him better access, then turned my head and bit down on his forearm.

He groaned low and whispered, "Have you ever been tied up, Bella?"

He trailed licks and bites down my chest to my nipples.

"No," I whispered hoarsely. "But I saw the rope and vibrator in your drawer."

"Yeah? What else did you see that interests you?"

"Nothing, because I slammed it shut when I realized what was in there. I was looking for a t-shirt."

Grinning, he ran his hand up my sides, then grabbed my wrists and raised them over my head. "Snoop away. When I get the chance, I plan to go through your drawers too."

My face flushed and mortification rolled through me. "What? No!"

He grinned, then rolled his hips and ran his cock across my wet core. "What's in there that has you so worried, sweet girl?"

"None of your business, big man."

He laughed and tightened his hold on my wrists. "How about a friendly little game? You like games, right? You let me tie you up with that red rope, and I get to use the vibrating bullet on your pretty pink pussy. If you're not begging me to let you come in eight minutes, then I won't go through your nightstand."

I smiled, feeling supremely confident. I loved games, and I loved to win. "And if I do beg you? What happens? Just in case."

"Then you tell me exactly what's in your nightstand or personal toybox, and you let me use them on you."

"What? That's a shitty deal," I laughed and bucked my hips. When I felt his hard cock press against my cleft, I groaned and ground myself along his length, forgetting our conversation.

Rubbing his shaft even harder against me, he leaned in and bit my lip. "I'll make it good for you, even if you lose. Say yes."

My eyelids drooped and I arched into him. "Yes."

Less than two minutes later, I found myself tied spreadeagle across his bed with the little vibrator pressed tight against my clit. I tried to squirm and wiggle away, but he unerringly followed me. And then he shoved two thick fingers inside me, and started to pull back and take the vibrator off my clit when he felt me tense up. *Mother fucking son of a whore.*

He tsked me. "You have a dirty mouth. I'm going to have to wash it out--with my cum."

Oops. I'd said it out loud. Four minutes later, when my head was thrashing and my juices were leaking all over his bed, he leaned in and sucked and bit my nipples. "Do you need to come?" His voice was muffled against my breast.

"Yes, goddamn it!"

"Then beg me, Bella. Tell me you want me to hold the vibrator to your clit while I fuck you hard with my cock. And I'll finger your ass if that helps you get off."

I froze, and my bottom clenched. "It would?"

He grinned and shrugged. "It might. We'll have to try it sometime and see. But for now, beg me to make you come." He put the vibrator on me for a few seconds, then pulled it off again when I thrust my hips. My head arched back, and I wailed in need. My insides ached and my legs shook.

"All right, I'm begging! I need to come." The last few words sounded almost like a moan.

I thought he'd gloat or laugh at winning our bet. Instead he smiled softly and climbed up my body. "You're fucking beautiful, tied across my bed, begging me to let you orgasm." He rubbed his length through the copious wetness between my thighs, then he angled into me and slammed inside. I arched up and tried to push my hips into him. I wanted it hard. I wanted him to hammer inside me and make me take every long, thick inch of him.

"Aw, God yes! Please, I need it hard."

By his fifth stroke, I cried out and came all over his cock. He didn't have to use the vibrator, his mouth, or even his finger at my ass. My orgasm smashed through me, and my insides clamped down so tight, I saw flashes of light behind my eyelids.

He leaned over and covered my mouth with his, taking in my loud cries. When I finally quieted down, he slid his palm around my throat.

"You orgasmed so hard, you almost broke my cock. You like being tied up, don't you?"

I realized he was right. My hands fisted, and lust swam through my veins. He'd tied me up, teased me, and made me come harder than I ever had. He leaned down and bit my nipple, then pulled and tugged on the other one. I arched up involuntarily, and my eyes lost focus. My breasts and nipples had always been sensitive, and I loved the feel of his mouth and hands on them.

"Be my good, sweet girl, and I'll make you come again."

He reached down and untied my legs, then he brought my knees up to my shoulders and spread me wide open. "I'm going to fuck you hard and deep, and then I'm going to put the vibrator back on you, and make you come until you beg me to stop."

"I want to touch you too."

He brushed my hair back. "Not yet."

I labored to breathe, struggling to draw in enough air. My sensitive clit tingled and pulsed along with my heartbeat. My arms were stretched out above me, and Connor had me pinned to the bed. I could only lay there and take what he gave me, and I loved every second of it.

When he found my core and thrust into me again, my body slid up the bed a little and my head flew back. He pinned me in place while he hammered inside me again and again. Lust and need coursed through my veins like a dark, addictive drug.

Connor tipped my head down and stared into my eyes. "I need to see your face. I need to watch you."

Then he reached down and put the vibrator on me again. I was so sensitive, the feel of it made me cry out, and my eyes closed.

He held it there anyway, right on my clit. Then he lightly slapped my flank. "Eyes on me, sweet girl."

I stopped breathing as my mind and body absorbed the swat, but I kept my eyes on him. He leaned in and sucked and pinched my nipples again. My body locked in place, and an almost painful climax built inside me. When he rubbed the vibrator against my clit and bit down on my breast, I let go and came again, long and hard.

He shoved inside me a few more times, threw his head back, and growled low as he orgasmed. Connor hung over me for a few moments, catching his breath. Then he turned off the vibrator and let go of my legs.

"My toes are cramping from coming so hard," I whispered in awe.

He barked out a laugh, then leaned down and curled me into him. My hands were still tied, and he reached up and undid the ropes.

Sitting against the headboard, he dragged me into his lap. "Let me see if I can rub your cramps out." He rubbed my wrists, then leisurely massaged my feet and calves. He grabbed his water bottle off his nightstand and handed it to me.

We sat there for almost an hour, talking and softly stroking each other. He asked how I'd liked being tied up and having a bullet used on me.

"At first, I wanted to rip your balls off," I admitted, sounding surly.

"What about now?"

Shifting in his lap, I sighed. "It... excited me."

"Good because I also need to gag you. You're a screamer and I don't want Elodie running in to rescue you while I'm paddling your ass or balls-deep in your cunt."

"Neither do I." I shuddered at the thought of trying to explain that to her. "Have *you* ever been tied up or gagged?" I ran my hand along his shoulder.

"I've been tied up, but I didn't like it." He took my hand and threaded his fingers through mine.

"Why?"

Connor shrugged. "I didn't trust the woman I was with." He grinned. "You lost the bet. What's in your nightstand?"

I froze. "Well, you see..."

"Tell me."

Letting out a long breath, I laid my head on his shoulder. "One of my best friends from high school started an online business a while back so she could work from home."

"Are you stalling? Because I can't figure out what that has to do with your nightstand."

I yawned and snuggled into him. "I'm getting there. Her online business is called the Cherry Box."

He stroked my hair and laid his head back on the headboard. "Why does that sound familiar?"

"The fact that you think it sounds familiar doesn't surprise me."

"And?" he prodded.

"She sells toys and other stuff online. She gave me a monthly subscription for my birthday last year."

"And? I'm still not sure how it relates to your nightstand."

"She sells *sex* toys. Her monthly subscription is called the Cherry Box."

Connor stopped stroking my hair and curled me into him. "One of your best friends owns an online kink shop, and she's been sending you a monthly subscription since last March?" His voice was low and scratchy.

"You remembered my birthday. That's nice," I teased.

"Answer the question, Bella." He nipped my chin.

"Yes."

"Who's been using the boxes with you?"

My shoulders slumped. "No one. Not one single person. I haven't even opened the last four boxes. It's too depressing, and I don't know what some of the stuff even is. I need to look it up."

He groaned into my hair. "Ho-ly fuck. I must be sleeping right now, and this is all one big wet dream."

"I'll pinch you to see if you're really awake," I told him helpfully.

He grabbed my free hand before I could follow through. "So your nightstand has a few items you can use on yourself?"

My face flamed. "Yes."

He leaned down and licked my lips. "And you have four boxes you haven't even opened."

"Our bet was only about what I had in my nightstand–"

He shook his head. "Uh-uh. You and I are going on a little field trip soon, and we're going to open those four Cherry Boxes. Then I'm going to make sure you know what everything is and how it all works."

I sat up. "No way. There are crops, and paddles, and a spreader–"

Before I could finish, he sat up and tossed me in the middle of his bed, then rolled me onto my stomach and pulled my hips up to meet his hard cock.

"This *is* a dream. And I've died and fucking gone to heaven." Leaning over me, he stroked down my back and cupped my wet pussy. "Are you ready for me? I need you again."

I laughed and wiggled my ass, then gasped as he slammed his hard cock back inside me.

# Chapter 20

On Saturday morning, I took Connor and Elodie to the skate park and tried to teach Elodie how to skateboard a little.

"Bend your knees a bit, and try to stay on." She wore one of my spare helmets, but it was too big for her.

"Like this?" she asked, practically squatting in half on the skateboard.

"Pretty close. Let me show you." I got on and balanced, then bent my knees a little. She backed away and watched me. I tic-tacked to face her, then stepped off the board.

She tried it a few more times, and when she balanced for a few seconds alone, she let out a little squeal. "I did it!" She got so excited, the board started sliding out from underneath her, and I quickly pulled her off and toed the board to a stop.

"You did! Nice work."

Connor watched us. "Can you do what they're doing?" He pointed to a couple of older boys riding around in the beginner bowl.

"Yeah."

"Show me."

"Alright." I popped my skateboard up, then did a throw-down and jumped on. Skating over to the intermediate bowl, I quickly dropped down and rode around for a few minutes to get a feel for it, then did a few tail stalls on the lip. After I'd warmed up a bit, I did a couple of simple ollies along the ledge.

Glancing up, I noticed a few of the other riders stopping to watch. This wasn't uncommon. Liam told me once it was fun to watch me skate since there weren't as many good female skaters. I'd learned to tune everyone out.

A few minutes later, I aired out of the bowl, grabbing the side of my skateboard briefly as I came out. Then just to show off a little, I did a kickflip not far from where Connor and Ellie were standing, rotating my skateboard underneath me, and came to a stop.

"That was fucking hot," one of the guys muttered to his friends.

Connor watched me. "You having fun?"

I raised an eyebrow, understanding the lust that was probably coursing through him. I'd felt the same when I watched him playing hockey for the first time with Titus.

"Yeah, I am," I grinned.

Elodie bounced beside me. "That was way better than dance. You have to teach me."

"Dance will help you with your coordination and balance. You could do both. But first, we need to get you a helmet that fits, and some pads."

She nodded happily. "Okay, it's a deal."

That night after we read with Elodie and tucked her in for the night, Connor grabbed a bottle of wine and we sat out on his back patio by the pool. We talked and gazed up at the stars. Honeysuckle and rosemary scented the air, and tall palm trees swayed gently in the breeze. I loved these desert evenings.

When we went to bed a little while later, Connor pulled the vibrator out of his drawer and took off my sweats. I grabbed his shirt and pulled it over his head. When we were both naked, he backed me into his bed and lowered me down. Then he knelt over me and nipped and sucked me from my lips to my ankles.

Tingles spread through me, and I shifted restlessly against him. He flicked on the vibrator and held it to my core. Then he pulled my head to the end of the bed. "Hold this on your clit while I fuck your mouth, sweet girl. Now open up."

He stood over me, sliding his cock inside. The reversed angle felt strange, and Connor gazed, transfixed, at my throat. As he pushed deeper into my throat, he laid his hand on my neck and squeezed. My eyes rolled back and the vibrator fell from my hand.

He reached over and picked it back up. Placing it on my clit again, Connor grabbed my hand and placed it over the vibrator. "Hold it there. Now loosen your throat and just relax. There you go, just like that. I can see my cock working inside your throat. What a fucking sight."

He worked himself inside again until he couldn't go any further, and my breath cut off. Then he pumped in and out a few times, and did it all over again.

Pulling out of my throat, he turned me around and positioned my hips at the edge of the bed. Then he pushed my thighs apart with his knees. "Beg for my cock," he demanded.

"Give it to me." I pushed my hips back.

"Beg me, and I'll give you what you want,"  he said through gritted teeth.

He rubbed his fingers along my clit, and I cried out. "Connor, oh God. Please!"

"There you go," he murmured, grabbing my hips. I cried out as he shoved inside me. He felt so big, and I was a little sore from last night. But desperation and need speared through me.

He leaned over and wrapped one hand around my mouth and used his other to knead and massage my clit. The vibrator fell to the floor somewhere, and his large muscular body pinned me to the bed as he pounded into me.

I blindly reached out and grabbed the bedding, trying to find purchase so I could push back onto him. My mind was awash in need and lust, and my vagina pulsed. When my climax hit, he muffled my wail with his hand as I convulsed around his cock. When I stopped pulsing, he let go and held my waist tight while he rammed his cock into me.

"*Fuuck,* Bella. You feel so hot and tight around my cock. Your little pussy is perfect." Growling low and long, he shoved inside me one last time and came.

He lay on top of me, breathing heavily before he finally rolled off.

I could hear a faint buzzing sound, and then it stopped. He'd found the vibrator and turned it off. Gathering me in his arms, he crawled into bed.

My body felt like dead weight, and my mind still buzzed from the remains of my orgasm. He haphazardly used a corner of the sheet to wipe us off, then pulled me into him.

"I want to be inside you all the time. We're going to fuck each other to death if this keeps up."

Maybe I mumbled a reply. I didn't remember, because I fell asleep seconds later with his hand curled around my chest and his leg pressed between my messy thighs.

Waking before Connor the next morning, I crawled out from under his arm and leg draped over my body. I used the bathroom and cleaned up, then went in search of coffee.

Elodie sang softly in her room. I looked in her doorway, and found her sitting on the bed with a book in her lap.

"Hey, you're up." I sat next to her.

She scooted over and handed me the book. "I can't read it."

"You can't read it *yet*," I corrected.

"Most of my friends can read."

She seemed a little upset, but I knew she'd just gotten a late start. "I know you can read some books. But if you want to read harder books, it's like everything else. It takes practice."

"Practice?" she looked at me.

"Yes. You need to read over and over and try to get better. Like your dad and hockey. He wasn't always an amazing skater who could score whenever he wanted to. So he practiced a lot. Probably every single day."

I searched for another example. "You know that trick I did with my skateboard when I twirled it around with my feet?"

"Yeah."

"It's a neat trick. But I practiced it for months and months. I tried it maybe a thousand times before I landed it. And I fell on my bottom a lot."

"Do I have to fall on my bottom to read?" she smiled.

"No, smart mouth. But you will have to read a lot."

She nodded, and we settled in with a book until Connor stumbled into the bedroom, laid down across our legs, and started fake snoring. Then it devolved into a pillow fight.

Later that morning, Dad came with us and we went to brunch and a Sunday stroll through the Old Town in La Quinta. There was a farmer's market, and we stopped and picked up some fresh produce. I'd never been to the area before, and I was utterly charmed by the little local shops, architecture, and bright flowering plants everywhere. The smell of brewing coffee and vanilla cones hung in the air as we walked through the square.

I noticed a thrift shop on the east end, and while my dad took Elodie to get an ice cream cone, I dragged Connor into the secondhand store. He watched, a little repulsed, as I thumbed through the books and clothes.

He stood behind me with his arms folded as I perused the book titles.

"What?" I finally asked without looking up.

"Do you shop in places like this often?"

I shrugged. "Not as much as I used to."

"That's probably good," he murmured, eyeing a rack of secondhand swimsuits. "It smells funky in here."

He wasn't wrong. Most thrift stores seemed to have that musty smell, but I'd just gotten used to it. He was a bit of a snob, I realized.

I set a book back and picked up another one. "I don't shop in places like this as much as I used to because I'm not working right now. So I usually don't shop at all unless it's for groceries. And maybe deodorant and toothpaste."

Holding up a very used copy of the first *Harry Potter* book, I turned to him. "But this is only twenty-five cents, and Elodie told me she's never seen the movie or had the book read to her, so I'm going to splurge."

Connor looked at the battered book. "I'll buy you the whole series."

I suddenly felt tired, and maybe a little ashamed that I was poor. I turned back to the bookshelf. We were different in so many ways. Could we really make this work between us?

"I know you can, and thank you for offering. But I'd like to buy this for her."

Tucking the book under my arm, I straightened. "Now I'm going to look through the men's section to see if I can find you a shirt. You look like you're ready to crawl out of your skin, so go catch up with Elodie and Dad. I'll meet you out on the bench in front of the ice cream shop."

He grimaced before he could catch himself, and I laughed. "Don't worry, I'll wash it twice before I give it to you."

Connor scowled, then leaned in and kissed me slowly, biting and licking my bottom lip. I heard a soft thud as I wrapped my arms around him and brought his mouth closer.

He eventually pulled back. "Fine. But that means I get to buy you something too." He leaned down and picked up the book I'd dropped when he kissed me.

# Chapter 21

"You don't need to leave. Sleep here," Connor said for the third time as I gathered my things from the nightstand on Sunday evening.

"No way. I need rest and actual REM sleep. I can't live on three hours of sleep smashed between all-night, mind-blowing sex."

He smirked and wrapped his arm around my chest, pulling me into him. "You can sleep when you die."

I shivered and almost caved. "How is it that you're ten years older than me, but I'm the  one who's worn out and being the voice of reason here?" I looked back at him. "I'm so tired, I'm having waking dreams."

He ran his nose down my throat and palmed my stomach. "Your body is telling me it wants you to stay."

I wrapped my arm around his neck and pushed back into him. "I have clinical hours this week."

He turned me around and licked across my lips. "Then stay next weekend. Starting Thursday night."

I rubbed my face across his chest and breathed in his heady scent. "I'm already planning on it."

Later that evening when I finally made it to my apartment, I was so overstimulated and tired, I crawled into my little bed and fell asleep almost before my head hit the pillow. I slept like the dead for the next nine hours.

On Monday afternoon, Connor came into the medical office as I finished up for the day. Titus had just gotten into the ice bath, and I was transcribing some last-minute notes.

When I glanced up and saw him, I did a double take. Connor looked like an actual CEO in well-tailored slacks, expensive dress shoes, and a gray button-down shirt that had probably been tailored just for him.

I leaned against the counter and folded my arms. "I've never actually seen you in business clothes before. You really do work here."

He walked up, leaned into me, and gave me a long kiss. "I missed you last night. And this morning. And in the middle of the night."

"For fuck's sake," Titus growled from the tub. Connor ignored him.

My knees went wobbly, but I pushed him back. "Behave yourself. How often do you work from your office here?"

He sighed and stepped back. "I can do most of my work remotely, so I don't need to come in very often. Thank fuck." He looked at my white consultation jacket. "I've never wanted to play doctor until now."

He grabbed my waist and backed me against the counter again. The man didn't seem to have any personal boundaries.

"We're required to wear the jacket, along with casual business attire, during clinicals."

"Hmm. I think just the white jacket, with nothing on underneath. And we can use your stethoscope to–"

Titus growled again from the tub. "Enough, asshole. I don't want to hear this."

Connor finally stepped back and turned to Titus. "You're just pissed off because you aren't getting any. And your biological clock is ticking."

"I already have a kid, and I'm only two months older than you. Do you really want to remind your twenty-something little skater girl here how old you are?"

Connor grinned smugly. "You have no idea, Tremblay. You should try it with someone besides a professional escort sometime."

Titus's lips twitched. "You probably have to take fucking Viagra to get it up."

"Okay," I said loudly. "You two behave like siblings." I turned to Connor. "Titus and I were going to grab something to eat. Do you want to come?"

Connor smiled. "Yeah, I always want to come. And food sounds good too."

Titus snorted and I rolled my eyes.

"You two are so inappropriate." They both laughed at me.

I started putting my things away, and Titus heaved himself out of the ice tub. I reached over, grabbed two towels, and threw them to him.

He caught them and dried himself off, then automatically stripped off his compression shorts.

Connor scowled at Titus. "If you weren't coming out of an ice bath, I'd rip your fucking balls off for stripping down in front of her."

Titus chuckled. "You'd have to find them first. Damn, that's cold."

"Way too much information," I complained.

A text message vibrated on my phone, and I looked down at it.

*Laurel: We're having Martini Monday at my house again tonight. Come by if you're not busy. Friends welcome*

I'd been to two Martini Monday parties since I moved here, and I thought Connor and Titus would enjoy them.

Looking up, I noticed Connor watching me.

"Sebastian's girlfriend, Laurel, invited me to Martini Monday at her house again. It's basically a poolside cocktail party."

"Are you going?"

"Maybe. She told me I could invite friends. Do you guys want to come?"

Connor's shoulders loosened. "Elodie has dance class tonight. If Javier will pick her up and watch her for a couple of hours afterward, I'm in. I like those guys, even if they did enjoy my twenty-year-old whiskey."

Titus shrugged. "The only thing waiting for me at home is Call of Duty. Who are they?"

Connor briefly explained how we knew them.

Titus smirked. "So this Zeke guy is the one who saved your ass by putting up extra backup cameras?"

I'd already told Titus what happened that night. "He didn't actually save my ass, but Noah could hardly deny it when it was all on video."

Titus cocked his head. "The video didn't save your ass?"

I glanced at Connor. "My apartment complex has cameras and an electronic gate. So I already had proof I was at my apartment when the robbery occurred. Noah didn't know I hadn't stayed overnight with my dad."

Connor folded his arms. "Why didn't you just say so when you came over to my house that night? Or when your dad called you the day before?"

Turning away, I started packing up my things. "Because I didn't want to. And I wasn't the one with the burden of proof. That was on you and your asshole brother."

"Damn it, Bella," Connor growled.

But Titus barked out a laugh. "She got you there, fucker."

Dad agreed to watch Elodie, so both Connor and Titus came with me to Laurel's Martini Monday party. We dropped my car off at my apartment and grabbed something to eat at The Ace Hotel restaurant close to Laurel's house beforehand.

They followed me inside my apartment so I could change clothes, and I saw Titus glance around and scowl. But he didn't say anything. I breathed a quiet sigh of relief.

At the restaurant, Titus and Connor ordered the roast chicken blue plate special.

When I ordered a house salad, Connor stared at me. "That's it?"

I shrugged. "Yeah. I went over my food budget again last week."

"Bella, I'm paying. Order real food, for God's sake."

I added a cup of soup to my order.

When the server left, Titus stared at me. "You have a food budget?"

"Of course. I have a budget for everything. I've been a struggling student for almost six years."

Titus pointed at me. "She's a fucking unicorn, McCoy. No one I know has a budget. But watch your fries around her. I keep trying to tell her, there is no 'we' in fries."

Connor hooked his arm around my neck and kissed my temple. "You can steal all the fries you want from me, but there'll be consequences later."

I squeezed his thigh under the table. I knew what kind of consequences he was talking about.

When the food came, Connor cut off a large piece of chicken and set it on my salad plate without saying a word. For some reason, the gesture caught me off guard. It was something my dad or my brother would have done. Or my mom when she'd been alive.

I set my fork down and wiped my lips with my napkin to give myself a minute.

"Thank you."

He glanced over and smiled, but he and Titus were deep in discussion about the Seattle team and how they were doing this season. I was glad he didn't notice how much his small kindness affected me.

Zeke answered the door at Laurel's house. When he saw who I'd brought, a big grin spread across his face. "Hey, Bells. I see you brought The Hammer *and* The Spartan."

I'd learned during the season opener that Titus's nickname was The Spartan. When he made a goal, the crowd chanted "Spar-tan, Spar-tan." The nickname fit him.

And of course, Connor was known as The Hammer. And now I knew what Wyatt had been talking about when he'd said the nickname referred to him off the rink too.

Titus shook Zeke's hand. "It's a pleasure to meet a Californian who knows shit about hockey."

When we walked into Laurel's kitchen, Harley and Damien sat at the bar. Martina stood across from them, and a huge man with a craggy, arresting face stood behind her. His name was Iz, and he owned The Cockpit.

Laurel waved from the kitchen sink. "We're making Manhattans if anyone wants one."

Connor nodded at Sebastian and Damien. "Hey."

Sebastian grunted back. He was one of the coaches on Elodie's soccer team, and I noticed he was even a little gruff with the five-year-old kids. But they seemed to eat it up, and Elodie loved him.

Martina smirked. "Titus thinks you know 'shit' about hockey, Zeke. Are you going to give them your philosophy about the amazing versatility of the word 'shit'?"

Damien groaned and Harley started laughing.

Zeke rubbed his hands together. "These guys give me a hard time because I believe the word 'shit' is the most versatile word in the English language."

Martina nodded. "And we've had a 'shitload' of conversations about it too."

"For the love of God," Damien pleaded. "Don't get him started, or they'll be at it all night."

Titus shook his head. "I think the word 'fuck' is more versatile, and it has an interesting history."

"What's the history?" Zeke asked.

Sebastian slid a perfectly prepared Manhattan over to me. I noticed a bottle of Angostura bitters on the counter next to the whiskey, and my drink was garnished with a dark, fragrant Luxardo cherry. I didn't like whiskey, but even I could appreciate a sip or two of a perfectly prepared Manhattan. The man took his bartending seriously.

"This should be interesting," Sebastian muttered.

I snickered and held up my drink in thanks.

Titus started in. "Some historians think the word originated from the term 'Fornication Under the Consent of the King,' giving us the acronym F.U.C.K. And that's where the word fuck came from. Some historians think the fornication rule started after the plague to try and control the population."

Iz spoke up. "I heard it was based on the medieval law 'For Unlawful Carnal Knowledge' or something like that. Either way, I'd rather be doing it than talking about it."

He gave Martina's ass a small pat, and she narrowed her eyes.

Zeke shrugged. "They sound similar. Isn't that a Van Halen album title? I still think 'shit' is *the* shit' but I can see your point about 'fuck.' I mean, the base meaning of the word *is* fucking awesome."

Harley and Laurel groaned.

Sebastian pointed to Connor and Titus. "Do you two fuckers want your whiskey straight, on the rocks, or in a Manhattan?"

"Straight. Thanks," Connor smirked.

"Straight, and I'll take two fingers," Titus added. When he got his drink, he took a sip. "It's the utility word of our generation. Fuck can be used as almost any part of speech–a noun, verb, adverb, or adjective. And just the way you say the word gives it meaning."

Martina glanced back at Iz. "That's true. My favorite is 'fuck off', or maybe 'mother fucker.'"

Iz winked. "I personally enjoy the verb form the most. The act of fornicating in its purest, dirtiest, form."

Iz's voice was a low, rumbling purr. Martina breathed heavily as she stared up at him.

Harley snorted and turned to Zeke. "It's probably good my sister, Olivia, isn't here. She'd add 'fucked up', 'fuckhead', 'fucktwit' and 'fucking nuts' to our growing list."

Zeke smiled a little. "Yeah, I'd like to hear her input on this conversation. There are all the acronyms too. Like FUBAR, WTF, SNAFU, or my personal favorite, MILF."

I set my drink down and patted Connor's stomach. "You're my favorite DILF," I said quietly in his ear.

He grinned and grabbed my hand, then licked the inside of my palm. My vagina spasmed.

Martina held up a finger. "There's also just TF, BFD, or OMFG. And FFS, or GTFO. This is all FYFI."

Laurel shook her head. "What does that say about me that I understood all those?"

Martina smirked. "It means we're part of the texting generation."

"My ears are bleeding," Damien groaned.

Harley patted Damien's shoulder. "I'll end our litany with 'holy fucking shit', I can't believe we're having another one of these conversations. And that brings it back full circle to the shit conversation. Let's end it here."

Just then Ramone and Jonathan walked in with a beautiful appetizer tray.

Ramone set it on the counter and looked around. "Sorry we're late. What'd we miss?"

Zeke held up his glass. "Not a fucking thing."

I'd just sipped my Manhattan, and some of my drink sloshed down my chin when I laughed. Connor grabbed a napkin and patted my face. I smiled up at him, then looked around at my new friends. Life was pretty great.

# Chapter 22

*M y life sucks*, I thought as I stared down at my car on Tuesday afternoon. When I'd walked out to the arena parking lot, I saw my front tires had been slashed and someone had scratched the words "whore" and "cunt" into the driver-side door of my car.

Anger and fear swam through me as I looked at the damage. Quickly scanning the lot, I pulled out my phone in case whoever did this was still around. I didn't see anyone. Letting out a breath, I tried to think.

Dad would be picking Elodie up from school, and Connor was… I actually didn't know where he was. I could text Jackson or Titus, but they'd probably call Connor. And I didn't want to drag Connor into my problems. So I called a local tire store and talked to the man on the phone.

"Ma'am, unless you have two spares I'd recommend getting a tow truck to bring your car over, and we can change the tires out for you."

"Okay. Any idea how much a tow truck would be?" When he told me a ballpark figure, I blanched. "Well, that gives me some ideas. Thanks."

"One more thing. If you were my sister or wife, I'd tell you to call the police and make a report. It seems targeted."

"I think you're right," I sighed. "They scratched two crude words into the paint on my door too."

The man went quiet. "Where's your car at?"

"At the ice hockey arena where I work."

"My name's Tyler, and I'm the general manager here. Tell you what, I'll send someone over with another spare, and he'll change both tires so you can drive the car back here. I'll only charge you for the new tires."

Emotion climbed up my throat. "Thank you, Tyler. I'm Isabella. If your store could do that for me, I'll see if I can get a few tickets to the next Thunderbirds home game, okay?"

"No worries. Someone will be there in about thirty minutes."

When I got off the phone with Tyler, I called the police. The officer who took the call also recommended I let the arena know since it happened in their parking lot. A police officer pulled up ten minutes later.

I was finishing up with him when a truck with a Tires for Less logo pulled up. A thin young man with gauges and a baseball cap came over and looked down at my car. His nametag read "Kirk."

"Looks like they did a number on your paint job too," he said.

Wincing, I studied the scratches. "I'll have to call a body shop and see if I can get them buffed out. The car isn't much, but it's paid for."

Kirk and I got to work. It was after eight when I finally made it home that night. The employees at the tire store had been the silver lining in my otherwise shitty day.

Connor called me a few minutes after I got home. "Where are you?"

I was tired, dirty, and a little cranky.

"I'm just getting to my apartment. A few problems came up after work. Where are you?"

He was silent for a moment. "At home. What kind of problems?"

I didn't want to tell him. Somehow I knew he was going to make a big deal out of it.

"I had some car problems, and I had to get two tires replaced. It's also late, and I'm tired and hungry."

"What aren't you telling me, sweet girl?" he asked quietly.

How did he know these things? And why did him calling me "sweet girl" in his deep, quiet voice make my vagina wet?

I yanked open the fridge and studied the contents. I had two tortillas and a block of cheese. Okay, good. I could make a couple of cheese quesadillas. Then I noticed mold on the cheese. Damn it.

"Why do you think I'm not telling you something?"

I pulled out a carton of almond milk. It lasted forever, thank goodness. Looking through my cupboard, I found a box of corn flakes. I desperately needed to go to the grocery store. I'd become too reliant on eating at my dad's or Connor's house.

He sighed heavily. "Because you had to replace two tires, and the chances of that being an accident are low to none. You also sound pissed and annoyed. Now what the fuck happened?"

"Someone slashed my two front tires and scratched a couple of bad words into my car door. And my cheese is moldy." I tossed the cheese in the garbage, then I poured myself a bowl of corn flakes and took a big bite.

"For the love of God, Bella. Why the fuck didn't you call me?"

I took another bite. "Because you were working, and it's not your problem."

"Where was your car parked?"

"In the arena parking lot."

"What do the words say?"

I winced and put my bowl down. "It doesn't matter."

"Bella," he growled.

"Whore and cunt."

"I'm coming over. Don't open your door unless you know who it is. No, don't open your door unless it's me or your dad." He hung up.

I set my phone down on the counter and stared at it. After finishing my cereal, I straightened up my apartment, folded some laundry, and then got ready for bed. The doorbell rang as I finished putting my laundry away.

When I let him in, Connor locked the door behind him and scanned me. "Are you all right?"

"Just annoyed and mad. What's wrong?"

His jaw clenched and he looked up at the ceiling.

I tried again. "The tire store helped me out, and I reported it to the police. I figured it out."

He scowled down at me.

I put my hands on my hips. "Why are you so angry?"

"Why didn't you call me?"

His quiet voice didn't fool me. "I didn't call you because I handled it myself. It was my problem to solve. This isn't about you, okay?"

"Bella, this *is* about–"

I interrupted him. "I'm the one who had my front tires slashed and filthy words scratched into my car. I'm the one who has to pay to get the tires replaced and the words buffed out."

"You need to–" he started again.

"So excuse me if I'm not up to soothing *your* temper or making *you* feel better. It's been a long, shitty day and I'm tired."

Connor stepped into my space and took hold of my arms. "Stop interrupting me. Someone told me a few months ago it's rude and annoying. And this *is* about me. Noah did the same thing to one of my cars in the same parking lot in December."

I stared up at him as I processed this news. His large, muscular body pressed against mine, and I absently rubbed against him, then stopped when I realized what I was doing.

"Well, shit." My anger morphed into lust.

"Yeah, 'well, shit' is right."

"It's still my car, so it's my problem."

He shook his head. "Bella, I know you can take care of yourself. I know you're independent and fully capable. It drives me fucking crazy, but it's also one of the things that drew me to you."

I stilled in his arms. "Okay."

"I want to be the one you call if something like this happens. Are we together?" He searched my eyes and waited for an answer.

Nodding, I relaxed against him a little. "Yes."

"Good. Because I need to fuck you or spank you. Right now."

When he said he needed to fuck me, my insides tightened. When he said he wanted to spank me, my insides contracted.

Rolling up on my tiptoes, I put my lips on his mouth. "How about both?"

He groaned, then slanted his head and kissed me until I was dizzy and short of breath. Grabbing my wrist, he pulled me to my bedroom. The room was small, and my nightstand and double bed took up most of the space.

Connor sat on the edge of the bed and pulled me onto his lap so I straddled him. He brushed his thumb over my mouth, then ran his lips across mine again. My mouth throbbed where he'd kissed me.

"Your lips are so pink and soft. Just like your sweet pussy."

My stomach tightened and I moved restlessly against him, rubbing my core over his hard length. He grabbed my ass with his large hands and squeezed almost to the point of pain. Excitement and a little apprehension slid through me. Everything was still so new, and I didn't know if he really wanted to spank me. My emotions were a hot, jumbled mess.

Connor broke the kiss and pulled off my shirt. I didn't have a bra on, and he held my ribcage and buried his face between my breasts, inhaling me. Goosebumps broke out across my skin.

"Where are your Cherry Boxes?" he asked against my skin.

I froze, then pulled back and glanced toward the closet. He smiled and set me to the side.

"What are you doing?" I asked in a high voice.

"Getting your birthday gifts." He opened the closet and looked up on the top shelf where four dark red, unopened boxes sat.

He pulled them down and sat on the bed. "Let's see what you've got."

I stared at the boxes with big eyes and chewed on my thumbnail.

Connor's lips twitched, but he set the boxes aside and stroked my back. "How about this? I'll open two and you open two, and we'll look through everything together. Then we each pick three items from the boxes to use."

His hands felt so good on my skin, and I relaxed into his strokes "Okay. But we each get to eliminate two items from the other person's pile."

"How about if we eliminate one item each."

Unfolding my arms, I slowly nodded. "Okay. One more thing."

"What's that?"

"What's your safe word?"

He grinned. "Lemonade. What's yours?"

"Penalty."

He laughed. "That's a good one. You ready?"

I nodded. We opened the boxes one at a time, and I blushed and stammered as I pulled out an anal plug, a flogger, and massage oils, among other things. He chuckled as he chose a heart-shaped paddle, cuffs, and a violet wand.

"What's a violet wand?" I asked, turning the package over.

"It's low level electricity play. It can be stimulating, but not everyone likes it. I'm eliminating the anal plug."

"Smart choice. I'm eliminating the violet wand then."

Moving the boxes off the bed, he stood up and stripped. Then he grasped my ankle and pulled me toward him. "Give me your wrists."

My heart sped up and my insides fluttered. The wrist cuffs were black with little red hearts stitched into them. I lowered my arms and held my wrists up.

"You remember your safe word?"

I nodded.

"Say it."

"Penalty."

Grinning, he ran his hand up my leg and pulled off my shorts and panties. "Alright then. Let's play, sweet girl."

He watched my face as he buckled the cuffs on my wrists and pulled my arms above my head. Then he leaned in and sucked and nuzzled my breasts until I was squirming underneath him.

"You look so fucking hot. Let's see how you're doing." Connor ran his fingers down my stomach to my wet passage. Then he massaged my clit.

"Oh, God. That feels so good." I arched into his hand.

He pressed his finger inside me. "Why are you telling God again? You need to tell me."

His touch sent tremors racing through my center, and I wanted to feel him skin to skin. I was so wet, I could hear the suction when he pushed his finger in and out of my channel.

He straddled my torso. "If you want me to spank you, you have to ask me. Nicely." Then he eased back and pulled my thighs apart so I was spread out to him.

I felt completely open and so turned on. "*Ask* you to spank me?"

He rubbed his thumbs slowly across my nipples, then pinched and tugged on them. "Your eyes are heavy and your slit is soaked. So after I eat you out for a few minutes, I'm going to turn you over and give you a few well-deserved smacks with that cute little heart-shaped paddle, and then my bare hand. But you're going to beg me first."

I shook my head in denial while my insides contracted.

"And when your cunt is dripping and your mind is confused with the mix of pain and pleasure, you're going to say please. And *then* you can have my cock inside you."

"Or, I'll laugh in your face."

"We'll see." He smirked and leaned in to lick the side of my neck. I shivered. Then he trailed his mouth slowly down my chest, barely skimming my breasts and stomach. Connor finally latched onto my clit, and I bucked underneath him.

I instinctively brought my hands down to hold his head to me, but he grabbed the cuffs and put my hands above my head again.

"Keep them there." He put his mouth back to my clit.

Connor licked and sucked me, then drove two fingers inside. When my breath sped up and I started panting and moaning, he pulled back. "Not yet. I want to be balls deep inside you when you come."

"Then put your cock in me," I panted.

He leaned back in to give my pussy a nice long lick. "Uh-uh. Not yet."

Burying his mouth deep in my slit, he hummed, pulled back, and blew softly. Then he slid two fingers back inside me.

My breath whooshed out of me. His mouth felt better than anything I'd ever done to get myself off. My mind went blank as my core tightened in anticipation.

He licked and sucked me, then pulled back when he felt me tighten again. After repeating the process until I was mindlessly begging him to spank me, fuck me, and for a few other things that probably weren't anatomically possible, he stood and pulled me up.

I wobbled, but he steadied me and positioned me on my knees facing away from him. Pulling my hips back to the edge of the bed, he folded my torso over until my forehead pressed against the bedspread. Then he stood behind me.

"Wider." He ran his hand down my back to my ass cheeks, and I shifted a little and spread my legs further apart. I felt moisture drip down my leg.

He ran his finger up the inside of my thigh to catch it, and rubbed it into my skin. "Your cunt is dripping. We're almost there. Push your ass out toward me."

I blushed, and my body tightened in need. Then Connor leaned over me and tweaked my nipple while he slid two fingers inside me. He pumped them in and out, and rubbed against my clit.

"Are you ready?" he asked softly. I gave a short, quick nod.

He picked up the paddle and delivered a few blows to my ass cheeks. I froze and tried to process the sting. He ran his hands over my thighs for a moment, then delivered several harder slaps, some to my upper thighs. I panted and shifted, and he set the paddle down to give me a few quick slaps with his hand right on my pussy. Sharp pain and pleasure radiated through my core. My mind blanked for a moment and I moaned. The heat built as I panted and whimpered. Maybe even sobbed a little.

He arched his body over mine and caressed the area he'd just spanked. "How're you doing?"

I couldn't speak, so I just nodded.

He cupped both my breasts, then whispered in detail what else he wanted to do to me. My breath sped up and I pushed back against him. Connor lined himself against my opening, grasped my shoulders, then shoved me back onto his hard cock while he thrust his hips forward.

I cried out as he slapped against my sore bottom, his thick length stretching my tight walls. He pounded into me and I held my breath and struggled to process all the overwhelming stimulus.

My mind spun like a stripped gear, and I started pleading again. "Connor, please. Oh, God, please! I can't... you feel so good."

A few bites of pain and the cuffs had intensified my pleasure, and I mindlessly shoved myself back on him.

Stroking my sweaty back, he hammered into me. "That's it. So tight around my cock."

He reached around and rubbed my clit, then lightly slapped it a few times. My head flew up. I was so close to coming, my limbs locked up as my climax crawled up my body. Connor leaned over and bit my shoulder, and I cried out as an orgasm ripped through me.

He shoved himself inside me so hard, he sent me skidding across the bed before he grabbed my hips and held them tight against his own as we came together. I finally drifted down, my head hanging as Connor held my limp body against him. When he quit coming and caught his breath, he laid us on our sides, still lodged inside me.

The spanking, my climax, and the stressful day had wrung me out. I was barely coherent when he finally pulled out, sending fluids running across the backs of my thighs.

He unbuckled the cuffs, then went to the bathroom to grab a warm, wet towel to wipe us both down.

I grazed his thigh. "I have no words. I came so hard I think I broke something."

He let out a quiet breath. "Tell me what you thought of being cuffed and spanked."

My face went hot and I let go of his thigh. "Do we have to talk about this?"

He grinned and kissed me. "Absolutely. Sometimes I forget how innocent you are. And I fucking love that you're doing all this with me for the first time. But I also worry I might scare the shit out of you."

I poked his side. "I'm okay not verbally processing everything."

"I need to know where your head's at because I want to keep tying you down, spanking, and then thoroughly fucking you. But only if you want it too."

A blush spread across my whole body, and I groaned. "I like it, okay? I liked reading about it, and now I know I like doing it. Is that good enough for you?"

He lay on his side. "Not even close. But we're both tired, so we'll finish this conversation tomorrow. I tucked Elodie in before I came, and Javier is staying at the house tonight." He pulled me into his side, and I snuggled against him. "We'll talk in the morning."

"Or how about never?"

He squeezed me. "If by 'never' you mean tomorrow, that works for me."

# Chapter 23

Early morning sunlight poured through the window when Connor rolled me over. "Good morning." He kissed and palmed my breasts. "It's tomorrow. Let's finish our talk."

I groaned and arched into his hands. "I need coffee. And the bathroom."

"We'll get coffee in a few minutes. Go use the bathroom, then let's talk."

After we cleaned up a little, he pulled me back to bed and started quizzing me. Connor asked me what I fantasized about, what I'd done in the past, and what I wanted to try. He also wanted to know what type of erotica I liked to read.

At one point, I was sure even my toenails were blushing. "Are you always this thorough with your partners?"

He chuckled and kissed my hot cheeks. "No. But I plan to keep you."

"Lucky me."

He laughed, then continued going through sexual positions and kinks. There was quite a laundry list of positions he put on our "to try" list. But we did cross a few things off. And I found out coulrophilia was clown play.

I shook my head. "I didn't know coulrophilia was even a thing,"

"Yep. To each their own, eh?"

There were several other sexual positions and fetishes I'd never heard of or considered.

"Are you just making stuff up now? What exactly is klismaphilia?"

He grinned and reached down to pat my ass. "Enema play. Some people like the extreme pressure. I hear others just like having their bowels cleaned."

I groaned in disbelief. "Holy mother of God, my ears are burning. I think I've had enough for one day."

He kissed my eyelids, then licked across my lips. "You're amazing, you know that? I've never trusted anyone enough to go through a list of extreme kinks and get their uncensored, funny-as-shit opinions. And I'm not sure how some of it works either."

"You haven't tried everything we talked about?"

He laughed. "Fuck no. We just had a five-minute discussion about necrophilia."

"Okay, I figured you haven't had sex with a dead person. But the rest?" I wiggled my eyebrows at him. "Not even clown play?"

"I think Pennywise from *It* turned me off clown play long before I knew it was a thing." His grin faded and he sighed. "We need to talk about Noah before you go to work today. You're not safe here by yourself."

I sat up and pulled the sheet over my breasts. "I didn't think Noah was in town anymore."

"Until a week ago, he'd been squatting at my house in Vancouver. He's also been talking to Amelia. Amelia's sister let me know."

I leaned over the side of the bed and grabbed my shirt and sleep shorts. "I'll take extra precautions. This complex has cameras around, and the property is gated. He'd need a code to get in."

Connor grabbed my pajamas and threw them across the room. "A ten-year-old could sneak into your complex. You shouldn't stay here by yourself, and there's not enough room for Elodie and me to move in with you."

I knew he was being diplomatic. He hated my apartment, and even if there was room, he'd never move here.

Sighing in frustration, I swung my legs over the bed to get my clothes again. I had to push the Cherry Boxes out of the way.

"I'll be fine. And I didn't invite you to stay–" My body stopped short when his arm wrapped around me.

Connor pulled me to him and leaned down. "Do you need me to spank and edge you again until you change your mind?" I could hear humor in his voice.

I shivered but held firm. "You can't do that every time I don't agree with you."

He sighed and let go. "I know, but I want to. Please, make it easier on your dad, me, Elodie, and everyone else who loves you. Come stay with me until this thing with Noah is resolved."

"I'm fine here."

He laid his chin on my shoulder. "Bella, it's not safe here for *two* reasons. There's also a slow leak in the ceiling. Your water stains are spreading, which means there's probably mold."

My body froze. I'd also noticed the water stains spreading over the last few days, and I'd already contacted my landlord. He hadn't called me back.

"Damn it," I sighed. "Alright."

"Look on the bright side, it'll be like a sleepover every night. And we still haven't gone through your nightstand. A bet is a bet."

Letting go of me, he started toward my nightstand. I squeaked and dove after him.

Connor held me off with one hand while he shuffled through my drawer. He found a vibrating dildo, nipple clamps, and cherry-flavored sensitizer gel.

Grinning like a kid in a candy store, he finally let me up. I scooted away when I saw the gleam in his eyes.

Connor tossed the dildo back on my nightstand. "We won't need that. Now come here so we can play some more before we have to get up."

I tried to scramble off the bed before he grabbed me again, but I was laughing too hard. After he fastened the little clamps and twisted them until I was crying out and squirming, he used the clit sensitizer on me. I quickly went from laughing to panting.

He held my hands above my head and watched me squirm. "How're you doing?"

"Like I want you to put your dick inside me and make me come. Or you can hand me my vibrating dildo, and I'll do it myself." I tried to buck him off.

He leaned down and licked my breasts around the nipple clamps, then blew on them.

My nipples tightened under the clamps, and pain and pleasure shot through me. "Oh, come on!"

Teasing me for a few more minutes, he finally positioned his length at my opening.

Connor worked his swollen cock inside me and stilled. "God, we make it fit every time. I fucking love being inside you." Then he started thrusting.

On Wednesday afternoon, Jasper came into the pediatric clinic for a routine checkup. I knew he was coming, and I'd asked Titus to get me some tickets for the next home game. He and Jackson came through with half a dozen tickets, and I sent some to the manager at the tire store who'd helped me out. But I kept two for Jasper and his dad.

"Hey, how're you doing today?" I asked him.

"Better now." Jasper looked me up and down with a smirk that didn't belong on a thirteen-year-old's face.

Shaking my head, I nodded at his mom.

She smiled. "He's had a good week. I think the oxygen treatment helped."

I checked Jasper's vitals and asked a few more questions. "Before you go, I have something for you."

He grinned. "I have something for you too."

I couldn't help it. I laughed, even though I knew I shouldn't. "Your attempt at flirting is acknowledged. Behave yourself. And don't go around saying things like that to girls your age. You may get your ass kicked."

His mom chuckled. "He did get his ass kicked. But I think he liked it because she's his girlfriend now."

"Huh. Okay, maybe it worked that one time. I have two tickets to the next Thunderbirds home game. The games are crazy, so I bet you'll love it."

For once, Jasper didn't give me a flirty comeback. "No shit? My dad loves them, but we haven't been able to go to a game yet. Thanks."

I knew he and his dad loved the hockey team, and I suspected they didn't have extra money to spend on things like hockey tickets.

Early that evening, Connor helped me move some of my belongings into a spare bedroom at his house. He'd wanted me to move my stuff into his bedroom, but I was feeling a little cornered, and he could probably tell he'd pushed enough.

"Okay, I get it. We'll make this room yours, and I'll move a desk in for you so you'll also have a place to study. But I want you in my bed."

I nodded. "And I want to be there, so that works for me."

Later that evening, I walked over to talk to my dad. He wasn't happy either that I hadn't contacted him about my car or the water stains in my apartment.

"You don't have to do everything yourself."

"You were picking Elodie up. It's okay, I took care of it. And that's what you get for raising an independent daughter."

"It's a blessing and a curse." He shook his head. "I'm worried. The words scratched into your paint seem personal."

I didn't argue. That's what the tire store manager and Connor had both said.

I patted his arm as we made dinner together. "If it makes you feel better, I didn't call Connor either."

"That makes me feel worse. I'm glad he dragged you out of that crummy apartment."

"Are you okay with me staying at his house?" I asked carefully.

"It's not up to me." He rubbed his forehead. "I worry that he can be relentless when he wants something. But I like him, and he got you out of that apartment."

"Are you okay to watch Elodie while the team comes over tonight?"

He nodded and smiled. "We have plans. We're going to make homemade pizza then read a few chapters of the *Harry Potter* book you gave her. I've never read it before, and I'm probably enjoying it as much as she is."

Around seven that night, the team started showing up for our Wednesday team-building potluck whiskey night. We'd have to work on the name, I decided.

Rudy looked around the living room. "Hey, Isa. This is some place, isn't it?" He came over and put his arm around me.

I stood awkwardly as he squeezed my shoulder. "Hi, Rudy. Yes, it is."

"How would it be to live in a place like this?"

Connor walked in and glared at Rudy. "She does live here, so she knows exactly what it's like. Would you mind getting your hands off her?"

I squinted at him. "Be nice. And I'm living here *temporarily* because my apartment ceiling has a leak, and my stuff is in a guest bedroom."

Connor folded his arms. "I don't give a shit where you put your clothes, Bella. But you're in my bed at night."

My face went hot and my temper ignited. "I can't believe you're saying this in front of the team."

He leaned into my space. "And I can't believe you're ashamed to have them know."

My head jerked back. "Ashamed? I'm not ashamed. But I *am* concerned about Coach Bailey finding out and telling me I can't come back to finish my hours."

Titus cleared his throat. "It's hard to believe I'm the voice of reason here, but are you two sure you want the whole fucking team to know your business?" He nodded at several players who were avidly watching us from the living room entryway.

"We do not mind," Mikael said, and a couple of them chuckled.

I waved awkwardly. "Hey, guys."

A few grinned and waved back.

Mikael looked pained. "Can you argue with her later? I want to start our game so I can win this time."

Jackson smacked his shoulder. "Do you have a death wish or something?" He turned to the other players. "Come on, let's go get drinks and food. There's good whiskey and grilled meat. It also looks like someone brought homemade brownies."

Whiskey and grilled meat seemed to be a big motivator. They headed toward the kitchen while Connor and I stared at each other.

I sighed. "I'm not ashamed of you. At all." I grabbed my hair and pulled a little. "Frustrated, confused, and annoyed sometimes? Absolutely. Ashamed? No."

He wrapped his arms around me. "Okay, I can work with that. And I don't give a fuck about Coach Bailey. He was the club's third choice."

"Be patient. I'm not used to having a… boyfriend." I rubbed my forehead against his chest. "I've never had one before."

He stilled. "You've never had one before?"

"Nope."

Connor squeezed me to him and groaned low in my ear. "I *know* I'm a perverted, depraved, cradle-robbing son of a bitch because now I want to mark your sweet little body with my teeth *and* my cum."

Shivering in his arms, I ran my hands over his shoulders. "You can't keep saying things like that."

He smiled into my neck. "Oh?"

Then he leaned in and told me a few other things he wanted to do. I put my hand over his mouth to stop the images from frying my brain.

Mikael almost eked out a win that night, mostly because I was so distracted and turned on, I couldn't concentrate. But it had been another successful team-building night.

By Thursday afternoon, I just wanted to curl up somewhere and sleep for twenty-four hours straight. I carefully drove to Connor's house in the late model Mercedes Connor insisted I use while my car was in the shop. When I pulled into Connor's huge garage and parked the vehicle, my shoulders slumped in relief.

No one was home. I changed into one of his t-shirts and fell asleep in his bed, spooning his pillow. It felt like minutes later when I woke with a long, hard body curled around me. Connor nuzzled my neck and pushed his hard length into my backside.

"Elodie is with your dad for the next hour. Are you up for an orgasm or two?"

My vagina was sore and still getting used to his thick length, but I languidly pushed back and rubbed myself against him as he slid his hand under the t-shirt and cupped my breast. Then he pulled my bra down and pinched and worked my nipple.

"I'll take that as a yes," he murmured.

I reached back and cupped his shaft, and Connor growled and slid his hand into my panties to test my center. When he felt the wetness there, he moved my hand away from his cock, freed it, and pulled my panties down to my thighs.

Then he worked himself inside me. The position made my channel even tighter, and he groaned as he thrust his way in. When Connor finally bottomed out, he rolled us over on our stomachs and brought my hands up to the headboard.

"Keep them there, unless you want the paddle tonight." My vagina spasmed around him, and he chuckled in my ear. "The paddle it is."

"I didn't say I wanted the paddle." My voice was hoarse and sleepy from my nap.

"Your pussy did, but we'll save it for this weekend. I think you're worn out from being tied up and fucked hard every night this week."

His words made my vagina spasm and contract again. My legs were trapped by my panties and his thighs, and his cock was lodged tight inside me. I felt every inch of him.

Connor knelt up, pulling my hips with him as he continued to hammer inside me. When he reached around and rubbed and plucked on my clit, an orgasm started to build. Then he pressed his thumb against my anal opening.

I froze. "What are you… Oh, God!"

"I plan to fuck you here too. We'll work up to it."

Gasping, I pushed back frantically on his cock, and the dark image tipped me over the edge. I climaxed hard, and a long wail broke free.

His thrusts became sporadic, and he brutally drove into me. Then he came on a low groan. After a moment, he laid my hips back down and draped over me.

"I keep forgetting to gag you. We'll take care of that this weekend."

I raised my head. "No, thank you," I wheezed out. His weight smashed me into the mattress.

He chuckled and rolled off, taking me with him. "Aw, sweet girl. It's cute you think you have a choice."

I poked his side. "Did I tell you about the time I shaved my brother's right eyebrow off in his sleep?"

Connor was quiet for a few seconds, then he shrugged. "To gag you, then paddle and fuck you? I'd be willing to lose an eyebrow."

# Chapter 24

On Friday afternoon, we went to the auto body shop to pick up my car. Connor insisted on paying to have the scratches buffed out, and I noticed my car had also been washed and detailed.

"I don't see why you won't keep driving the Benz," he grumbled for the third time as we drove to the shop.

"Because it's not mine, and driving it makes me nervous and gives me hives."

"What are hives?" Elodie asked from the back seat.

I turned around. "It's like a red rash or bumps people might get when they're nervous or upset."

"Why are you upset?" she asked.

"Because the car is worth so much money, if anything happened to it while I was driving it, I'd be paying your dad for the rest of my life."

She looked confused. "Why?"

"Why what?"

"Why would you pay Daddy?"

"Because if I broke it, I'd want to fix it. And fixing a car like that is expensive."

"My mom broke lots of cars."

I had no idea what to say, so I looked at Connor for help. He just shrugged.

Straightening up, I looked back at her again. "Your mom probably needed a car to help take care of you. I also don't want to take advantage of him."

"Belly, I think he *wants* you to take 'vantage of him."

Connor smiled at Elodie in the rearview mirror. "That's right, Els. I do want her to take 'vantage of me."

Watching them grin mischievously at each other, I just shook my head and looked out the window.

We decided to take the team to see the Zoo Lights for our team-building activity the next week. More accurately, Elodie and I wanted to see them, so we dragged Connor and the team along.

Titus and Jackson strong-armed the players into going, and Connor made the club buy tickets for everyone. But I did get the club a group discount.

We met everyone at the front gate, and they moaned and complained like they were there for a colonoscopy.

Mikael took his ticket from me. "This team-building activity would be more appropriate if we were in the kindergarten league, *vännen.*"

"You're all whining like little babies, so it does seem appropriate."

"I want to play Catan again so I can win this time."

I smiled sweetly at him. "You'll have to get in line. My dad and brother have been trying to take my title away for years."

Mikael frowned. "Your lack of modesty and humility makes me want to beat you even more."

Rudy leaned in and took his ticket. "I haven't been to the zoo since I was a kid."

Jackson grinned. "When was that? Last year?"

"No, it was two years ago."

I couldn't tell if he was joking or not.

Titus walked up. "I got them all here except Wyatt, and no one will miss him. I'm calling in a favor, *choux*."

"Why does that make me nervous?"

He shrugged and pulled me aside. "Because you know I wouldn't ask if it wasn't important. I'll talk to you tomorrow."

"Let go of my girlfriend, asshole," Connor called from the cotton candy booth where he was in line with Elodie.

Ignoring Connor, I studied Titus. "Okay. But if it's something that could cause me bodily or emotional harm, or get me thrown in jail, I reserve the right to say no."

"Fair enough. Now let's go get this Zoo shit out of the way."

He let go of my arm as Connor strode over with Elodie, who was stuffing blue cotton candy in her mouth.

"Jackass," Connor muttered as he peeled a piece of cotton candy off Elodie's stick, then offered me half.

"Prick," Titus growled back as he pulled a piece off when Elodie held the stick up to him. "Thanks, El."

Titus looked at Connor's white button-down shirt with tiny pink flamingos on it. His head cocked to the side. "Where'd you get that shirt? I kind of like it."

I smiled wide. "Thank you."

"I like it too," Elodie said. "It has 'mingos on it."

"You're close. Flamingos," I told her.

"Bella got it for me at the thrift shop in La Quinta," Connor told Titus. "I thought this'd be the perfect place to wear it."

Titus stared at Connor. "You went into a thrift shop?"

"Yeah, and he lasted about three minutes," I told him.

We headed inside. It was still a little light out, so the guys hit the outdoor beer garden first. I was surprised to see it, but looking around I realized there were as many adults here as children.

The large, illuminated lanterns started to glow in the twilight, and a few of us pulled our phones out and started taking pictures.

Some of the other zoo-goers recognized Connor and Titus, and even a few players on the team. Several of them approached for photos and autographs. Pretty soon, word spread and the crowd swelled.

I glanced at Jackson. "Maybe I'll take Elodie and go look at the zodiac lanterns."

Titus and Connor stood in the thick of the crowd, and I waved at him and pointed to Elodie, then at the lanterns. He nodded and mouthed *thank you.*

Jackson looked around and grimaced. "I'll come with you. I've never been good at the public relations bullshit."

We wandered through the exhibit and bought bubble tea.

Elodie gazed at the glowing, ten-foot lanterns. "They're beautiful. How do they get so big?"

I pointed to the small fans hooked up to a few of them. "They're similar to big, blow-up hand-painted puppets."

"How do they move?" Several of the lanterns were automated, and an enormous whale slowly moved back and forth as if it were swimming.

Jackson pointed to the mechanism underneath the whale. "They use those machines. It looks like magic, doesn't it?"

Just then, a bubble machine behind the whale spewed bright opaque blue bubbles and fog all over the walkway. Elodie gasped and darted around, trying to pop them. I laughed and tried to catch a couple with her.

A few other kids ran over and played with the bubbles for a few minutes.

Jackson watched her. "I'm glad you and Connor are together. They deserve someone like you who makes them happy."

I looked over at Connor and the team, who were slowly extracting themselves from the crowd.

"I don't know what to think," I admitted. "We're different in so many ways. He's a hockey superstar, and I'm an intern. He's ten years older than I am, and has a dating history I can't get my head around."

"Yeah, but it's been almost five years. He seems settled and happy, and I don't think he's messing around this time."

Elodie ran over and tugged my hand. "Let's go see the rest."

A few of the players caught up with us, and they stared at the big moving whale.

"Okay, I'm not gonna lie," a player said. "That's fucking cool."

Just then, another stream of fog and blue bubbles floated out from behind the whale, and several of the younger players started trying to pop them, just like the little kids.

Connor and Titus extracted themselves from the crowd and caught up with us.

Connor draped an arm across my shoulder. "It's been a while since that happened. I don't miss it."

We made our way through the exhibits and pointed out the animals to Elodie as we wandered around together. A couple of hours later, Elodie got tired and Connor picked her up and carried her to the exit.

Most of the players took off, and Mikael turned to me. "I must eat my words, as you Americans say. That was an incredible display of artistry, mechanical ingenuity, and creativity. I will admit when I am wrong."

Jackson chuckled. "What he's trying to say is this was the shit, Isa."

Elodie lifted her head from Connor's shoulder. "Yeah, Belly. It was awesome." She laid her head back down. "And you owe me two bucks, Jack."

I chuckled and patted her little back as Connor gazed down at me with a soft grin. My heart slowly turned over in my chest; I was so screwed.

# Chapter 25

Dad, Connor, and I sat in undersized folding chairs at Elodie's elementary school auditorium that Friday night, watching her Spring dance recital with the other parents. Before the recital started, Elodie's dance teacher, Ms. Sissy, came over to Connor about ten seconds after we walked in.

"I'm so glad you could make it. Elodie is such a precious little girl," Ms. Sissy gushed at Connor as she took hold of his arm.

I'd been standing next to Connor as we looked around for seats, and she'd slid right in front of me. I stepped back so I wouldn't get trampled. She didn't acknowledge either me or my dad.

Dad tapped my shoulder. "I'll go save us seats."

I turned to follow him. "Good idea. I'll go with you."

Before I could take a step, Connor reached around the dance teacher and grabbed my arm. "Javier, we'll meet up with you. I want to introduce Bella to Miss Sandra."

The big, bright smile on Ms. Sissy's face slipped a little. "It's Sissy."

Connor stared down at her but didn't respond. She finally took a hint and stepped back, letting go of him.

He pulled me next to him and put his arm around my shoulder. "This is Bella, and I think you know Javier. He's Bella's father."

Ms. Sissy stared at Connor and me, then watched Connor lightly run his fingers along my collarbone.

She pursed her lips. "It's nice to meet you. Bella, is it? I'm going to say hello to the rest of the parents." She turned away and marched over to the stage.

I watched her go then looked around. "Let's find Dad."

Connor scowled. "Don't abandon me to the likes of Ms. Sissy again, eh?"

I patted his hard stomach. "It's kind of sad seeing their faces when you call them by the wrong name."

He wrapped his arm around my neck. "Should I be bothered you don't seem to care she was hitting on me?"

I shrugged philosophically. "If she's your type, then I'm not. Same with the secretary at the arena."

Connor's smirk turned into a real smile. "You're the most blunt, straightforward woman I've ever met. And you don't play games. It's refreshing. And so you know, I *do* get jealous."

"Oh, I'm well aware of that. And I never said I didn't get jealous."

We found our seats, and searched for Elodie among the little dancers lined up onstage. She crinkled her brow and looked anxiously through the crowd until she saw us in the audience, waving enthusiastically at her. She broke out into a big smile, then waved back and giggled nervously behind her fingers.

The dancers were young and enthusiastic, and their costumes were so adorable I had to hand it to Ms. Sissy. She'd put together a cute recital. I pulled out my phone and took several photos and videos.

The next morning, I went with Connor to Elodie's soccer game in Palm Springs. On the sidelines, I recognized a parent from the opposing team who'd brought his little boy, Tyler, to the pediatric clinic with a broken finger a couple of weeks ago. He'd been in a month before when the flu was going around, and Tyler couldn't keep anything down.

Daniel, the dad, was probably in his late twenties and looked like he spent a lot of time outside or at the gym. While I'd treated his son, Daniel mentioned a couple of times he was divorced.

He walked over and stood in front of me, grinning. "Hey, Isabella. It's good to see you again. Who're you here to watch?"

I waved half-heartedly. "Hello, Tyler's dad. How's his finger doing?"

He stepped closer. "It's Daniel, and Tyler's finger is fine. We have a follow-up appointment next week. What're you doing for lunch after the game?"

Connor came up behind me and wrapped his arm around my chest. "She's eating lunch with my daughter and me."

I clasped Connor's forearm. Daniel straightened and studied Connor, then glanced down at my empty ring finger.

He nodded at me. "It was good to see you. I'll talk to you at the clinic next week." He glanced at Connor. "Enjoy the game."

When Daniel walked across the field, Connor tightened his grip. "He's a fucktwit."

I rolled my eyes. "You don't know that."

"Even after I told him we were eating lunch together, he still looked at you like that. And he reminded me he'll be seeing you next week. That's a fucktwit move."

"You have no room to talk. There was Ms. Prissy last night."

"It's Ms. Sissy."

"Oh, now you can remember her name."

He grinned and took my hand.

Laurel came over and stood by us during the game. Sebastian and Matías coached the team together, and Matías's little girl, Sophie, was the best player on the field. She ran circles around the defenders, and she had good instincts.

Laurel started chuckling and pointed to the goalie on the other team who was picking his nose in front of the goalie box.

"So far, he's done the 'pick and flick' and the 'pick and rub.' Which he rubbed on the front of his shirt. But it looks like..."

I wrinkled my nose. "Oh, gross. That's disgusting."

Connor grinned. "That was the classic 'pick and eat.' If you watch enough kids' sports, you'll eventually see it."

Laurel grimaced. "It still makes me want to gag."

Connor shook his head. "That's one thing about hockey. Kids have to hold a hockey stick, so their hands aren't free to pick their noses. Or other places."

"This is an obvious subject change," Laurel said, turning to Connor. "But what do you think about hosting a Martini Monday party at your house sometime? No worries if it's not your thing. But both Damien and Zeke said you have a beautiful home, and we'd love to see it."

Connor shrugged. "We have the entire hockey team over every Wednesday night for what I call Whiskey Wednesdays. I think we can handle a Martini Monday party." He glanced at me. "You okay with that?"

I smiled. "It's your house. But I'm happy to help."

"Deal." He leaned over and kissed me.

"How about a week from Monday? We're having it at Scott's house this Monday, and you're invited, of course. Titus too."

"Sounds great. Scott lives on your street a few doors up, right?" I asked.

Laurel nodded. "Yeah. He's the house with the pink door. You can't miss it."

Just then the referee blew the whistle, signaling the end of the game. Players on both teams erupted into cheers and ran around the field, hugging each other.

Connor watched in bemusement. "The other team knows they lost, right?"

Laurel grinned. "They did this last season too. It's a kids' recreational soccer league, and they're five. No one but the parents care who wins."

Connor stopped to talk to Sebastian and Matías, and I continued walking toward the parking lot with Laurel.

Daniel, Tyler's dad, caught up with us and took my elbow. "Hey, can I talk to you?"

Laurel looked at me questioningly.

"I'll just be a minute," I told her.

She nodded and stayed close.

He pulled me a little further away. "So you're seeing that guy, huh?"

"Yes."

"Look, I know things happen. If you ever want to meet up for lunch, or even just get a coffee sometime, let me know. I work at the Desert Regional Medical Center as an assistant director."

Stepping back, I put up a hand. "I may not be in town much longer, but it was nice to see you and Tyler again. Have a good weekend."

"You too." He studied me then turned and walked away.

When I looked around for Connor, I saw him walking toward us with Sebastian. He didn't look happy.

He met up with me and took my hand. "See? Total fucktwit."

# Chapter 26

The Thunderbirds had another home game on Sunday. I nervously watched the action from the front row next to Ben.

Mikael played starting goalie, and he was a machine. Titus and Wyatt still didn't seem to trust each other, but Wyatt passed a little more often, and both he and Titus scored.

The Thunderbirds were up by one at the beginning of the third period, when an opposing player hooked Jackson in the face from behind with his hockey stick, and the stick got under his face shield.

Jackson's head jerked back, and blood flew. He went down on his knees, and Ben and I both jumped up. When the official stopped the game, we ran out on the ice. Jackson was bent over, bleeding and holding his face with his gloved hands. When he straightened up, I saw the deep slice along his lower cheek. It reminded me of the scar on Connor's face.

An official called a minor penalty against the player who'd hooked Jackson, and the Thunderbird players and fans erupted into angry shouts.

Ben gave Jackson a clean towel to stem the bleeding, and he skated off the ice unassisted while the crowd applauded him and booed the opposing player who skated toward the penalty box.

I glanced over at Elodie, who was standing between my dad and Connor. I gave them a quick thumbs up, and Connor put his arm around Elodie. Her face looked pale, but she waved back.

Ben took Jackson to the medical office to treat his face and stitch him up, and I stayed to finish the game. I fervently hoped there wouldn't be any more injuries, and when the final buzzer sounded, relief coursed through me.

Jackson's injury and the questionable call seemed to energize his teammates. They played hard during the third period and ended up winning the game four to one. I was a sweaty, nervous wreck by the end of the game.

The locker room buzzed as the players laughed and shouted at each other while they re-hashed their win. Jackson sported eight stitches across his right cheek, and he laughed when someone called him Scarface.

Connor walked into the locker room not long after, and he grinned at a few players who called out to him. He nodded to me but headed over to Jackson. I breathed a relieved sigh, picturing Coach Bailey's head exploding if he saw Connor come over and kiss or hug me in front of the team.

My dad and Elodie were waiting outside the locker room.

When Elodie saw me, she grabbed my hand. "Is Jack okay?"

Then she zeroed in on a few spots of blood on my jacket, and her eyes went wide. I hadn't realized I'd gotten Jackson's blood on me. Quickly shrugging the jacket off, I squatted down next to her.

"He's fine, Ellie. He got a cut on his face, but my friend gave him stitches." I smiled even though I was upset Jackson would probably have a permanent scar on his face. "He looks kind of like a pirate."

When I stood up, Dad patted my shoulder. "That was one of the few times I regret having such good seats." He shook his head. "It was a little graphic for her."

A couple of players started filing out of the locker room. Connor and Jackson walked out a few minutes later, and Elodie grabbed Jackson's hand. "Are you okay? There was blood everywhere!"

Jackson knelt next to her and smiled. His stitches pulled, and he grimaced a little.

"I'm fine, Els. It looks like I might have a scar like your dad. Cool, huh?"

Elodie didn't agree. She hugged him and patted his shoulder. "You scared us. Don't do that anymore."

Connor took her hand, wrapped an arm around me, and we all walked out together. The game had been exciting, and the players were pumped up from the win. I just felt shaky relief that Jackson was okay.

On Monday, Titus and I went to lunch to discuss his important issue. We picked a Tex-Mex place, and I tried to talk Titus into splitting a burrito with me.

"I can't eat the whole thing by myself," I argued.

"I can, and I'm paying so order what you want. And don't be stingy, for fuck's sake. You always order a little salad then end up eating my food."

"That's not true, I only eat *half* your food."

He rolled his eyes.

We got our order and sat down. "Tell me what's so important," I prodded.

"Max's mother might agree to share physical custody with me."

I grabbed his arm. "That's wonderful! But what do you mean, she *might* agree?"

He sighed. "I have to go before a family law judge and prove I have adequate income and a stable environment. And an appropriate family setting."

"Hmm. You have most of that. What do they mean by an appropriate family setting?"

"Fuck if I know. I may need some help to make sure I have whatever the hell that is."

"Okay. When you figure it out let me know." I picked up my taco and took a bite.

The next day, Titus texted me a link to an article.

*Titus: Thought you should know.*

The article had been posted on a prominent hockey news website, and there were two photographs included. The first photo showed Ben and me kneeling over Jackson on the ice, and he had blood dripping down his chin. I held a towel to Jackson's cheek and had a concerned look on my face. The second photo showed Connor and me walking out of the arena together after the game. He held Elodie's hand, and his other arm was draped around my shoulders. His head was tipped toward me, and I was turned toward him, smiling.

The headline read "The Hammer Hooks Up with Thunderbirds' Medical Assistant." My stomach dropped and my mind froze for a moment. I started imagining all the worst-case scenarios as I read the article. It was sparse, and they must have thought the photos were enough.

A few minutes later, I settled down a little. My internship was actually with the sports medicine clinic. I also wasn't technically "employed" by the Thunderbirds or Connor. Hell, I was even paying tuition to be there.

I needed to call Ben and let him know. There might be fallout with Coach Bailey, but it wasn't like I'd been trying to hide anything from the team or the staff. I'd even walked into the arena office with Connor to grab some skates a couple of months ago.

Everything would be all right, I reasoned. Feeling a little better, I forwarded the article to Connor, then I pushed the whole thing out of my mind.

# Chapter 27

Everything was not all right. Coach Bailey called Ben and me into his office the next day.

"What is this, Ms. Cruz?" He pointed to the article and photos on his laptop. "I specifically tried to avoid something like this happening when you started working here."

"Coach Bailey, my relationship with Mr. McCoy doesn't affect my work with the team."

He scoffed. "We're a professional organization, and employees should not be fraternizing with the players."

My hands clenched and my temper started to boil. "Connor and I knew each other before I started my internship with Doctor Rasmussen and Doctor Singhal's clinic. And Connor is not a player on the team."

Coach Bailey's eyes narrowed. "Yes, it's actually worse than that, isn't it? He's one of the *owners*."

I tried to keep my voice calm. "I'm not an employee of the team. My clinical internship is through Dr. Rasmussen's office, and I frankly don't see why this is an issue."

"Is Mr. McCoy how you got your internship here, Ms. Cruz?"

My spine straightened. Did he think I'd slept with Connor so I could get this internship?

Ben shifted next to me. "That's uncalled for. Connor McCoy didn't factor into us choosing her in any way. Isabella came highly recommended, and her grades and scores are top-notch."

Coach Bailey shook his head. "It's unprofessional. I'm going to contact her school and report this."

My heart thudded and my stomach lurched, but I tried to keep my expression neutral. "I've done nothing wrong. You have nothing to report."

I wanted to rage at him, and then go somewhere private and cry. But I knew that wouldn't help my case.

Ben studied him. "Do you think that's a good idea?"

"Are you threatening me?" Coach Bailey asked softly.

Ben shook his head. "No. I'm just reminding you who you actually work for. If anyone has a right to be upset about this, it'd be Dr. Singhal and myself, and we don't see a problem. I think we're done here." He got up and walked out, and I followed him.

As we walked back to the medical office, I glanced at Ben. "I'm sorry for involving you in this."

"Confidentially, Coach Bailey isn't well-loved. And in my opinion, he's a narcissistic, egotistical prick." He looked down at me. "Be careful, Isa. I don't want to see him undermine all your hard work."

I didn't either.

When Connor got home that night, he greeted Elodie and my dad, but he avoided my eyes. Throughout dinner, he was quiet.

"How was your day?" I asked him after Dad headed home and we'd tucked Elodie in together. I wanted to tell him about my run-in with Coach Bailey, but he seemed so distant.

He finally looked at me, but didn't smile. "It was fine. I have some work I need to finish up tonight though."

I took the hint and left him alone. When he finally came into the bedroom, I pretended to be asleep. I didn't tell Connor about Coach Bailey, and we didn't talk about the article because he became quiet and withdrawn over the next week. But he often woke me up in the middle of the night to have sex.

As the week wore on, I wondered if he was embarrassed about his business colleagues and former teammates knowing about me. Then I wondered if he'd gotten bored and wanted me out of his house. I even worried that maybe he'd gotten sick and didn't want to tell me.

On Friday night after we'd tucked Elodie in, I asked him again. "Tell me what's wrong."

He glanced at me. "Nothing. I just have a few things on my mind. It doesn't concern you."

He was lying, and we both knew it. When I stopped in the middle of the hall, he took my hand and started pulling me.

I dug my heels in. "You've barely spoken to me since that article came out. What's bothering you? Are you embarrassed to be with me?"

His jaw clenched. Connor pulled me into his bedroom and backed me against the door. He'd accused me of the same thing not long ago.

"I'm not embarrassed, and don't say that again. Nothing's bothering me except you still have your clothes on."

He started taking off my shirt.

"Connor, talk to me. You can't keep using sex to avoid whatever this is."

He froze, then laid his forehead against mine. "I don't want to lose you. I should have…"

"What? You should have what?"

When he didn't answer, my stomach dropped. "I'm sleeping in the other room tonight. When you're ready to tell me what in the actual fuck is going on, let me know."

For the next two days, I slept alone. Connor finally came into the guest bedroom on Sunday night and picked me up. He carried me back to his bed and tucked me under him with his arm and leg hooked around me.

I lay still for a few minutes and listened to him breathe, then turned my head into his shoulder. His warm body smelled so good, and I wanted to run my hands up and down his chest. But there was a wall between us I couldn't breach.

"Please talk to me."

He pulled me closer but didn't say anything. Long after he'd fallen asleep, I looked out the window at the early morning light, tears sliding down my cheeks.

Work dragged on Monday. I tried to hide my melancholy, but Titus cornered me in the medical office as I got ready to leave.

He leaned his hip against the counter and studied me. "Talk to me. You haven't teased any of us all day. You're starting to worry us."

Pretending to study whatever was on my laptop, I gave him a small, distracted smile. "I'm fine. Just a little tired is all."

"Bullshit. You look sad." He reached over and grasped my shoulder. "What's wrong?"

I slid my computer into my backpack. "I don't know what's wrong. Connor stopped talking to me."

Titus nodded toward the door. "Let's get lunch."

"I'm not hungry." My appetite had fled a few days ago, and I seemed to have a constant ache in my belly.

"Now I know something's wrong. Let's go get coffee then."

We went across the street to a little coffee and bakery shop near the arena, and I ordered a tea.

Running my thumb along the lid of my drink, I brooded. "Since that article you sent me? The one with the two photos? Connor hasn't said more than a handful of words to me. And he's distracted and quiet."

Titus leaned back in the booth and grunted. "Are you still living at his house?"

"Yes. But I can't stay there." I looked away. "He won't talk to me, but he still wants to... have sex all the time."

Titus's hand clenched on the tabletop. "I'm sorry, *choux*. How's your apartment?"

"The landlord finally texted back last week. And then only when I sent photos of the leaks to both him and the HOA. He said he's working on it."

Reaching over, Titus grabbed my hand and squeezed. "You can stay at my place if you want. Connor will be pissed, but he deserves it."

Something about Titus's comment struck me. "What do you mean? What does he deserve?"

He shook his head. "I'm not getting in the middle. But if you need a place to stay, you're always welcome. Connor can go fuck himself."

On the way home, I stopped and picked up a few items to make a charcuterie board for the Martini Monday party at Connor's house that night. We'd agreed to host it together when he'd still been talking to me. Then I started worrying he'd forgotten or changed his mind, so I texted him.

*Me: Are you still okay with having Martini Monday at your house tonight?*

*Connor: Yes. Why wouldn't I be?*

My temper rose, and I fired off a reply.

*Me: Hum, I don't know. Maybe because you've been moody and silent over the past week.*

He didn't text me back.

Two hours later when Connor still hadn't come home, that sinking feeling grew in my stomach.

Connor walked in around the time guests started to arrive. I didn't look at him. Dad had strung café lights around the pool area, and he'd turned on a few heaters so we could enjoy the courtyard and the gardens. He and Elodie had helped me get ready, then they'd gone to his house to watch the newest episode of *Ada Twist, the Scientist.*

Martina, Sebastian, and Laurel arrived first. Sebastian helped prep the drink station, and Martina stood by with her arms crossed. "What drinks did you decide on?" she asked.

"Well, this group seems to like whiskey, so I thought an old-fashioned and a whiskey sour would work. There's also beer and wine."

"Sounds good. Sebastian can mix those up in his sleep."

Sebastian grunted. "Good choices."

She turned to me. "I need to talk to you. I ran into Connor's former assistant a couple of days ago. We had a strange conversation."

"What'd she tell you?" I asked as I laid out cheese wedges.

Martina glanced around and lowered her voice. "We need to talk in private. Harley mentioned you're living with Connor right now because your apartment flooded."

I grimaced. "There's a slow leak spreading across my ceiling. I'm pretty sure there's mold by now."

"You should come stay with Laurel and me. I already talked to her about it, and she's got an extra bedroom. It would give me someone else to bully into going to karaoke night with me."

"That's a nice offer, and I appreciate it." I put the cracker box down. "But you're scaring me. What is it?"

Martina sighed and rubbed her forehead. "You and Connor may have already talked about it." She studied Connor with narrowed eyes. "But men can be bastards. And if it were me, I'd want to know."

Titus and Jackson arrived just then, and we made drinks and talked about their out-of-town game. They'd won, but Wyatt had gotten in a fight afterward with some girl's boyfriend, and Jackson had to bail him out of jail.

"What did Coach Bailey say about it?" I asked.

Titus shrugged. "Don't know, and don't care. He found out about it after we'd already bailed his ass out. If Wyatt weren't such a good player, we would have left him there."

Sebastian and Zeke made the cocktails, and I decided I liked the whiskey sour best. It tasted the least like whiskey.

Connor didn't approach me, but I caught him staring at me a few times. When most the men were playing a game of cutthroat pool in the entertainment room, Martina pulled me outside.

We walked through the courtyard into the back garden area, and she turned to me. "I'm not going to beat around the bush. Last week I ran into Rachel, Connor's former assistant. She told me all about Noah. You were right. He did hit on her, several times."

"That's not surprising."

"She also said he manhandled her when she turned him down. And threatened her."

I sighed. "She needs to tell Connor. I think Noah has done this before."

Martina looked out into the garden. "Probably. Rachel also said Noah warned her away from Connor, and told her Connor's already married."

My body froze. "Married?" I whispered. I wasn't sure I'd heard her right.

She studied me. "Yeah. Married. Noah told her he's been married to Elodie's mother since Elodie was born."

My stomach wanted to rebel. "Oh, my God."

Martina took my hand and led me to an outdoor seating area. "I take it he didn't tell you."

Shaking my head, I sat down hard. "I didn't know. He never said a word." My stomach churned and acid rose in my throat. "I've been living with and having sex with a married man."

Martina sat down next to me. "It depends. His divorce became final about a month ago."

I sat still and counted the weeks we'd been together. He'd come back from Canada last month in a terrible mood, but he told me he was done fucking around. And Titus asked him if he'd gotten his shit taken care of. My mind worked sluggishly to grasp the fact that Connor had been married. For years.

And the worst part was he'd never told me. I thought back to the conversations and discussions we'd had. He never said a word.

Squeezing my hand, Martina kept going. "Rachel said Noah told her Connor only married her because of Elodie. So she'd have his last name and he'd have a better chance of keeping her safe and getting custody."

"What else did Rachel say?" I was so angry that Martina was the one telling me these personal details about Connor's life.

"She said Noah actually laughed about Connor being stuck in such a bad marriage for so long. I think Noah gets the prize for the world's shittiest brother."

My mind tried to process what she'd told me. "Connor hates Elodie's mother, but it doesn't matter. I can't stay with someone who keeps things like this from me. He wants me to tell him what's happening in my life, and be honest with him. But he keeps this from me? Men are such fucking assholes." My voice broke.

"They definitely can be. Did I ever tell you about my ex-husband?"

"No." I brushed a few tears away. "I didn't know you'd been married before."

"When I was nineteen. When we met, he was cute and funny. And he said he loved me."

I squeezed her hand. "What happened?"

"He turned out to be a manipulative, controlling bastard. The short version is he started belittling and criticizing me. Then he complained whenever I wanted to see my friends or family. Finally, he hit me. That's when I left him."

"I'm so sorry."

"Me too. Having an abusive partner can really fuck you up." She stared out into the garden.

"I can't stay with him," I whispered.

Martina's head tilted back, and she looked up at the starry sky. "There's more."

"I'm not ready for more."

She smiled a little. "We never are. After I talked to Rachel, I may have asked Zeke to do a little digging for me. He has more... elastic morals than the rest of them."

"What did he find out?"

She looked at me. "You may already know, but Zeke said Connor has a thing for spanking and ropes. And other interesting, kinky shit."

I looked up at the sky too.

She pushed my shoulder and chuckled. "So you *do* know about that. When I start having sex again, I'll have to get a few ideas."

"I'm not sure what you're talking about," I lied. "I thought you and Iz were a thing."

She sighed. "Iz is a story for another day."

"I'd like to hear it sometime."

"When I figure it out, I'll tell you all about it."

I wrapped my arms around myself. "Tell me the rest."

"Connor is loaded. His ex-wife is also unstable and has a string of assaults and disturbing the peace convictions. It's gotten worse over time, especially when she goes off her meds. That scar on his cheek?"

"Yeah?"

"He did get it from a skate blade. But it wasn't during a game. Amelia went to his house, they got in an argument, and she swiped him across the face with one of his skates."

I flinched. "Oh, God."

"She split his cheek wide open, and he had to go to the emergency room. That's when he started fighting for full physical custody."

"When was that?"

"Right before he decided to retire."

We sat in silence for a few minutes, lost in thought.

"I don't know what to do," I whispered.

"Come stay with Laurel and me while you figure it out. For as long as you need."

I turned to her. "Thank you. For being my friend, and for telling me."

"You're welcome. My life is messed up right now too." She smirked. "Most of it I did to myself. But if you like Connor and think something could come of it, I have one piece of measly advice."

"What's that?"

She sighed. "Don't do what I did. Or what Connor did, for that matter. Be honest, talk to him, and don't hide anything."

My jaw clenched. "That's going to be a little tough since he stopped talking to me last week. And right this minute if I told him what I was thinking, it would be a big 'screw you' with a side of 'you fucking bastard' thrown in."

She squeezed my shoulder. "Fair enough."

# Chapter 28

When we walked back inside, a hot ball of rage simmered in my chest. Connor not telling me hurt more than finding out he'd been married when he started pursuing me.

The party was breaking up.

When Titus walked over to say goodbye, I pointed a finger in his face. "You knew. You knew he was married, and you didn't say a word," I snarled in a low voice.

He studied me for a minute, then put his hands on his hips. "*Choux*, I know you're angry. And probably want to knee us both in the balls."

"No. I want to go back to Seattle and pretend I never met Connor. Or you."

He winced, then let out a long sigh. "Talk to him, and get his side. You can still stay with me if you need to." He squeezed my stiff shoulder and walked out.

Connor and Jackson were in the game room, but everyone else had left. I didn't dare go to the bedroom and pack my things, but I wasn't staying here a minute longer.

Quietly, I grabbed my purse and car keys, then went over to my dad's house. He and Elodie were just walking out.

"How was the party?" he asked.

"Good. You guys could have come over."

Elodie yawned, and I knelt down next to her.

"Sorry for keeping you up. You ready for bed?" I asked.

She nodded. "I read some books. And you know what?" she asked.

My heart hurt a little. I already loved her so much.

"No. What?" I asked softly.

"I'm reading really good now."

"I know you are. I love you. Have a good night."

When I stood up, Dad studied me. "You okay?"

"I'm going to grab a few things I left at your house. If you talk to Connor, tell him... I'll contact him in a few days, okay?"

Dad glanced at Connor's house, and his brow furrowed. But he nodded.

Hurrying inside, I grabbed some clothes and toiletries and stuffed them in an old gym bag. I also picked up one of my skateboards. I must have known on some level not to leave all my things at Connor's house.

When I pulled up to Laurel and Martina's place, I let out a long, shuddering breath. Checking my phone, I noticed Connor had called me twice, and he'd left a few texts.

*Connor: Where are you?*

*Connor: Bella, where the fuck are you?*

I steeled myself, then called him back.

He answered on the first ring. "You better have a good reason for sneaking out."

"I do." Rage and anger morphed into hurt and pain. "You were married. Up until a month ago, you were married. I called you my boyfriend, we lived together, and we fucked... so many times. But you never said a word."

He was silent for several seconds. "Come home so we can talk."

"*Now* you want to talk? That's ironic, isn't it?" I laid my head on the steering wheel. "How could you not tell me something like that?"

"Bella, it's not what you think."

"Were you married to her for the last five years?" I asked.

"Yes," he clipped.

"Then it's *exactly* what I think. And you know what sucks? If you would have just *talked* to me, I probably could have dealt with it."

"My divorce was final the night I dragged you out of Titus's house. And I never lived with Amelia or fucked her while we were married. I did it for Elodie. To give her my name, as leverage for custody, and to keep her safe."

A few tears slipped out. "Why didn't you tell me? Why did you—"

"Because I thought you'd never give me a chance if you knew I was married when we met. And half the Goddamn hockey team would love to have you in their bed. Titus is right. You're a fucking unicorn."

"That's not true," I argued.

"It's absolutely true. Bella, come home."

"I can't. I don't trust you anymore. I never wanted to be that woman." A sob slipped out, but I shut it down. "Maybe I don't even know you."

He sighed. "Promise me you won't shut Elodie and me out."

"That's not fair. You can't bring her into this."

"I *can* bring her into this. Elodie is the only reason I married Amelia, and she's one of the reasons I fell for you."

Tears slipped out, but I tried to will them back. "I need time. I have to think."

He sighed, long and hard. "Okay. And when you're ready, I'll tell you anything you want to know."

"Now you'll talk to me."

"I'm going to tell you the truth from now on. Where are you staying? Not at your apartment," he growled.

"With friends."

"Please fucking tell me it's not Titus."

"He knew you were married and he never said a word." My voice rose. "I'm almost as mad at him as I am at you."

He chuckled mirthlessly. "Well, that's one good thing that came out of this mess. Sooner or later, you and I are going to talk. Stay safe, eh?" And he hung up.

On Tuesday at the arena, I didn't look at Jackson or Titus. Jackson finally approached me toward the end of my shift.

"I know you're mad."

"You think?" I continued typing notes on my laptop.

Jackson rubbed the back of his neck. "Titus told me what happened. I'm sorry I didn't say anything. I don't know if this makes it better or worse, but I kind of forgot he'd married her. I was still in high school."

I stopped typing. "Really?"

He shrugged. "I figured he'd gotten a divorce long before now."

Sighing, I put my laptop aside. "He should have told me, and now I don't trust him. And I worry about how this will affect Elodie if I disappear from their life."

"Elodie loves you. I think that's one of the reasons he didn't want to tell you. And Connor probably worried you would've friend-zoned him if you'd known."

"Connor is too much of an ass to friend-zone," I retorted.

Jackson laughed as Titus walked in.

Titus scowled. "You're talking to him, but you won't talk to me?"

"Jackson explained and then apologized. I also confided in you, but you didn't say anything."

Jackson raised his hand. "Although I'd love to stay and watch you hand Titus his balls, I'm taking off." He hugged me. "Give Connor a chance. I don't want to lose you either."

He walked out, and Titus stepped in front of me. "First, Connor is also my friend. I told him to tell you, but he said he didn't want to lose you. That was his call. It was a fucking stupid call, but still his to make. Second, you two are good together. You know it, he knows it. Even your dad knows it. And he's divorced now, so if you think he's worth it, cut him a break. God knows, the man needs one. Even if he's a fucking idiot sometimes."

I stared at Titus and thought about my life before Connor came into it, and how alone I'd been. My choice had mostly been about school, but now I loved having him and Elodie around.

"He was married for five years, and he didn't tell me. I don't know if I can trust him again. And does he really want to be in another relationship so soon now that he's free?"

Titus cocked his head and studied me. "It's been years since he's been in an actual relationship. Amelia isn't a relationship, she's a fucking tragedy. He was alone for a long time, and then you came along. Think about that."

The rest of the week dragged by. It was cold and flu season, and we had a rash of kids come into the pediatric clinic. I called my dad to make sure Elodie was okay.

"She has a little sniffle, but nothing to worry about. Now what's going on with you and Connor? He looks like he hasn't slept in a week, and you sound like your dog died."

"I've never had a dog, so how do you know what I'd sound like?"

He sighed. "You know what I mean. Now what's going on?"

I cleared my throat. "Connor and I aren't seeing each other anymore."

"I suspected something like that. Are you okay? What happened?"

"Up until about a month ago, he was married. I found out on Monday."

Dad sucked in a sharp breath. "What? Who in the world was he married to?"

I told him what I knew. "The thing that hurts the most is he didn't tell me."

"If I'd known, I never would have encouraged him." Dad sighed. "He and I are going to have words."

"You don't need to defend me. I can do it myself."

He ignored me. "I don't understand. He doesn't even like Elodie's mom."

"He said he married her so Elodie would have his last name, and he'd be in a better position to get custody. But it doesn't change the fact that he was married when we met, and he never said a word."

"Why didn't he just tell you?" Dad sounded baffled.

"Because he's an idiot?"

"I can't argue with that. It's a damn shame because you seemed to make each other happy."

"I miss seeing you every day. And I miss Elodie." I missed Connor too, but I also wanted to scream at him.

"Maybe Elodie and I can meet you at the park, or for lunch sometime. She asks where you are. She misses you too."

"Let's meet at the park. Give her a big hug for me."

The next afternoon, Dad brought Elodie to the skate park closest to Connor's house so we could hang out together. She had her own helmet, pads, and a sweet little SkateXS board with a purple and green flower design.

Elodie jumped up and down when she saw me. "I have my own stuff now. And you know what?" She put her hands on my cheeks.

"I practiced with Daddy. And I only fell off four times the last time."

My heart squeezed when I thought of Connor patiently working with her on her little skateboard.

"Are you wearing your helmet and pads every time?"

"Yeah. And look at my pink shoes. I love them! They match yours."

Her little pink suede lace-up high tops didn't look like my beat-up black ones. But they were the same brand, so I guess that counted.

She patted my shoulder. "I miss you. Where have you been? Daddy said he made you sad. Are you mad at me?"

"No, sweetheart. I'm not mad at you at all. I need to think about a few things, and I need to do it while I'm not at your dad's house. I love you. Don't ever think me not being there has anything to do with you."

She studied me, as if looking for the truth. "Okay. Can you help me skate?"

"Absolutely. Remember, it takes a lot of practice. So don't get frustrated, just go slow, and have fun."

I stood up, and my dad put his arm around me. "I brought a few of your things from the house, something from Connor, and some lemon bars. You look like you've lost weight. I don't like it." He set a large bag down by my backpack.

Sighing, I hugged him back. "Thanks. The lemon bars will help. Let me work with Ellie, then we'll break them out."

We skated, talked, and ate lemon bars for an hour or so. When they left, I skated alone for a while, working my way in and out of the intermediate bowl. A few younger boys came, but they just watched and left me alone.

I was able to turn off my mind and enjoy the movement and rhythm. It worked until I sat down and looked through the bag Dad had left by my backpack. There was a pair of suede pink lace-up high-top shoes in my size that were almost identical to Elodie's shoes. Now I knew what she meant when she said our shoes matched.

A note was tucked in with the shoes. *You promised I could get you something in return for the flamingo shirt.*

I slowly pulled the shoes out and tried them on. They were perfect and I loved them, damn it.

On Sunday morning, Laurel, Martina, and I sat down for brunch on her back patio. They were great roommates and had become good friends, but I didn't want to take advantage.

"I want to pay rent. At least let me pay for the utilities."

I'd recently stocked up on groceries since Laurel still refused to let me pay her for anything.

She waved her hand. "I've told you a million times, I'm good. You're welcome to stay as long as you need."

"My apartment should be done soon. It'll just be temporary."

Martina raised her coffee cup. "Or until Connor talks you into moving back in with him."

Laurel gave Martina an exasperated look. "Really? You can think it, but don't say it right to her face."

"What? Anyone who's seen them together knows that's probably what will happen."

Laurel glanced at me. "Yeah, but right now isn't the best time to say it."

Martina rolled her eyes. "She's not dumb. We don't need to baby her."

I raised my hand. "I'm sitting right here. And thank you for not babying me."

Laurel studied me and set her glass down. "Talk to us. We've both been through some stuff, and I'm a good listener."

"What am I?" Martina asked, sounding offended.

"You're blunt and a little crazy. Which is as important as being a good listener." Laurel turned to me. "Talk."

So I told them about how Connor and I met, Elodie, and how I started falling for him.

"We're so different though. He's rich, and I'm definitely not. He's ten years older than me, and he can be... overwhelming."

Laurel nodded. "I get it. I have a man like that myself."

Martina shook her head at both of us. "But the sex is fucking fantastic, isn't it?" She turned to Laurel. "No specifics!"

I rubbed my forehead. "Sometimes I have to fight his possessive nature, and it's an uphill battle. But he's protective and loyal, and he loves Elodie and tries so hard to be a good dad. He also gives me the tingles." I glanced at them and cleared my throat. "Sex with him is hot and dirty. And fun. He makes it fun." My mind drifted. "Sometimes I just want to bite his ass, and grab... Well, you get the idea."

They both stared at me and nodded. Martina seemed to shake herself. "I need to get laid," she muttered.

I sighed. "I don't know what to do."

"Well, you better figure it out," Martina said. "Harley overheard Connor talking to Damien yesterday. He said he's done fucking around."

My heart lurched, and I sucked in a breath. Connor told me that the day his divorce was final. It didn't bode well for me.

# Chapter 29

On Friday afternoon, I met Dad and Elodie at Elmer's Café for an early dinner. When she saw me, Elodie hopped up and down and hugged me tight.

"Belly, I miss you. Come home!"

I hugged her back, then studied her. She had on green striped leggings, a red print shirt, and her pink Vans. Her outfit clashed spectacularly, but her hair was arranged in a beautiful rose braid with little wisps floating around her face. I smiled and felt a sharp pain in my heart.

Dad studied my face. "Are you getting any sleep?"

Shrugging, I took Elodie's hand and led her into the restaurant.

"Have you ever had their German pancakes?" I asked her.

"No, but Daddy made pancakes this morning. He burned them and said the f-word twice!"

"You sound happy about it."

"Yeah, 'cause I'm rich."

We ordered German pancakes and strawberry milkshakes. Elodie bounced next to me and talked my ear off.

"How many best friends do you have now?" I asked her.

"Lots. 'Cause everyone should have a best friend."

"You're right."

She put her sticky hand on my thigh. "Daddy is sad. He said he misses you. Are you still his best friend?"

My eyes filled with tears, and I squeezed her hand. "We're trying to figure a few things out, Ellie, and I need some time."

"Okay. How much time?"

Smiling a little, I gave her a side hug. "I don't know. But I'm coming to your game tomorrow, so we'll see each other there." God, I missed them so much.

The next day, I was a bundle of nerves before Elodie's soccer game. I rode with Laurel to the park, and as we walked to the soccer field I saw Connor standing on the sidelines watching the kids warm up. He looked so good, and I'd somehow forgotten how tall he was.

He turned and spotted us, then stared at me as we walked toward him.

I held up my hand. "Hello."

Laurel looked out at the players. "How do they look today?"

"Young and uncoordinated. Except Sophie." He grimaced as a kid kicked at the ball but completely missed it.

Laurel smiled. "Believe it or not, they're doing much better this season."

"Did you two drive together?" he asked.

Laurel nodded. "Yeah. It made sense."

Connor turned to me. "Where are you staying, Bella?"

Before I could say a word, Laurel answered. "With Martina and me. But you already knew that since Sebastian told you the morning after she got to my house."

Connor stared at me. "Are you still there?"

"Yes. Not that it's your business."

He narrowed his eyes and stepped closer. "You'll always be my business. At least you aren't back in your shitty apartment. Or at Titus's house."

"Hey! My apartment isn't shitty."

"It's a complete shithole."

"It's just old."

He ticked a list off on his fingers. "The ceiling leaks and has water stains, you've probably got mold, the flooring is disgusting, and the kitchen is a nightmare."

Laurel stared at me, her mouth open. "He's right. You can't move back there, and your landlord sounds like a slumlord."

I threw up my hands. "It's affordable, and it's a roof over my head, okay? Trust me, I've lived in worse."

Connor swiped his hand over his face and swore under his breath.

Laurel shook her head. "I'm going to talk to Sebastian before they start." Then she mouthed *good luck* to me before she walked off.

I started following her, but Connor took my wrist and drew me in.

"Look at me." He waited until I met his face. "Are you all right?"

"I'm fine. Why wouldn't I be?"

"Because Javier said you haven't been sleeping, and Elodie said you cried at the restaurant yesterday."

Standing this close to him, I could smell his scent and feel his warmth.

I stepped back. "It may take a little time, considering you lied to me since we met, and you were married to another woman and I had to hear it from someone else."

"I'm sorry I didn't tell you. You don't know how sorry. And my divorce was finalized before we started having sex and you moved in. Now when are you coming home?"

I shook my head. "It's not that simple."

He carefully took hold of my wrist and slowly pulled me closer. "It's as simple as you want it to be, Bella."

I shook my head. "I don't trust you. I can't just decide to come home and everything will be better, And you just got your freedom back. You can be with anyone you want, and I can't do this again. I don't want to hurt like that again." My chest heaved, and my heart ached.

He clasped my shoulders and pulled me into him. "Are you listening to yourself? You called my house 'home.' And you know damn well I don't give a fuck about other women." He let out a long breath. "You can sleep in the guest bedroom. I just want you there."

I stood still and finally admitted the truth, to him and myself. "I'm scared. I don't know if I can do this."

"We miss you." He leaned down and murmured in my ear. "Come to Vancouver with me and Elodie next weekend. We'll stay at my house there, and I'll show you around. We can visit the botanical garden, see downtown, go to a show. Whatever you want."

The referee blew the whistle a few times to signal the game would be starting.

He held my chin. "What kind of life do you want, Bella? What makes you happy? Because you make me happy, and I want you in my life."

I gazed up at him, his words echoing my own thoughts. I started a little when I heard someone squeal my name. Elodie skipped over and threw her head back to look up at me.

"Yay, you came! Eat lunch with us."

I smiled down at her sweet face, and my heart let go of some of the hurt. "That sounds wonderful, and you can pick where we eat."

Sophie called her to get into position.

"Coming!" She squeezed my hand and ran back onto the field.

I stared at her, then turned to Connor. "You don't play fair."

He grinned. "When it comes to you, I don't give a fuck about playing fair."

The game went by in a blur. Connor stayed close, and my mind raced from one thought to the next. During the game, Elodie went from running after the ball to dancing around and talking with the little girl from the other team who stood next to her.

Connor shook his head. "I don't think she's cut out for competitive sports."

I watched her hug the opposing player. "Probably not."

After the game, we walked over to Laurel and Sebastian.

Connor took hold of my elbow. "Isabella is coming to lunch with us. You guys are welcome."

I blushed and looked up at the sky.

Laurel smiled. "Thanks for the offer, but the twins need to get home." She turned to me. "I'll see you at the house later. Or not."

Before I could reply, Elodie came up and grabbed my other hand. "Bye, Coach!" She waved at Sebastian and we took off.

Connor looked down at her. "You seemed to enjoy yourself out there. Where do you want to eat lunch?"

"Just home."

I stared at her, panicking a little. "Are you sure you don't want to eat out? It's your pick, and we could even do McDonalds."

Elodie shook her head. "Nah. Let's go home."

Connor grinned. "Good choice, El. Home it is."

My leg bounced and my thoughts churned on the drive to Connor's house. We walked into his kitchen together, just like we had a hundred times before. I was quiet as I tried to figure out the best way to extract myself after lunch.

Elodie ran to her room and changed out of her soccer clothes while I stood awkwardly in the kitchen with my arms folded.

Connor stuck his head in the fridge. "We have leftover chicken pasta, sandwich stuff, or a frozen mac and cheese casserole we can heat up. What sounds good?"

I shrugged. "I don't care. I think Elodie would like the mac and cheese best."

He nodded and stuck the casserole into the microwave. Then he leaned against the counter and watched me. "Are you and Titus talking again?"

"Barely. He's still on my shitlist."

Connor nodded. He pulled off the counter and walked toward me. I backed up quickly and hit the oven.

Smiling, he leaned into me. "Are you nervous?"

"No, of course not," I lied. Hell yes, I was nervous.

"You're lying. What do you need, sweet girl?" he asked softly in my ear.

Swallowing, I shifted nervously against him. "I need space. You're smashing me."

"No, I'm not. But I'd like to be."

I rolled my eyes and was about to tell him to fuck off, when Elodie came running down the hall. Connor reluctantly stepped back, and I breathed out a sigh.

Connor smirked down at me. "Don't get too comfortable."

We ate lunch together, and Elodie chattered away. She had so much to tell me, and I loved and hated it. Connor stared at me through most of the meal.

Dad came over as we were finishing up to take Elodie to her friend's birthday party.

Before they left, she took my hand. "Will you be here when I get back?"

I tucked a small wisp of hair behind her ear. She'd changed for her party, and she matched today. Mostly because she wore a one-piece blue romper. She looked so adorable with her hair done up in Princess Leia buns.

"Yes. I'll wait for you," I promised helplessly.

Dad glared at Connor for a few seconds, then let out a long sigh. "I'll pick her up, and we need to run a few errands afterward. We'll be home around five."

That was four hours from now. "I'll come with you," I blurted out.

"Fuck no," Connor growled.

Dad shook his head. "You two need to figure a few things out." He turned to me. "Remember, I love you. And no matter what you decide, I'll always support you." And then they were gone.

# Chapter 30

I slowly turned to Connor. "What just happened?"

"Elodie set you up like an experienced card shark, and your dad just walked out with her."

Nodding, I started backing up. "I think you're right."

Connor smirked and folded his arms. "I'd prefer to have sex now and talk later, but I can be persuaded."

My temper flared to life. "How about if I yell at you, and we *not—*"

He was on me before I knew he'd even moved. He wrapped his hand around the back of my neck and pulled me to him, devouring my mouth. Connor swept his tongue inside and tilted my chin.

My brain emptied, and I grabbed his shoulders. I felt like a junkie needing a fix, and my skin buzzed where he touched me.

Then he pulled back. "Tell me you want me to fuck you."

"I shouldn't."

"Bella, tell me or say no."

"I want you to fuck me, okay? You're still a son of a–"

Cupping my head, he kissed me again, long and hard. Then he pulled back. "You feel so good. I need to strip you, bend you over the kitchen table, and paddle your ass for leaving."

My pussy contracted, and I pushed my breasts against his grip, then wedged my hand between us, palming his cock.

"You're delusional if you think I'm going to let you spank me. I'm still so mad at you." Reaching up, I grabbed his hair with my free hand, pulling his mouth back to mine.

When we finally came up for air, his grin was dark and feral. He took hold of the hem of my shirt and ripped it over my head. I returned the favor and pulled his shirt off, then leaned in and bit his pectoral. He growled and scooped me up, laying me out on the kitchen table and knocking over a chair.

Palming my stomach, he pulled my leggings and panties down and ripped them off. Then he caged my head between his hands and looked down at me. "Spread your legs. Wide."

My heart hammered and my mind melted into a white hot haze. Connor's eyes scanned my body, and his jaw clenched. I spread my thighs.

"That's it. My good, sweet girl."

"I'm not your sweet girl today, McCoy. I'd just as soon rip your balls off."

He grinned and pulled his cock out, then ran it through my wet slit, snagging it at my opening. "I need them first."

"Oh, God," I panted. My head arched back.

"No." He put a hand behind my head and pulled me up a little. "You're going to watch me pound into your hot, wet cunt until you scream my name and beg me to go harder."

Then Connor bent his legs and surged into me. I cried out. He let go of my head and pulled my bra down under my breasts as he thrust into me over and over.

I propped my elbows up on the table so I could watch him slam into me. He leaned over and wrapped his mouth around my shoulder blade and sucked and bit.

The bite of pain pushed me higher. "Please. I need to feel you deep."

His hips crashed into mine, and my body jolted with each savage thrust. He paused to pull up my hips, giving him a better angle. Then he stroked my clit. My orgasm started building, and I thrust back at him. The sight of him holding me up so he could pound into me made my stomach clench and my thoughts scatter, as lust and need coursed through me.

His teeth worried my nipples, and he pulled and licked at them until they were tender and aching. He wasn't gentle, and I knew he'd leave marks. But I wanted him to mark me.

Before I orgasmed, he pulled out and lifted me off the table to turn me around. I pushed him back a little, and bent down to take his cock in my mouth. I could taste myself on him. Connor threw his head back and groaned. I sank to my knees and cupped his testicles while I sucked and licked him. I wasn't gentle either. After taking him in the back of my throat a few times, he pulled me off.

"That feels so fucking good. But when I come, it's going to be deep inside you," he hissed.

He pulled me up, then turned my body around and positioned me over the table. Placing his palm in the center of my back, he pushed my legs further apart with his knees and slammed into me again. My feet came off the floor, and I cried out as pleasure and a little pain surged through my core.

Leaning over my back, Connor wrapped his large hand around the front of my throat and squeezed gently. "You're going to tighten around my cock when you want to come."

Our scents mingled and surrounded me, and the feel of his hand at my neck, his chest at my sweaty back, and the slapping sounds of his hips powering into me overwhelmed my senses. Then he worked his hand between my legs and rubbed on my clit.

An orgasm surged through me, and I keened high and long as I locked around him. He snarled and thrust into me almost brutally until his hips locked, and he shot his hot semen deep inside.

We lay across the table for a few moments, panting into the silence. When he finally lifted off me and helped me stand, I grabbed the table for a minute to steady myself.

He held me until I caught my breath. As the lust faded, reality started creeping in.

Sighing, he set his chin on the top of my head. "Will you come back and work this out with me?"

I tensed in his arms, remembering my anger and hurt. But I wanted to try, and I'd missed him so much.

"I can't promise that, but I'll try. And we do need to talk. I'll come back until my apartment is fixed, and we'll see what happens after that." I needed to protect my battered heart.

He let out a quiet breath, nodded, and hugged me to him.

That evening, we ate dinner with my dad. While Connor helped Elodie put her birthday party loot away, Dad and I got dinner ready.

He studied me as I set the table. "Are you okay? You look a little better."

I blushed but nodded. "We talked, and I think we're going to try and work things out."

"You think? Or you know?" he asked.

Sighing, I set the silverware down and leaned my hip against the table. "I don't know anything anymore, Dad. I feel conflicted, and just so... mad at him for not telling me. But when I'm with him I feel happy, like I belong. I'm so confused."

He walked over and wrapped an arm around me. "That sounds a lot like love. If you didn't love him, would you be so mad?"

I blew out a breath. "Probably not."

He smiled gently. "Sounds about right. He may be older than you, but I don't think he's had a lot of love in his life. He's probably learning too."

We ate dinner together, then Connor and I went back to his house to watch a movie with Elodie. She fell asleep halfway through. While Connor woke her up enough to brush her teeth and get her tucked in, I got ready for bed with the toiletries and clothes I'd left behind when I'd fled Connor's house a few weeks ago.

Everything was exactly where I left it. I stared at his massive bed and looked around his bedroom, smelling his sandalwood scent and seeing a few of his small personal items scattered around. I wasn't ready to share this room with him.

After putting on a t-shirt and sleep shorts, I padded to the bedroom where I'd stored some of my things. Connor told me if I came back I could stay in a guest bedroom, and I was going to take him up on it. I tossed and turned for almost an hour. When he didn't come after me, I finally drifted off to sleep. Only to wake up when the bed shifted.

Adrenaline and lust hit my system, and I was suddenly wide awake. "You said I could sleep in the guest bedroom if I came back," I whispered.

He sat on the bed next to me. "I did. But I never said I wouldn't be sleeping in it with you," he murmured back.

"Huh. I missed that big, fat loophole." I sat up and started swinging my feet off the bed. "Then I'll go sleep in my dad's spare bedroom."

He laid a hand on my thigh. "I won't stay. I just want to talk."

After a minute, I pulled my feet back on the bed. "Okay."

"I'm sorry I wasn't the one to tell you about the marriage. I was married on paper, but that's it. She was never my girlfriend or wife. And she sure as fuck wasn't anything to Elodie."

I tried to study his face in the darkness. "You hurt me. You lied by not telling me."

"I did. And I'm sorry I hurt you. I was afraid after the way we met, you wouldn't have given me the time of day if you knew I was married. God, you were this beautiful, angry, innocent woman. You're so different from anyone I've ever been with. You didn't give a single fuck about my money or hockey career. I sometimes think my own goddamned family cared more about it than me."

Old wounds echoed in his voice.

"They were stupid then," I murmured.

"You also love Elodie like she's your own daughter even though I royally fucked things up. I couldn't stay away, and I didn't want to lose you."

A few tears leaked out, but I ignored them. "You let me start falling…" I trailed off.

"Say it, Isabella. Say it." He leaned over me.

"No, damn you."

"Elodie and I have been mired down in craziness and hate for five fucking years. So I *need* you to love me. To love her. I fucking crave it."

My shoulders shook, and I tried to cover my face with my hands. He gently pulled them away and wrapped his arms around me. "I'm sorry, love. I'm so fucking sorry. Please stay with us."

His soft words seeped into the aching hole in my heart as he sat there rocking me.

When I finally quieted down, I slowly wrapped my arms around him. "Don't freeze me out, or lie to me again. Or I swear to God, I will make you rue the day you ever met me."

He squeezed me hard against him and let out a long sigh. "I promise."

# Chapter 31

Titus brought me coffee and a chocolate doughnut on Tuesday morning as a peace offering. "I'm sorry I made you mad, *choux*," he said as he set them down on the counter next to me.

"Would you do it again?"

"Yes," he said without hesitation. "But just remember, I'd keep your secrets too."

I picked up the doughnut, contemplated that for a few seconds, then took a bite. "Okay."

Coach Bailey still wouldn't talk to me or make eye contact. I didn't care, but I noticed he used some of the same tactics with the players. In my opinion, it was an asinine way to coach.

After practice, Titus lay on his stomach on the massage table in the medical office with a towel draped over his hips. Phyllis, the trainer, worked a few kinks out in his lower back with her elbow, and Titus groaned in pain.

She smirked when he started swearing in French. "You'll thank me later, Tremblay."

"*Baise-moi.* I doubt it," he grumbled.

Patting his shoulder, she finished up. "Make sure you ice it, and stretch out a little this afternoon." She waved at me and walked out.

Titus groaned. "Honest to God, I don't know which is worse. A deep tissue massage from Phyllis or an ice bath."

I smirked. He wasn't the first player to complain. "Well, at least her massages don't leave you with cold, tiny balls."

He grunted out a laugh and slowly sat up. "I heard Coach Bailey is giving you shit about Connor."

"Bailey's giving me the silent treatment now, but when that article with the photos came out, he told me in front of my supervisor he plans to complain to the University." My stomach clenched just thinking about it.

"What a fucking prick. What did Connor say?"

"Nothing." I turned and started typing on my laptop.

"Did you tell him about Bailey's threat?"

"Mmm. Hey, do you still need help with your custody case?"

"Yes. And you're a shitty liar."

I shrugged, giving up any pretense. "He wasn't talking to me when it happened. And then I wasn't talking to him. It hasn't come up yet."

"You need to tell him."

"Yeah, I'll be sure and get right on that."

Titus winced. "You two give me heartburn. I have shit to do this afternoon, Let's meet for lunch tomorrow."

We met at Booze Hound for lunch on Wednesday. It was close to the pediatric clinic, offered some good lunch specials, and had that great retro Palm Springs vibe.

I sighed when I slid into the booth across from him. "I like kids. I swear I do. But if I have to listen to another parent tell me how wonderful and exceptional their child is, I'm going to lose my mind."

Titus smirked. "You don't think Elodie's an exceptional child?"

"I don't *think* she's exceptional. I know she is."

Titus laughed. "Yeah, I think Max is too."

"Okay, point taken. Now tell me how I can help."

He set his elbows on the table. "Max's mother finally agreed to joint custody."

"Oh my God. Titus, that's wonderful. When is he coming?"

Titus rubbed the back of his neck. "I have to go to Vancouver first, and take my girlfriend with me so the judge and Max's mother can meet her. That's how I'll convince Max's mom and the judge that I have an appropriate family setting."

The server came and took our order. When she left, I stared at Titus. "I'm not sure I heard you right."

"You heard me right."

I blinked slowly. "You don't have a girlfriend. And you lied to your family law judge."

"Yep."

"What are you going to do?"

"I'm going to find a 'girlfriend' in the next two weeks. And you're going to help me."

Laughing, I grabbed my water glass and took a sip. "No problem. One girlfriend coming up. Really, what are you going to do?"

Titus stared at me. "You could be my fake girlfriend."

"You're serious, aren't you?"

"Yep."

"You realize how crazy you sound, right?" I set my water glass down.

"Yeah."

"What's Max's mother like?"

Titus sighed. "She's a nice woman, but we've never been together. She's a hookup. A puck bunny."

I gave him the stink eye. "Didn't you tell me you steered clear of them? I guess that's better than Connor's situation."

Titus smirked. "That's a pretty low bar."

"I'm trying to make you feel better, okay?"

"Her name is Trixie. And, yes that's her real name. She's from Vancouver, and she's a hairstylist." He rubbed the back of his neck. "After my injury, I had a few weak moments."

"We all have them. If she's a puck bunny, how do you know Max is your biological son?"

"I didn't, but she was pretty sure. When she found out, she told me she was pregnant but planned to get an abortion because she couldn't afford to raise a child on her own. She was crying and pretty broken up. I asked her if she'd be willing to have him, and promised I'd pay child support whether the child was mine or not."

I stared at Titus. "Wow. I did not see that coming. Did you do a paternity test?"

"Yeah, and he's mine. I've always wanted kids, but I don't think I'd make good husband material."

The server brought our food, and I absently grabbed a few of his fries as he forked the tomatoes off my salad and put them on his plate. I hated tomatoes unless they were in ketchup or marinara sauce.

"Is she good with Max?" I asked after a few minutes.

Titus put his half-eaten burger down and sighed. "Yeah, she is. She's a decent mom, but Max loves me too. I miss him."

"Huh. That sucks." I leaned back. "I might have an idea."

"Thank fuck. Because I don't want to bring some stranger into this."

"Well, that's actually my idea."

He slid his plate away. "How about if you pretend to be my girlfriend for the day, and I owe you a favor?"

"No way. Connor would freak out. And there's that article with pictures of Connor and me."

"Shit, I forgot."

I pulled his plate toward me. "Aren't you going to eat this? You shouldn't waste food." I plucked his burger up and took a bite.

He watched me eat. "You're the most frugal person I've ever met. Do you have any idea how much Connor is worth?"

I shrugged and stuck a fry in the blob of ketchup on his plate, then shoved it in my mouth.

"Who cares? Even people who are loaded shouldn't waste food."

He grinned and watched me eat. "What's your bright idea, *choux*?"

# Chapter 32

Connor met me in the kitchen when I got home that evening. He still had his work clothes on, and he looked good.

"What are you and Titus plotting?"

"Why do you think we're plotting anything?" Those hockey players were the biggest gossips.

"Because two players texted and told me he met you for lunch. And he told me he might be getting joint custody of Max."

I studied Connor. "How would you feel about me pretending to be his live-in girlfriend for a court hearing in a few weeks?"

He stared at me, and I swear his left eyelid started to twitch. "No. Fucking. Way."

"That's what I thought. I told him it'd probably blow up in his face."

"So what's your plan? I can hardly wait to hear what you're cooking up." Sarcasm dripped from his voice as he pulled me into his arms.

I held up my phone. "I'll tell you in an hour. I need to make a phone call first."

He kissed me and let me go. I walked into the back patio area and looked up Abigail's number, hesitated for a few seconds, then called her.

She picked up. "Hi, Isa. How're you doing?"

"Good. How about you and Stella?"

"We're hanging in there. When do you come back for graduation?" Abby sounded subdued and tired.

"In a few weeks."

"I'm so happy for you. And a little envious."

"Don't be. My apartment has a leak, someone keyed my car and slashed my tires, and I'm living with Connor McCoy."

"Sorry, I thought you just said you're living with Connor Mc-Coy."

Sighing, I sat down. "Yeah, that's because I did."

"We need to talk more often. The last time we spoke, he'd accused you of burglary, and you hated him with a burning passion."

"It's complicated. But I'm calling about you. I have a friend who needs a girlfriend."

"Uh, sorry again. I thought you said you have a friend who–"

"I did."

"What does that have to do with me?" She asked carefully.

I told her about Titus and his situation.

She sighed. "I'm not sure how I can help. We live in two different states, with a few states in between."

"Well, you see, he needs a *live-in* girlfriend. You'd, uh, need to come here and stay at his house. He's a good friend, and I trust him."

Abby was silent, so I kept talking. "He has a beautiful house, and you'd have your own bedroom and so would Stella. He'll pay you a monthly wage for living there and helping him with Max when you can."

"I don't know," she said hesitantly.

"And he'd pay for Stella's daycare and preschool so you can work or go back to school if you want."

I hadn't thought of that until just now, but I knew Titus would agree. Abby going along with our scheme was far-fetched, but maybe with enough incentive, we could persuade her.

"Oh God. Isa, be honest with me. What's the catch?"

I sighed. "You'd have to tell a family law judge in Canada that Titus is your boyfriend."

"So I'd have to commit perjury."

"Well, if you and Titus got to know each other a little bit and decided to *become* a couple before the hearing, then *technically* it wouldn't be perjury."

Abby exhaled. "I must be completely bonkers because I'm actually considering it. My parents are unbearable, and they've started to take it out on Stella."

"I'm so sorry. Are you guys okay?"

"No," she murmured. "Isa, I found bruises the size of fingerprints on Stella's arm last week. And she's afraid of them." Abby's voice broke. "My father watched her when I had to work and she was sick and couldn't go to daycare."

My heart lurched, and I sucked in a breath. "Is she okay?"

"Physically, yes. I learned to suck up their digs and my father's temper, but I can't stay here anymore."

"Come and meet Titus at least. He'll fly you and Stella out. The sooner the better. Tell them you and Stella are coming to visit me in Palm Springs. Or don't tell them and just come. Even if things don't work with Titus, you can stay with me."

I didn't know how I would manage since I was living with Connor and my apartment was out of commission. But we'd work it out.

Abby sucked in a breath. "I'm sorry. I never wanted to be a burden on anyone, but I don't want this for Stella. She deserves to be around people who love and cherish her. I don't want her to grow up like I did."

"Come to Palm Springs. We'll help you. I'll get you plane tickets."

"No."

My heart sank. Abby and Stella needed to get away from her parents. "Let me help you."

"I'll drive. I need my car there."

I breathed out slowly. "How about if I fly to Seattle, you pick me up from the airport, and we drive together? You shouldn't drive all that way alone."

She sobbed softly. "Okay. Thank you so much. But I'm paying for your airfare."

"I have more airline points than I know what to do with," I lied. "Now when can you leave?"

After we said goodbye, I stared unseeing out at the garden. My heart hurt. Abby was one of those rare friends. Even if I didn't see or talk to her for a while, when we got together it was like no time had passed. And she'd been there for me when my mom died.

I knew what her parents were like, but I hadn't known the extent of it. I found Connor in his home office working on his laptop. He looked up when I walked in.

"What's wrong? You look upset." He pushed his chair back and patted his thighs.

I didn't hesitate. I sat on his lap and wrapped my arms around him.

"I just got off the phone with my best friend since middle school. She has a little girl, and she lives with her parents. They're horrible."

I told him about my conversation with her, and my plan to have her be Titus's "girlfriend" at the upcoming hearing.

He sighed. "I wasn't wrong when I asked what you two were hatching up. What's your friend like?"

"She's kind and funny, and has this dry sarcasm, despite her parents. I don't know how to describe her. She's quiet until she gets to know you and trusts you. Abby has an old soul."

"Do you think she'll be okay living with Titus?"

"Yeah. But it'll take some time for her to feel comfortable around him."

Elodie walked into Connor's office and saw me sitting on his lap. "Are you best friends again?"

"Yes, we are," Connor answered before I could get a word out. "Come here."

Elodie walked over and crawled on my lap.

I hugged her to me, then sniffed. "You smell like peanut butter. Did you make yourself a sandwich?"

"Yep. A cracker sandwich. I can make you one."

"I'm good. Let's get you ready for bed so we can read."

Before we could jump off his lap, Connor sniffed us. "You two smell like peanut butter and coconut. I don't know who to eat first." He growled and started tickling us.

Elodie squealed and wiggled off. "She's bigger, eat her!"

Connor grinned and nuzzled my neck. "That's a good idea. I think I will."

# Chapter 33

Connor and Titus tried to talk me into taking a private jet to Seattle to pick up Abby and Stella, fly us all back, and pay someone to drive her car to Palm Springs. But I knew Abby wouldn't agree to that. They didn't seem to understand how regular people lived sometimes.

When Abby picked me up at the SeaTac airport early Friday morning, I noticed fresh bruises on her face. And her black eye.

"Did your father do that to you?" I asked through clenched teeth.

Abby looked thin and beaten down. Her chin wobbled. "Please, just get in the car. I can't talk about it right now."

I bit my tongue and hugged her. "Okay. But I'll drive." After a moment, she nodded.

Stella sat in her car seat, studying me with sleepy eyes. The last time I'd seen her, she'd been just over two years old. Stella had gone from a toddler to a little person.

"Hi. I'm Isa." I waved, and she shyly waved back.

There were a few garbage bags of clothes and toys in the trunk and backseat. It looked like Abby planned to stay in Palm Springs for a while. Judging by her bruised face and black eye, the conversation with her parents hadn't gone well.

Looking at her, I sighed. "You and Stella sleep for a few hours, and I'll take the first leg."

Abby nodded, avoiding my gaze. "Okay, thank you. We didn't get much sleep last night. I ended up staying in an airport motel after I told my parents I was coming to see you."

I drove and silently stewed for almost five hours while they slept, and finally stopped when Stella woke up and started shifting in her seat. I pulled into a gas station, and while Abby took Stella to the bathroom, I filled her gas tank. Based on the condition of both her and Stella's coats and shoes, they were destitute.

Her fucking parents. I knew they lived in a decent middle-class house in a Seattle suburb, and they both worked.

We took turns driving. The first night we stayed at a cheap chain motel in Yerka, California just below the Oregon border. The room came to just over sixty dollars, and I saw Abby hold her breath when the hotel clerk swiped her credit card.

"Abby, I can help pay," I told her quietly. "At least let me pay for half."

She raised her chin and shook her head. "No, Isa. I need to do this."

I understood, and I didn't bring it up again. Luckily, I'd brought along a Ziplock bag full of granola bars and dried fruit, and she had a box of Cheez-Its.

We dragged what we needed for the night into the small motel room, and Stella followed behind us with her little backpack. She seemed so quiet after being around Elodie. I worried about her. After freshening up a little, we went outside to walk around and get some fresh air. It was drizzling, but the motel had a small play area.

I turned to Abby when Stella ran over to the little climbing bars. "Tell me what's going on."

Abby sighed. "You know Stella's father never wanted anything to do with her. And my father's temper is explosive, but I don't have anywhere else to go. He's always been scary, but he's gotten worse over the past few months."

"What about your mom?" Her black eye had turned purple. I didn't know how a mother, or grandmother, could just stand by and let that happen.

"She doesn't want to be his punching bag, so she mostly stays quiet. They're both still religious fanatics, and I guess we make easy targets."

She looked at Stella with a sad, tired smile. "I wanted so much more for her. But I live in grinding poverty, and I can't seem to get out from under my parents' thumb."

I put my arm around her and laid my head on her shoulder. She was a little taller than me and she used to be curvier. Not anymore.

"Did your father do that to your face?"

"Yes."

"Did he do anything else?"

She stilled, and I knew my hunch was right. Abby had been favoring her left side.

"My ribs are bruised."

"Is anything broken?"

"No, I don't think so."

Her motherfucking asshole parents. I hated them so much. "You and Titus need each other, so use his free rent and monthly pay to figure out what you want to do. It'll give you some breathing room. How does that sound?"

Stella ran over to us, and Abby reached down to brush her hair out of her face. "It sounds... safe."

My heart broke to think Abby equated moving to another state to live with a man she didn't know as "safe." I wanted her to dream about her future again, and talk and laugh with me like she used to. I put up a silent prayer that she and Stella would be safe, and maybe even a little happy, in their new home.

The motel had a continental breakfast, and the next morning both Abby and I took extra fruit and cold cereal boxes from the buffet to have for lunch.

We took turns driving for another seven hours until we reached our next pit stop. I pulled into a discount grocery store, and we bought a few items for dinner that night. Then we found another cheap chain motel to stay in.

Early Sunday evening on the third day, we finally reached Titus's house. We were strung out, and Stella was fussy and tired of being in her car seat. But she'd been a little trooper. I'd also heard her say a few simple words, but no full sentences.

When we pulled up to Titus's house Abby looked a little green, and I saw her swallow a few times.

I turned to her. "Like I told you, Titus looks a little scary, and he growls a lot. But he's like a coconut——hard on the outside but soft in the middle."

She turned to me. "Coconuts aren't really that soft inside."

I shrugged. "You know what I mean."

Things went downhill from there. When Titus saw Abby's bruised face, he looked like he wanted to kill someone. Abby took an involuntary step back, and Stella started whimpering.

I sighed and smacked Titus's arm. "Quit looking like a serial killer. You're scaring them. Let us in, I've needed to pee since Riverside."

Two hours later, after I'd introduced them and helped Abigail and Stella settle in, Titus ordered an Uber to take me home. They needed to figure things out on their own.

Abby still shot wary glances at Titus, and he still looked like he wanted to kill someone. But Stella inexplicably decided she liked Titus, and when I hugged Abby goodbye and waved at Stella, she was sitting next to Titus at the kitchen bar eating cold pizza and drinking apple juice.

"Bye, Stella Bella. Come see me in a few days, okay?" Stella waved back at me and stuffed more pizza in her mouth. Well, at least one of them seemed to be settling in.

I texted Connor and my dad on the way home, and let them know I was coming. When I walked in, I smelled something delicious.

Elodie met me at the door. "Your birthday cake looks yummy. Can we eat dinner now?"

Connor smiled, kissed me, and handed me a glass of wine. "Welcome home. Happy Birthday yesterday."

I hugged Elodie with my free hand and stole another kiss from Connor. "Thank you. I'm now officially just ten years younger than you."

He smirked and patted my butt. "I'll have to give you your birthday spankings later." He sobered and studied me. "How's she doing? And how did it go with Titus?"

I'd told him about Abby's condition when I'd found a private moment to call him yesterday.

"The drive sucked, Abby looked scared when I left, and Titus was glaring like he wanted to kill someone. So worse than I hoped, but about what I expected."

It was so nice to be home. I watched my dad and Elodie set the table and Connor pull food out of the oven. An overwhelming sense of contentment and gratitude washed through me. This was my tribe; these were the people I loved most. I suddenly felt so lucky and blessed.

On Wednesday afternoon, I slipped into Molly's hospital room. Her mother slept on the reclining chair next to the bed, and Molly looked up from her book, giving me a weak smile.

She was on book twelve in the *Wings of Fire* series. I'd broken down and bought her the last four books when the library couldn't get them in for a few months. I didn't know if Molly had that long to wait.

"Hey, how're you doing?" I whispered. She sat up a little and set her book down.

"I'm still sucking air, and the chemo's done. So not bad. Thanks for the books."

Molly had a disconcerting bluntness to her that I liked, especially for an eight-year-old. She probably knew her chances of reaching adulthood were marginal. Or maybe she would have been like that even if she'd been born healthy.

"You're welcome. I won't stay long so you can get back to your book."

She nodded. "I'm at an exciting part. Do you have anything to eat? Lunch was chicken and broccoli again."

I pulled out a container of orange glazed cookies my dad had given me this morning, grabbed a paper towel from her bathroom, and set a few on her tray.

"Save one for your mom, okay? She looks worn out."

Molly nodded. She was using a blue origami whale I'd given her a couple of months ago as a bookmark. It looked worn out and frayed, so I pulled out a green jumping frog and set it on her book.

"I'll see you in a few days."

"Okay," she said around a mouth full of cookie.

On Thursday afternoon after I got done at the pediatric clinic, Connor, Elodie, and I flew to Vancouver B.C. together. We headed to the private jet terminal at the Palm Springs airport. Connor didn't own an airplane, but he used a private charter jet service whenever he flew. I shuddered when I thought about the cost.

"Why can't we just fly coach?" I asked again. My anxiety ratcheted up as we boarded the jet.

"Because I don't do coach, and first class isn't that much less than a charter flight. Besides, I can get the club to pay for it."

"Uh-huh. You're kind of spoiled. You know that, right?"

"Come on, it'll be fine." He wrapped his arm around me while the co-pilot gathered our luggage and stowed it away.

Elodie didn't seem to care how we got there, she was just excited to see her Mémé. As soon as we took off, the attendant brought us drinks and food as Elodie chattered excitedly.

The flight was just under three hours, and we landed in Vancouver in the evening. The damp, rainy weather seeped into my bones, and I was grateful for my wool sweater and black puffer jacket left over from my time in Seattle.

We took a taxi to Connor's house, and as we drove through the upscale area to his exclusive neighborhood, it reminded me again of the gaping disparities in our lives and income brackets.

Connor's home sat on a bluff in the high-end West Vancouver area. The taxi pulled up to a gated, sprawling Pacific Northwest home. The professional landscaping and outdoor lighting showcased the house well, and I knew the home was worth millions.

I'd gotten used to his large house in Palm Desert, and even secretly thought of it as my own home occasionally. But here was yet another large estate he owned. I pulled my jacket closer as I shivered in the damp, foggy weather.

We grabbed our bags, and Connor punched in the code to the front gate. As we walked up the drive, I paused and looked up at the house again, wondering what I was doing here.

Connor turned. "Come on. Sherrill said she had my housekeeper stock the fridge and get the house ready for us. It should be warm."

When we walked inside, I noticed the gleaming wood floors and expensive, tasteful furnishings. He also had art gallery paintings on his walls.

I cleared my throat. "It's spectacular. You must have missed it over the past few months."

He looked around with a small smile. "Yeah, I did."

We put our luggage away, and Connor gave me a tour. Elodie followed us until we got to her bedroom. The room was painted a soft blush color, and the furnishings were tasteful and white. It looked like Connor had hired a talented interior decorator to furnish and decorate it.

"Hello bed, hello stuffed animals. Hello chair. I missed you." She walked around the room and greeted her things.

That evening, we ordered gourmet pizza and watched a little TV, then called it an early night. Connor did some work in his office, and I was fast asleep when he finally came to bed.

The next morning, Connor let me know that Elodie's aunt, Geneviève, planned to pick her up to go see her Mémé.

"Doesn't Amelia live with her?" I asked.

"Yeah, but Geneviève isn't anything like Amelia. And Elodie adores her."

Connor worked in his home office most of the morning, so I did Elodie's hair. She asked for braids, so that's what I gave her.

The doorbell rang a few minutes later, and Elodie ran to unlock it while I waited behind her. The woman on the doorstep wore stylish cold-weather clothes. She was tall and lean, and gave me a penetrating look.

Then she smiled down at Elodie and opened her arms for a hug. "There's my favorite niece. I missed you, bug."

"Aunt Genny!" Elodie cried. "Where have you been? I missed you too." She wrapped her arms around the woman's waist and squeezed.

I smiled, but my heart clenched a little. Connor and Elodie had a life here, with friends and family who loved Elodie.

The woman patted Elodie's back. "I've missed you too." She glanced at me, and her eyes cooled. Straightening, she looked me up and down.

Connor walked into the foyer. "Hey, Gen. Thanks for taking Elodie to see Mémé."

Geneviève smiled and kissed Connor on the cheek. "It's no problem. I'm happy to spend time with her. How are you doing?"

"We're good. How about you?"

She rolled her eyes. "Oh, you know. Mémé is looking forward to seeing Elodie. Is it alright if I take her to lunch, and maybe over to my house afterward?"

Connor tensed. "Lunch is fine, but bring her home after that."

He hadn't introduced me, and I thought he might want some privacy.

"I'll grab Ellie's coat." I looked at Geneviève and was about to say it was nice to meet her, but I hadn't officially met her, so I just lifted my hand. "I'm Isabella Cruz, by the way." I glanced at Connor, then quickly walked down the hall.

Elodie ran after me and grabbed my hand. "Do you want to go with us?" she asked tentatively.

For the first time since I arrived in Vancouver, I smiled. "Thank you for inviting me. But I think your dad just wants you to spend time with your aunt and see your Mémé. But I'll be here when you get back."

Elodie walked with me to her room to grab her coat. I hugged her and sent her back alone. Heading to the kitchen, I poured myself another cup of coffee, and sat down at the kitchen bar.

Connor walked in a few minutes later, his brows furrowed. "You didn't come back."

Setting my phone down, I studied him. "You didn't introduce me. I got the feeling you wanted some privacy."

He rubbed his neck. "She's a good aunt, but she can be a bitch sometimes. I'll make sure I introduce you from now on."

I nodded jerkily. "It didn't seem like you were happy about having Elodie go home with her."

"If Amelia is at her house, then fuck no. The custody arrangement states supervised visitation with an approved adult present. So far, that's a professional supervisor or me."

"That makes sense."

He studied me. "I have a few things I need to take care of while I'm here. Will you stay here and be home for Elodie if she gets back before me?"

I kept my shoulders relaxed and my face neutral, but I felt out of sorts and anxious here. "Sure. I can work on my clinical writeups."

"You sure you don't mind?"

"No. We have Disney on Ice tickets tonight, so we can hang out together then."

He kissed me, long and slow. "Okay. Tonight I want you naked in my bed."

"That works out well because I want you naked in mine." I leaned in and nipped his jaw.

"Deal."

# Chapter 34

Connor changed into an expensive-looking suit, and he seemed distracted when he left.

Pulling out my laptop, I spent the morning and early afternoon getting my notes caught up on my clinical hours. Geneviève and Elodie arrived back a little after two, and when they walked in, I noticed Elodie seemed subdued and her little hands were clenched.

"Hey, Ellie. Was it nice to see your Mémé?"

"Uh-huh." Elodie didn't smile, and I could see shadows in her eyes.

I squatted down and took her hands. "What's wrong, sweetheart?"

Geneviève shifted awkwardly, and I knew something had happened. Elodie was usually full of questions or news.

But she shook her head. "Nothing. I'm going to my room, okay?"

"Alright." I stood up as Elodie walked out. "What happened?"

Geneviève folded her arms. "I didn't catch your name."

"Isabelle Cruz. Why does Elodie look sad and scared?"

"Where's Connor?"

"He's working this afternoon. What happened to Elodie?"

She shook her head. "I saw the photos of you and Connor, and we heard rumors you're living together."

I nodded. "We are."

"Connor was married until just a few months ago. And now you're living with him."

Her barb hit, but I uncrossed my arms and walked to the front door. I wasn't going to do this with her.

"I'll tell Connor to call you when he gets home." I held it open for her.

She stopped in the doorway and looked down at me. "You're a child, playing in an adult world. Connor is way out of your league, and he has a history you wouldn't understand. I'm telling you this for your own good."

Her words rubbed at my insecurities. But she'd hurt Elodie, and now she was deflecting.

"You let Amelia see her, didn't you?"

Her flinch gave her away. "She's her mother."

"You exposed Elodie to your sister when Connor told you not to. And you went against the court order. Now you're trying to hide your fuckup by attacking me."

She narrowed her eyes. "You don't understand."

"You're her family, for God's sake. You should be watching out for her."

She blanched, and I knew I'd scored a hit as well. "You don't know–"

"Yes, I do. You need to leave so I can go console Elodie and try to undo whatever damage Amelia, and you, did to her."

"I didn't do anything."

"You didn't *protect* her."

She studied me, her eyes going a little glassy. "I just want Elodie to know her mother."

"And we want Elodie to be happy and safe. I think that's more important. Call Connor and talk to him if you have anything else to say."

She stared at me, then slowly walked out the door. I locked it behind her and went to find Elodie. She was curled up on her bed.

"Hey. I take it you saw your mom and it didn't go well."

Elodie turned her head, and I saw tears in her eyes.

"I'm sorry, sweetheart. Grown-ups can be real assholes sometimes." I looked at her worriedly. "Am I going to owe you two, or three bucks for that word?"

Her lips twitched, and she scooted next to me. "I don't have a bet with you."

"Do you want to talk about what happened?"

She shrugged. "I guess."

"You don't have to, but sometimes it helps me to talk about what hurts me." I was bad at it, but it did help sometimes.

"Mom came to the lunch place."

"Huh." I wanted to punch Geneviève.

"She started saying mean things about Dad. And then about you. Then she said mean things about me."

I squeezed her shoulder. "She didn't mean what she said about you. She's mad at me for being with your dad. I think she wants to be with him."

"But Dad doesn't like her," she whispered. "I don't like her either."

She sounded heartbroken, and I didn't know how to make her feel better. So I just held her.

After a while, I talked Elodie into seeing if Connor had the ingredients for cookies. We were rummaging through the cupboards when I heard the front door unlock and open.

"Hey, we're in here," I yelled, thinking it was Connor.

I heard a shrill female voice, and turned to see a woman who looked a lot like Geneviève walk into the kitchen. She was gorgeous and reminded me of a Botticelli painting with her perfect pale complexion and long, flowing hair.

Noah walked in behind her. My stomach dropped and I quickly took my phone out of my back pocket to speed-dial Connor. He didn't pick up so I called Titus next.

"Hello again, you little bitch." Noah leaned against the wall and stared at me, then looked down at my phone. I lowered it to my side, hoping he wouldn't try to take it away, and prayed Titus had picked up.

Glancing at Elodie, I held out my other hand. "Come over here sweetheart. I don't want you near him."

Noah sneered. "You don't want her near *me*? You're the dirty, poor hired help."

"So you think anyone who works for a living is dirty and poor?"

He scoffed. "Where the fuck is Connor?"

"What are you doing in Connor's house? You aren't supposed to be here."

"Who are you to tell me I can't be in my own brother's house?"

I tried to reason with them. "Amelia, you aren't supposed to be here either. You can't have unsupervised contact with Elodie, and you've already violated that order once today."

Her eyes were flat and vacant. It was eerie. "Don't talk to me. You're just one of Connor's sluts he likes to fuck and throw away." She looked around the kitchen.

My temper got the better of me. "You both need to watch your mouths in front of Elodie."

Amelia's eyes snapped to mine and she marched around the counter to face us, her high-heeled boots clicking on the tile. She stared at me for a few seconds, then slapped me hard across the face. Then she hit me again with a closed fist.

My head snapped to the side, and my vision blurred. The attack was so sudden, I just stood there for a second in shock.

Liquid slid out of my left nostril, and Elodie started screaming. I backed away and patted Elodie softly. I didn't look down at her, hoping she couldn't see my bloody nose.

"Shhh, sweetheart. I'm okay." I pulled a dish towel off the stove handle and held it to my face. Blood slid down the back of my throat.

Noah smirked. "So now you're freeloading *and* fucking my rich brother, huh? Are you hoping he'll marry you, and you won't be a poor little whore anymore?"

"Elodie is right here."

Amelia cocked her head and watched me curiously, her eyes skittering between Elodie and me. She scared me the most, and that was saying something.

"Where is Connor?" Noah demanded again.

"On his way home," I lied.

"Don't bullshit us. Did he dump you off to babysit so he could go fuck one of his puck bunnies?"

"You both need to leave. Elodie shouldn't have to listen to this."

Noah glanced down at Elodie, who stood shaking beside me. I instantly regretted bringing her up again.

Shifting in front of her, I tried to draw his attention away. "Aren't you already on probation? I thought you were supposed to stay away from Connor. And his houses and workplace." My hands were shaking and my face hurt, but the bleeding seemed to have slowed down.

Noah looked around the kitchen. "I just need to talk to Connor to explain what happened. Maybe tell him I'm sorry. He'll forgive me. He always does because I'm his only family." He didn't sound contrite or sorry.

Elodie whimpered and wrapped her arm around my waist. I hugged her to me and turned away from them.

"Don't hide my daughter from me!" Amelia screeched. "You made her not love me. You told her to not love me." Amelia breathed heavily, her eyes darting around.

Noah turned to her and clenched his fists. "Shut the fuck up. You're always screeching. It hurts my fucking ears."

She turned her anger on him. "You're a stupid, crackhead asshole. Don't tell me to shut up, you whine all the time."

"You fucking crazy bitch. I've had to put up with your ranting and screaming for months. Just shut your fucking mouth!"

I set the bloody dishtowel on the counter, then carefully stepped back with Elodie glued to my side. Neither of them glanced our way. They sounded like a crazy toxic married couple, standing nose to nose, screaming at each other.

"Come on, sweetheart. Let's go."

I doubted Elodie could hear me over their screaming, but I tugged her hand and we quickly backed out of the kitchen together. Then I steered us to the front door, and when we ran outside I put the phone to my ear.

"Titus? Are you there?"

"You guys okay? Where the fuck are you?"

"We're at Connor's house. He's not here, and Noah and Amelia walked in together a few minutes ago." We ran toward the front gate. "One of them has his house codes."

"Holy fuck. How did those two get together? I texted Connor to let him know what I heard. One of us needs to call the police."

Looking down at my feet, I realized I didn't have shoes on. Luckily, Elodie was still wearing hers.

"We snuck outside when they started screaming at each other. I don't have shoes on, or my purse. I don't know where to go." I had to fight down the panic rising in my throat.

"*Putain de bordel de merde,*" Titus muttered. "Do you have the Uber or Lyft app on your phone? I'm texting you the address to my apartment in downtown Vancouver. You can go there until we track Connor down."

"Yes." I thought about calling the police, but I didn't know if nine-one-one even worked in Canada. I choked down a sob and tried to stay calm.

Titus let out a relieved sigh. "Okay. Get away from the house before those two come after you. Go to my apartment, and I'll let the doorman know you're coming."

"I'm so glad you answered." My voice broke a little so I cleared my throat. "Thank you. How are Stella and Abby doing?"

Elodie and I made it to the property gate.

He grunted. "They're safe. We'll talk when you get back. Now go. I'll call the police, but text me when you're clear."

# Chapter 35

My face throbbed and my heart pounded. I was afraid I'd lose the internet, so we paused at the gate and pulled up the Uber app, then plugged in Titus's condo address. It looked like the closest ride was six minutes away. Elodie and I were going through the gate when Amelia yanked open the front door.

"Where do you think you're going with *my daughter*?" she screamed. "You're trying to be her mother. You're trying to take her away from me." She stalked toward us.

It was cold outside, and my toes were going numb. I hustled Elodie out the gate and we started running up the road. I didn't see Noah anywhere, and I wondered if he was inside the house looking for things to steal.

I stepped on something sharp and felt a sting on the pad of my foot. I grunted but kept moving.

Elodie looked up at me with wide, panicked eyes. "Where are we going?"

"Someone's going to pick us up and take us to Titus's apartment. I couldn't get ahold of your dad, and I don't have a car or my purse." Or shoes, I thought.

"I'm scared," she whimpered.

"Me too," I admitted. "But if we can get away, we'll be okay."

My feet felt scraped and raw, and my toes started to tingle. Amelia ran after us, screaming and swearing. Luckily, her boots weren't made for running, and we had a head start. But she was gaining on us.

When I saw the black sedan matching the Uber app driving toward us, I waved frantically. The man pulled over, and I opened the back passenger door and hustled Elodie into the back seat.

"Are you Ahmed?" I asked as I got in beside Elodie and slammed the door.

He looked at my face and his eyes went wide. "Yes. Are you Isabella?"

"Yeah. Please drive. A crazy woman is chasing us."

To Ahmed's credit, he nodded and put the car in drive. As we passed Amelia, she lunged at the car and screamed at us. I leaned over and buckled Elodie up, then buckled myself in. Elodie panted next to me, and I put my arm around her.

"We're okay, sweetheart. I'll keep you safe."

She started crying softly.

I looked at Ahmed, who glanced back at me and silently pointed to my nose. Then he rummaged around and pulled out a packet of wet wipes.

"You've got blood on your face, ma'am. Are you and the child alright?"

Taking the packet, I pulled a few out and dabbed at my nose. "We'll be fine now. You've already helped more than you know by being early."

I tried to hand the wet wipes back to him, but he glanced down at my feet. "I think your foot is also bleeding."

Sighing, I pulled a few more wet wipes out and tried to clean the cut on my foot. I texted Titus to let him know we were clear. Just then my phone rang, and I saw Connor's name on my screen.

I answered and immediately started talking. "Elodie is safe. A little shaken up and traumatized, but fine."

She put her hand on my thigh. "Is that Daddy?"

I nodded. "She wants to talk to you. If I were you, I'd send police to your house as soon as you can. Noah and Amelia walked in together not long after Geneviève dropped Elodie off."

He let out a long low string of expletives. "I already called the police, and I'm on my way. Thank you for keeping her safe."

My throat threatened to close, but I held it together. "Here's Elodie."

I sat back, half listening to her murmurs and Connor's voice over the phone. My cheek and nose throbbed, and my feet tingled and stung as they slowly thawed out. Elodie nudged me and handed my phone back, then laid her head on my arm.

"Hey."

"Elodie said something about Titus."

"When you didn't answer, I called Titus. We're in an Uber headed to his apartment right now."

"No. Give me a few minutes, then meet me back at the house. I need to see Elodie–"

"No way." I cut him off. "We are not going back there. You don't know what happened, you weren't there. When you get done with whatever it is you need to do, we'll be at Titus's apartment."

"Isabella–"

I was scared, drained, and suddenly I'd had enough. Hanging up on him, I turned my phone to mute and shoved it in my back pocket. I felt it vibrate a few times, but I ignored it.

Ahmed double-parked and walked us into Titus's sleek, modern condo building, making sure the doorman was there to take care of us.

I turned to Ahmed and gave him a little bow, putting my hand to my chest. "Thank you for your kindness. And the wet wipes."

He smiled and bowed back. "It was my pleasure to assist you. Be safe."

He left us with the stocky, middle-aged doorman named Keith.

"Titus told me to expect you, Ms. Cruz." Keith looked down at my feet. "He also said you'd have Ms. Elodie, and you wouldn't have shoes on." Then he studied my face and shook his head. "He didn't say anything about you looking like you've been in a WWE match."

I smiled faintly, then winced. My face felt bruised and sore, and I worried I might end up with a black eye.

"I wish I could say 'you should see the other guy', but I just needed to get her out of there."

He looked down at Elodie and nodded. We took the elevator up to the top level, and walked out into a penthouse suite. Keith gave us the codes and told us he'd tell Titus we'd made it to the condo.

"Let me know if you need anything," he said as he walked toward the elevator.

"Elodie's dad, Connor McCoy, may be coming later. Can you let him in if he does?" I asked.

He smiled. "Yes, I know who he is. You two have a good night."

Elodie and I used the bathroom and got cleaned up the best we could. I grabbed a dishtowel and put some ice in it, then laid it on my face.

Titus's condo was modern and well-appointed, but it had a stale, unused feel to it. I grabbed one of his t-shirts to change into since my shirt had blood all over it, and we raided his pantry. I heated up a can of tomato soup and microwaved two frozen burritos.

I called Titus back while we ate, and gave him a brief explanation of what happened.

"You left out the part where Amelia hit you," he growled. "I heard Elodie screaming her head off. Where the fuck is Connor?"

Rubbing my eyes, I slumped on his couch. Elodie had fallen asleep a few minutes ago, and I'd taken off her shoes and covered her with a throw blanket.

"He left the house late this morning. We were supposed to go out tonight."

"What a goddamn shitshow," he muttered.

"Elodie's aunt took her to see her great-grandma and then have lunch together, and when she brought Elodie back, I found out Amelia had met them at lunch. It didn't go well."

"It never does."

"Then Noah and Amelia walked right in the front door. I thought it was Connor." I let out a shaky breath.

"How are you doing? And don't lie this time."

I walked into the kitchen and poured myself some water. Then I sat down at the kitchen bar.

"I hate it here," I admitted. "Not your condo. It's very nice, and thank you for letting us stay. But I've felt anxious and out of place since we got here. Vancouver is beautiful, and Connor's house is stunning. But..."

"His house is pretty spectacular. I thought he was fucking nuts when he bought it. But it's almost doubled in value since then."

I sighed. "It took me months to get used to his house in Palm Desert. Only to find out he has an even bigger one here. And he seems so distracted and distant here. I felt anxious even before Noah and Amelia walked into the house."

"What do you mean?"

I rested my head on my hand and struggled to explain. "I'm not sure we're meant to be together. I don't fit in, and I don't belong in expensive houses in gated properties. Maybe I don't belong with him."

"The fuck you don't," I heard Connor growl from the kitchen doorway.

I yelped and bobbled my phone. "Holy shit! Don't sneak up on me like that."

"Who are you talking to? And where did the blood come from in the hallway?"

Damn it, I'd forgotten to mop up the blood from my injured foot.

Glaring at Connor, I put the phone back to my ear. "Titus? Connor just walked in and scared the hell out of me. I've got to go."

Titus chuckled. "Tell him I said he's welcome and he owes me one. Good luck."

Connor studied me as I disconnected.

His gaze sharpened when he noticed my swollen, battered cheek. "What happened to your face?"

At least I'd been able to clean up my bloody nose. I didn't answer right away. "What happened at your house? Were they still inside when you got there?"

He walked over to me. "I came here first. The police and Sherrill are there, and she'll call me back when she knows anything." Carefully, he held my chin and turned my face toward the light. "Now tell me what happened to your face."

"Amelia hit me." Thinking about it made my hands shake all over again. "Geneviève and Elodie's lunch didn't go well. Amelia showed up. Then about an hour after Elodie got home, Noah and Amelia came to the house and walked right in. They had your codes."

He froze and stared at me, then he pulled his phone out to call his assistant. "Sherrill, where are you at? Are the police still at the house?" He paused. "Did they arrest Amelia too? Tell them Amelia assaulted Isabella, and I want her charged." He paused. "Someone needs to interview my girlfriend and daughter. We can go to the police station tomorrow."

I could hear Sherrill's voice on the phone, but I couldn't hear what she said.

Connor nodded and started pacing. "Okay. Give them my number, and make sure they know about the restraining orders on both of them. Also, find out how they got my fucking house codes. And get the codes changed *today*."

He hung up and stared down at his phone, then looked at me and his eyes softened. "I'm sorry, honey. I brought you here, then left you vulnerable."

My lips trembled, but I glared at him. "You were mad because Titus helped us. You can take your apology and shove it."

"I'm sorry. And for once, I'm grateful you and Titus are friends. Now tell me where the blood in the entryway came from."

"Don't worry, it's not Elodie's. When we made it out of the house, I didn't have shoes on. I stepped on a piece of glass or a rock when we were running. Luckily, Elodie was wearing hers." I pulled up my injured foot and showed him.

Connor scowled at the laceration. "You didn't have shoes on? It's ten fucking degrees out there."

It took me a minute to realize he was referring to Celsius, not Fahrenheit.

"Where did you go?" I asked quietly.

"To talk with my attorneys about Amelia. I want her charged for some of the things she's done over the last five years." He absently rubbed the scar on his cheek. "I also met with a realtor about selling my house here."

My eyes snapped up. "You're going to sell your house?"

"Yes. Because you live in California, and I can't see you wanting to move here."

He turned my barstool a little to face him.

I sighed and leaned my forehead against his chest for a moment. "Don't sell your house here because of me. You love it, and Mémé is here."

Before he could reply, Elodie walked into the kitchen rubbing her eyes. "Where were you?" She leaned her head against his hip. "It was scary. Mommy hit Belly in the face and made blood go all over."

Connor looked at me. "You didn't tell me about the blood."

I winced. "We just talked about it."

"That was from your foot."

"Your foot got hurt too?" Elodie asked.

"Yeah, but it's fine now. And you were so brave."

Her chin wobbled. "I didn't feel brave."

"Neither did I." I slid off the stool and hugged her. "But we didn't panic and we got away in one piece. I think that counts for something."

Connor wrapped his arms around both of us and let out a breath. "I agree."

# Chapter 36

We stayed at Titus's apartment that night. Connor left for a couple of hours to check on his house, and talk to his assistant. When he came back, he brought takeout Chinese food and our suitcases.

I looked around. "Do you think Titus will care if we eat in his living room? I don't want to get anything on his couch."

Connor pulled out cartons and put them on the coffee table. "I'll fucking buy him a new one if he does."

"Five bucks," Elodie chirped.

I shook my head. "You need to curb your prolific use of the f-bomb around her."

Connor shrugged and kicked off his shoes. I ran into the bathroom and grabbed a couple of towels to put over the couch, and we ate in front of the TV.

Elodie snuggled between us that night. I was afraid she would have nightmares, but she slept soundly through the night. My mind wouldn't quiet, however, and the day's events kept playing through my mind.

The next morning, we went back to Connor's house after he promised the codes had been changed. Police Officer Teasdale stopped by around eleven to take our statements, saving us a trip to the station. He was probably in his mid-thirties, and had an intense gaze. He wore a typical police uniform, except the insignia on his shoulder had a red seal and crown, and a Canadian flag underneath.

"So you did not invite them in or open the door?" he asked me for the third time.

"No. And I know I locked it after Elodie's aunt left. I've been a little anxious since I got here."

Connor searched my face.

Officer Teasdale turned to Elodie. "Did you see your mom hit Isabella?"

She nodded, and her lower lip trembled. "Belly didn't even say anything mean or bad, and Mommy screamed and hit her twice. Really hard. And you know what?"

The corner of Officer Teasdale's mouth twitched. "What?"

"Her nose bled. And she sneaked me outside, but she didn't have shoes on. Then we ran from my mom, and we went to Titus's house."

His eyes went wide. "Titus Tremblay? The Spartan? One of the greatest centers of all time?"

Elodie nodded. "We just call him Titus though."

He glanced at Connor. "Any chance Tremblay is coming back to play in Vancouver again? We could sure use him. It was a tragedy when you retired. And then we lost Tremblay." The officer shook his head glumly.

"You'd have to ask him that," Connor clipped out. "Now back to my girls."

"Right." Officer Teasdale straightened and turned back to Elodie. "Is there anything else you want to tell me?"

"Yeah. Can you tell Noah and my mom to leave us alone? They're mean and they might scare Belly away. We need her."

I swallowed thickly.

Officer Teasdale glanced at me and smiled a little. "I'll certainly try. And I understand why you'd want to keep her."

Later that night, Connor curled around Elodie as she slept between us again, with his arm draped across both of us.

"I talked to the police officer who interviewed Noah this afternoon," he said softly. "He said Noah told him they rang the doorbell and you let them in."

I sighed. "Did they believe him?"

"No, because Amelia told another officer she's my wife and had every right to be there. She also said Noah bribed my cleaner for the codes, and that's how they got in."

"If you don't sell your house, you need to get security cameras installed here."

He nodded. "I do. I have an alarm, but no cameras."

I cupped his cheek and admitted the truth. "I want to go home. Vancouver is beautiful, but I don't think it's safe for us right now, and I don't belong here."

He squeezed my hand to his cheek. "I love Vancouver, and I'm going to bring you back someday so I can really show it to you. But we'll fly out tomorrow. And you belong wherever we are."

The next morning, we went to see Elodie's great-grandmother before flying back to Palm Springs. The senior apartment community where Mémé lived seemed sunny and cheerful. There were several elderly people in wheelchairs and walkers in the main atrium when we walked in, and a few assistants in bright scrubs mingled among the residents.

We found Mémé in her suite, sitting up in a recliner.

Elodie ran over to the woman and patted her hand when we walked in. "I brought Belly to see you, like I promised."

Mémé looked frail, but I could tell she'd been statuesque and striking in her prime.

She gazed at me, then turned back to Elodie. "Good morning, sweetheart. Thank you for bringing her here to see me."

"You're welcome. And you know what? Mommy hit Belly in the face and made her bleed. And we had to go outside and run, and she didn't have any shoes on. But we got away. And guess what?"

Mémé frowned and her forehead crinkled. She glanced back at me, looking closely at the bruises on my face.

"What, sweetheart?"

"I can read good now. And Javy makes cookies with me and has a one-eyed cat. And I want Daddy to marry Belly so we can keep her."

I choked and shifted around nervously, looking up at the ceiling.

Mémé cleared her throat, sounding like she was stifling a laugh. "Well. It sounds like you've been a busy bee in California. What's this about a one-eyed cat?"

For the first half of the flight back home, Elodie sat between us and chattered away. When she eventually fell asleep, Connor took off her shoes and laid her chair back. I covered her with a lap blanket while he spoke quietly to the attendant who disappeared into the cockpit.

Then Connor took my hand and led me to a small, private sleeping area in the back. He slid the door closed and pulled me to him.

Leaning in, he nuzzled my cheek and softly bit my neck. "It's been days, and I need to be inside your sweet little pussy like I need my next breath."

My breath whooshed out, and I shivered. Shifting closer to him, I wrapped my arms around his waist. He cupped my face and kissed me, licking my lips, then thrusting his tongue inside.

His mouth felt so good, and his hot, hard body made the cold inside me dissipate a little. I'd felt chilled for days, and I wanted to crawl inside him and bask in his warmth. Sliding my leg up, I wrapped it around his hip, then wound my arms around his neck.

He growled in his throat, and shifted me to the small berth. The backs of my knees hit the edge, and he laid me down, then broke the kiss. His eyes were hot as he stared at me. Pulling off my shoes, he reached up and stripped off my jeans and panties. I matched his impatience, and I unbuckled his belt then untucked his shirt.

Leaning over me, Connor pulled off my sweater and un-clipped my bra. "I fucking love unwrapping your beautiful, round breasts."

Sweeping his thumbs across my nipples, he grinned when my hips involuntarily bucked. Stepping back, he yanked the belt out of his belt loops, then undid his jeans. "Are you going to be my good girl and keep quiet, or do I need to gag you?"

I smirked. "You can try–"

He grabbed my ankle and pulled me to him. "A gag it is."

Connor laid his belt on the bed next to me and pulled my hands down. Then he wrapped my wrists tight and pulled the end through the buckle, giving him a nice lead. Leaning over me, he took a pillow off the small bed and pulled the pillowcase off. Then he rolled it up.

My eyes went wide. "I can be quiet!"

"Too late." He grinned and quickly wrapped it around my jaw, tying the ends across my mouth. Then he patted my uninjured cheek. "And this way you can scream all you want while I hammer into your tight little pussy."

My eyes narrowed, and I called him a cock sucking whoreson. It came out garbled and muffled.

He laughed softly, then reached down and palmed my wet core. "This doesn't lie. You're hot and soaking for me."

Bending down, he spread my legs wide and licked up my slit. I let out a low moan, and his hands squeezed my thighs.

"That's it. Let me taste you."

He lapped at my clit, and plucked my swollen nipples. I closed my eyes and saw white bursts of light flash behind my eyelids. The sound of him sucking and licking my slit, and the mingled smell of our arousal assaulted my senses. I instinctively rocked against his mouth.

Sliding two fingers inside me, he pumped his hand. My back arched and my legs locked. I wailed softly behind the pillowcase as my orgasm built. Connor bit the inside of my thigh, and I jerked at the nip. Then he bent over again and sucked my clit deep into his mouth, working it with his tongue.

He knew exactly how to make me beg. I whimpered when I felt the oncoming climax, and he relentlessly and rhythmically lapped at me. A red film ripped across my mind as my orgasm rose. My insides clenched and I cried out behind my gag and came all over his mouth. He slammed two fingers inside me, and I contracted around him.

When my breathing slowed, he pulled back and wiped his mouth across my stomach, leaving a trail of my juices. He grinned down at me, then flipped me over on my stomach and pulled my hips up to meet his thick, hard length.

Spreading my legs as far as he could, he strained my thigh muscles. "Your cunt and ass are a fucking work of art. I want to mark you up, make you come, and ruin you for anyone but me."

He smacked my right cheek, then slid his finger across my openings. I whined and tried to shift, but his hands clamped down on my hips. My body was completely open and vulnerable to him, and he could see how wet he made me.

My hands were still tied together with his belt, and he reached underneath and pulled the belt end between my knees. My upper body collapsed down on the bed, and I turned my face to the side so I could breathe. He tucked my bound wrists between his knees, then slid his hands up my thighs and groaned.

"You're *mine*, sweet girl."

I growled and pushed my ass back against his groin. He had me immobilized and gagged, but I could still communicate my displeasure.

He laughed, then he ran his cock between my folds. My moisture coated his shaft. Positioning his tip at my opening, he relentlessly pushed himself inside, then started thrusting into me until he was fully seated and pushing against the end of my channel. I whined with lust and discomfort.

He breathed heavily in my ear as he leaned over and squeezed my breasts, which were smashed against the bed. When he pinched my nipples, I gasped and started rocking back against him. He leaned up and slowed down, then pulled halfway out several times to prolong his pleasure.

I struggled to get enough breath through my nose and tried to process all the stimulation. Connor's heavy thighs held my legs firmly open, and I smelled his musky scent.

Connor pushed his finger against my anal opening, then firmly pressed inside. My body locked up, and I started panting behind the gag. I was confused and frustrated by all the stimulation and my inability to move, but so turned on I bit down on the gag and screamed. An orgasm hit me, and I convulsed around his cock.

My climax triggered his, and he lifted my hips off the bed, holding me up as he furiously pistoned inside me. Then he slammed his cock inside, and came long and hard, sending hot spurts of semen deep inside me. When he finally stopped coming, he slowly lowered my hips, and my knees hit the bed again.

I collapsed onto my side, and he crawled next to me and cradled my body against him for a few seconds. Then he pulled off the gag and unwrapped his belt.

Shifting my jaw around, I opened and closed my mouth a few times. Connor reached around and ran his hands up and down my wrists, massaging the marks his belt had left.

"You good?" he asked softly.

"No." I grabbed his hand and squeezed. "I've temporarily died and gone to orgasm heaven. It's going to take me a minute to come back." My voice sounded hoarse.

He chuckled and wrapped his arms around me. "Welcome to the mile-high club. We're a mess. I wish this plane had a shower so we could clean up."

"You're the one who made me that way. And the plane has a freaking bed, don't be greedy."

We cleaned up with the damp, wrinkled pillowcase and then used the bathroom. Connor checked on Elodie, who was still sound asleep.

He came back and laid down next to me. "This trip didn't turn out like I'd hoped. Except the last part."

He studied my cheek and his eyes got hard. "Tomorrow I have a meeting with Zeke. We're also talking with an investigation agency from Vancouver. I'm ending this."

I wrapped my arms around him. "Amelia and Noah seem to hate me." I hesitated. "Maybe I'm putting Elodie in danger by staying with you."

He stilled, then hugged me back. "You're not, so get that fucking thought out of your head. You got her out of the house and protected her."

But the thought lingered.

# Chapter 37

When we landed and I took my phone off airplane mode, I noticed a text from my landlord letting me know my apartment had been repaired and renovated. I didn't know what "renovated" meant to him, but I suspected someone in the HOA had gone into my apartment to see the leaks, and figured out my landlord was a big, fat slumlord. I'd never admit that to Connor, though.

There was also a text from Abby.

*Abby: What happened in Vancouver? Titus said Connor's ex-wife assaulted you?! Call me!*

*Me: I'm fine, and it wasn't that bad. How are things with Titus? Let's meet for dinner tomorrow.*

*Abby: Sounds good. Things are fine. And you're lying.*

I smirked. She was probably also lying, but we'd talk tomorrow.

When we got back to Connor's house, I walked over to see my dad.

He took one look at my cheek and started turning red. "What happened to your face?" His voice sounded strangled.

I held up a hand. "Elodie's mom hit me. She and Noah came to Connor's house when he wasn't there, but I got Elodie away."

He stared at me for a few seconds, then roughly pulled me in for a hug. "I'm sorry. This is my fault. I never would have encouraged Connor if I'd known he'd been married, and his ex-wife would do something like that to you."

Shaking my head, I stepped back. "I blame him for not being honest with me, but this is all Amelia." I pointed to my face. "And better me than Elodie."

He still looked upset, so I stuck around and we spent some time together. He poured me a glass of homemade lemonade and put a few snickerdoodle cookies on a plate, then we walked out to his little back patio.

"What're you going to do when you finish school?" he asked.

I picked up a cookie. "Connor wants me to stay here and move in with him 'officially.' But I'm not sure."

"What about work?"

"I have a solid job offer in Seattle, and the pediatric clinic here also talked to me about staying on."

Dad bit into a cookie. "And the sports medicine clinic?"

"Ben talked to me too."

"What about Connor and Elodie?"

I put the cookie back on the plate and took a long sip of lemonade. "I don't know."

"Talk to me."

I sighed. "I'm scared, okay? And I'll deny it if you tell Connor. Because you have a big mouth when it comes to him."

"I only told him things when I thought it was for your own good."

"Yeah, well stop it."

"What are you scared of?" he asked.

"Of hurting Elodie. Or Connor deciding he could do better or needs more variety in a year or two. Of Amelia harming them because I'm in Connor's life." I glanced at him, and admitted my biggest fear. "I don't want to start loving them, and then have it all ripped away."

"You already do love them. And life is pain. Anyone who tells you differently is selling something."

I stared at him. "Did you just quote *Princess Bride* to me?"

He smiled a little. "Maybe. It's still one of my favorite books. Do you think Elodie's too young to enjoy it?"

"I'm glad you're taking this seriously."

"Oh, I am. I want you to be happy. And I also want grandkids, but the way you and Liam are going makes me think that's never going to happen." He leaned back and studied me. "Since your mom died, you've closed yourself off to avoid getting hurt. Maybe I have too."

I didn't deny it. "I miss her. Even now, I'll see something and want to share it with her. And then I remember she's gone."

"Me too. But I wouldn't trade the time I had with her for anything in the world. Whatever you decide, don't let your fear of pain stop you from living."

I left his house with a container of snickerdoodles and a lot to think about.

The next morning before I went into the clinic, I told Connor my apartment was habitable again.

He carefully set his coffee mug down. "Do you want me to go with you to pick up the rest of your things?"

"No. I'm moving back there while I finish up my clinical hours. Thank you for letting me stay here, even though I wasn't very grateful at first."

He started shaking his head, but I plowed on. "I'll still come over, but me moving in with you was just temporary until my apartment got fixed. We both knew that. I'm not trying to break up—"

"No."

"No, I don't have two weeks left? Or no, you do want to break things off?"

"You're not moving back there. And *fuck no*, we aren't breaking up. You already moved out once." He lifted his eyebrow, daring me to argue.

Instead, I walked over and cupped his cheeks. "I need to do this. And you know why I moved out before. Now that Noah is in jail and my apartment is habitable again, it's time."

"Bella, you don't."

Sighing, I dropped my hands and told him the other reason. "Coach Bailey contacted the University and made a formal complaint against me because I'm seeing you. Me living here doesn't help things."

Connor's eyes narrowed into slits. "You are fucking *kidding* me. How is this any of that asshole's business?"

"He said there's a no fraternization policy. I got an email from my academic counselor this morning." I shook my head. "Don't worry. I'm going to ask Ben to email them and let them know the sports medicine clinic doesn't have any issues with me."

He gritted his teeth and looked up at the ceiling. "I'm fighting the urge to go beat the shit out of Bailey, then come back and throw you over my shoulder, take you back to *our* bed, and fuck you senseless."

I crossed my arms. "Three things–I'm moving back to my apartment, you can't beat up Coach Bailey, and I'm up for being fucked senseless. But right now you have an appointment with Zeke, and I need to go to the arena."

"Meet me for dinner tonight then," he sighed. "If you're moving out, I want to see you every day. We're also doing dates, and sleeping in the same bed as often as I can manage it."

I stared at him. He was an excellent negotiator, and my panties were getting wetter by the second. "We don't have to rush this. I want to make sure it's right, and what we both want."

He curled his hand around my neck. "Say yes."

"Yes. We'll date, and I'll come over. But I'm meeting Abigail for dinner tonight. I need to check on her."

"Okay, tomorrow night then. And Bella?"

"What?"

He leaned in and whispered in my ear, "Game on, little girl."

When I got to the arena in the morning, I went looking for Titus. "So? How'd it go with Abby?"

He scowled and pulled on his workout jersey. "Fine."

I waited for him to say something else. He didn't. "Fine? Really? That's it?"

"It's fucking fine except I want to kill her fucking dad, and Stella is fucking adorable. But she should be talking at her age."

Based on his scowl, and him using "fucking" three times in one sentence, things were not fine.

"When's your hearing? Are you guys ready?"

"Soon. And we're getting there."

"Abby lied to me. And now *you're* lying to me."

He stood up and put his hands on his hips. "Speaking of lying, tell me what really happened at Connor's house in Vancouver."

"Why is it when it comes to *my* life, you have no problem talking? But when we start talking about yours, you suddenly clam up?"

Coach Bailey walked in and spotted me. "Ms. Cruz, haven't you caused enough distractions? Leave my players alone and stay out of my locker room."

The low murmur of players talking and getting ready for practice stopped; the locker room went silent.

Titus turned his bad temper on Coach Bailey. "She was asking me about my back," he lied. "That's her fucking job. And why don't you leave her the fuck alone? She's done more for this team's morale than you."

Ooh, damn. This was not good. I didn't want Titus to get kicked off the team, and I didn't want to get fired or banned right before I finished my hours.

"Titus, it's okay." I tried to pull him back.

Coach Bailey's eyes went wide. "What did you say to me, Tremblay?"

"You heard me the first time. You've been nothing but a sexist asshole to her since she started, and you play fucking head games with the players."

Jackson walked over and gently grabbed my arm, pulling me away. "Come on."

I resisted, but he pulled again. "This has been a long time coming, and it's not just about you. But I think it'd be better if you're not here." He pulled me out of the locker room as a few other players walked over and stood behind Titus. Even Wyatt. What the heck was going on?

Outside the locker room, I turned to Jackson. "I'm fine, but Connor will want to know what happened. Go back in."

He squeezed my arm and stepped back inside. I wanted to be a fly on the wall, but Jackson was right. Something had been brewing with the team and Coach Bailey all season, and they needed to hash it out.

I just hoped I didn't get blamed for lighting the match.

# Chapter 38

Early that afternoon, I went back to Connor's house and grabbed some of my things. No one was home, and I wondered if Connor might be dealing with the "Coach Bailey" situation.

Before leaving the house, I put a little purple origami flower on Elodie's nightstand and an orange fox on Connor's desk. I also left a note in the kitchen and told them I needed to see about my apartment, but I'd be over tomorrow. I didn't want Elodie to think I was abandoning her.

Abby and Stella came over to my place that evening, and Abby looked around curiously. "This isn't as bad as I've been led to believe. Titus said you live in a hovel."

A *hovel*? Titus and I were going to have words. "It's a lot better than it was. They fixed the leak in the ceiling and repainted it. There's new flooring too."

Stella wandered around, checking out the small space. Abby studied me. "Your face looks like someone smacked the crap out of you, and your concealer doesn't quite cover the bruising around your eye."

I grimaced. "It was a rough weekend. I'm happy to see your bruises are almost gone."

"We're quite the pair, aren't we?" She followed me into the kitchen. "I thought you were living with Connor. What happened?"

"It was temporary while my apartment was out of commission, and Noah was causing trouble. We're still together, but I want to make sure we're not going too fast."

We caught up as we ate dinner.

"How's it going with Titus?" I asked.

She shrugged, nibbling on her chicken wrap. "Fine. He scared me a little at first, and I think I offended him."

"Tell him to get over himself. And you have a right to be wary of men. So far all the men in your life have been complete assholes."

"I'm not like you. He intimidates me, and I'm living in his house. He could kick me out at any time."

"He'd never kick you out. And trust me, he needs you as much as you need him. Are you ready for the hearing?"

She winced. "We're working on it."

"You two are such liars. Abs, if the judge asks you basic questions about him and you can't answer, you're both screwed. I'm going to send each of you a set of 'getting to know you' questions, and you two need to sit down and answer them together. And *talk* to each other. Can you do that?"

"Yes, Mother."

I smacked her arm. "That's pretty damned rude. Your mother can be a raging psychotic bitch."

Her lip twitched. "You're right. Sorry."

My stomach unclenched a little. Her parents had tried to break her, but they hadn't succeeded. Now I just needed Titus to pull his head out of his ass.

Over the next week, I went to Connor's house most nights for our usual family dinners, and we went to Martini Monday at Ramone and Jonathan's house. That Wednesday night, the team met at The Cockpit. They'd agreed to hold a special karaoke night just for our Whiskey Wednesdays team-building party.

Martina worked at The Cockpit now one night a week DJing the karaoke, and somehow she'd talked me into thinking karaoke night with the team was a brilliant idea. I was having serious second thoughts.

Jackson, Wyatt, and a few other teammates were the first to arrive. They looked around and grinned.

Jackson shook his head at me. "You've come up with some pretty creative team activity nights, but this one is crazy. Wyatt didn't believe us when we told him he missed out on Zoo Lights."

Wyatt smirked. "It may be karaoke night, but a bar is still way better than the fucking zoo. At least there'll be drunk women here."

I sighed. "Wyatt, are you always this offensive, or are you making a special effort just for us?"

Rudy walked up with a beer in one hand and a shot of whiskey in the other. "I'm working on my liquid courage so I'll be ready when my song comes up."

"You're going to fucking sing?" Wyatt laughed.

Rudy blinked at him. "Yeah, because I'm not a chickenshit. That probably means you won't be getting up there."

I stared at Rudy, open-mouthed. He didn't flinch when Wyatt tightened his fists and glared at him.

"Did you really just call me chickenshit?"

Rudy nodded. "Absolutely. And I don't think you have the balls to get up there."

Wyatt rolled his shoulders. "I'd wipe the fucking floor with you."

Rudy set down his beer and threw the shot of whiskey back. "Let's make a bet, Wyatt. Whoever gives the best performance tonight wins. I'll bet a hundred bucks."

Martina held up her hand. "I want in on this. I may be the DJ, but I also sing occasionally." She cocked her eyebrow. "Unless you guys are afraid of a little competition."

Wyatt smirked. "The more the merrier."

Rudy slowly grinned. "You're on. Let's round up the boys and spread the word. Isa will keep track. The only rule is the crowd decides the winner. Agreed?"

Wyatt smirked. "Agreed."

Connor heard about the bet, and he bought a round of whiskey shots for all the players to get them lubed up. Martina announced the competition to the crowd, and they were more than happy to judge the performances. A few patrons even got in on the action.

The first player started off with a drunken rendition of Willie Nelson's "Blue Eyes," followed by another player who sang a credible version of "Rapper's Delight" while holding two shots.

One of the younger players sang "I Feel Like a Woman," and another butchered an Elton John song. His teammates started singing along just to help him out. Wyatt surprised us all by singing a decent rendition of "Thunderstruck."

But the clear winner—or winners—and the most controversial entry of the night, was a duet rendition of "Whiskey River" by Martina and Rudy. When they started singing, we figured out pretty quickly they'd sung together before. And they were fucking phenomenal.

I remembered Chris Stapleton and Justin Timberlake sang the song together at a music award show back when I was in high school, and it blew me away. Martina and Rudy were almost as good.

They were the last entry, and by the time they finished, the crowd was going nuts. Rudy had a deep, well-trained baritone voice, and he slid through the notes like a professional. And Martina had a voice that should have been on the Billboard charts. Wyatt watched them sing together, and I could tell he knew he'd been played.

When they finished and jumped off the stage, Wyatt went over with the rest of the crowd to congratulate them. He slapped Rudy on the back, then he hugged Martina, squeezing her a little too tight. I noticed Iz straighten off the wall where he'd been watching and make his way over.

"Holy shit," Titus muttered. "That was fucking phenomenal."

I agreed. It had been another interesting evening.

Connor wrapped his arm around my neck and pulled me to him. "I think that was the most successful Whiskey Wednesday you've had so far. And Rudy being able to sing like that? I had no idea." He turned to Titus. "We need to have him sing the National Anthem at the games sometime."

"Hell yes. It'd be great publicity," Titus agreed.

"You ready to go?" Connor asked me a little while later.

I smiled as I watched the team talking and laughing together. "Yeah, I think I am."

On Thursday night, Connor picked me up at my apartment for a date. We'd had mind-blowing sex and even lived together, but we'd only been on a couple of dates. I wore my black spandex pants with black sandals and a red gauzy blouse I'd bought at the second-hand store a couple of years ago. I'd even styled my hair and spent extra time on my makeup.

Connor looked me up and down and grinned. "I've never seen you in red before. You look extra fuckable."

I smiled and blushed. "Thank you. I think. We've only been on two dates, so that's not surprising."

"Two dates? Are you sure?"

"Yep."

He thought for a minute. "Huh. I'll have to rectify that. I guess I've enjoyed staying home with you and Elodie so much, I don't go out like I used to."

I took his hand. "Staying home with you guys is one of my favorite things too. You don't need to rectify anything."

Connor brought my hand up to his mouth and kissed it, then he leaned in and sniffed my neck. "Mmm. You smell good." He held up his other hand with a small gift bag in it. "And I brought you something."

When he ran his nose along my neck, goosebumps broke out on my skin. I shook myself and took the bag, then pulled out a package of Kami origami paper from the bag.

I stared at it for a moment. "Oh my God, this is some of the best origami paper." The beautiful two-sided colored paper was the perfect weight and folded easily.

Connor watched me curiously. "I'm glad you like it."

"How did you know?"

He smiled. "How could I not know? You leave us little origami animals, and you told me about your mom teaching you."

I stared up at him and my heart squeezed. "Thank you."

When the weekend came, Connor talked me into staying for a couple of nights at his house. He didn't have to try very hard. I missed him, especially when I went back to my apartment and crawled into my cold bed. But I also needed the quiet time to sort through my chaotic feelings and thoughts.

On Sunday night, I gathered up my things before heading back to my apartment for the coming week. Connor had set his cell phone down on the kitchen counter, and I glanced down and noticed the photo on his screen saver. It was the selfie he took several months ago with Elodie and me in his living room when we'd gone swimming together. We'd been smiling as we tried to fit us all into the frame, and we looked like we belonged together. It was a nice photo.

That week I didn't tell anyone at the arena that Tuesday was my last day. Connor and Titus knew it was coming up, but I hadn't given them exact details.

Connor came into the medical office just as I was finishing up for the day. He'd brought lunch with him.

"Looking at you in that white jacket never gets old. Come eat lunch with me in my office."

He looked at Titus and raised an eyebrow, probably daring Titus to invite himself.

I rolled my eyes. "That smells good. Titus can't join us though since he and Abby are going to sit down today and get their stories straight. I don't want my best childhood friend to end up in a Canadian jail."

Titus patted the top of my head. "Don't worry, *choux*, we'll be ready. Some of your questions are fascinating. I'm curious to hear what her answers are."

I swatted his hand away. "Yeah, just make sure you go through *all* the questions, not just the more intimate ones."

Connor and I headed to his office. Valerie looked up when we walked into the reception area.

"You have two new messages, Mr. McCoy, but neither are urgent." Then she smiled a little at me. "Hi, Isabella. Thank you for the birthday brownie last week. That was nice of you."

I'd brought her a brownie when I saw a generic mylar birthday balloon by her desk. I knew what it felt like to have a birthday and not have family or friends around to celebrate it.

I smiled. "You're welcome. My dad made it, so I know it was good."

We walked into his office and set the food down on his desk.

He nodded toward the door. "Are you two friends now?"

"Maybe 'friendly' is a better word. She doesn't have family around, and I think she's a little lonely. I talked to her a few times in the ladies restroom, and we got to know each other a little bit."

He smiled. "People are drawn to you. You have a habit of picking up strays."

"I'm probably a stray myself, so there may be some truth to that. Where's Coach Bailey? I haven't seen him around this week."

Connor's face went hard. "He's on suspension. The assistant coach is going to step up, and Titus will assist. Bailey's been playing head games with the players, and he isn't helping the team. They're winning despite him." He folded his arms. "I got an earful the other day about how he's been treating you."

I avoided his eyes, and started pulling out food. "Huh. I told you he reported me to my school. This smells good. Thanks for lunch."

He sat on the edge of his desk. "Bella."

"What?"

"Why didn't you tell me about him?"

"Because it was my problem."

He sighed. "That's what you said about Noah vandalizing your car."

"Okay, maybe that one wasn't just my problem. But Coach Bailey is."

"You're mine. I want to be there for you." He paused and seemed to collect his thoughts. "I want to hear about your problems and frustrations. And your successes. I'd like you to confide in me like you do your dad. Or even Titus."

I sighed and set my plate down. "There's a difference between listening and discussing, or listening then wading in and trying to fix everything." I looked up at him. "I want a partnership. I want to be valued and needed. And not just for sex." My face went hot, but I held his gaze.

"You don't think I value you?"

I jerked my shoulder awkwardly. "Maybe? I'm ten years younger than you, I'm not a famous athlete or a hockey legend, and I'm dirt poor." My eyes slid away. "But I like myself. I work hard, and I try to be a good person."

He grabbed my hand and pulled me to stand between his legs. "Do you have any idea how fucking wonderful you are? And what you mean to me? To us?" He cupped my jaw. "Do you know what you've given me? Before Elodie and you came into my life, I never knew what love was supposed to be like. To love so much that I worry about you, and want to be with you all the time. I'd fucking do anything to keep you safe and happy. You're not rich, but who cares? What you've given me is priceless. Do you understand?"

I stared at his magnetic, rugged face and slowly ran my thumb across the scar on his cheek.

"Maybe. Because it's what you've given me." I put my forehead on his shoulder. "I love you too. And I love Elodie. I also worry about both of you." I looked up again and my voice broke. "But

I'm afraid. Of losing you, or not being enough for you. And I'm scared of that pain."

He nodded and cupped my cheek. "I am too, but I'm willing to risk it. You're this warm ray of sarcastic sunshine that blasted into my cold life. I want you to come home. And be *mine*. My best friend, my girlfriend." He smirked. "My sweet, good girl. And eventually my wife."

Tears rolled down my cheeks, but a laugh escaped me. "How about if we start with me moving back in?"

"Fuck, yes." He rubbed the tears away and kissed both my cheeks. "And for the love of God, please don't move out again. Elodie's mad at me, and she keeps asking me what I did *this* time."

My laughter was cut off when his hard lips pressed against mine.

# Chapter 39

On Wednesday night, we invited both the Martini Monday and the Whiskey Wednesday crowds to Connor's house for a blow-out party. We found a babysitter for Elodie and Stella, and they hung out over at my dad's house.

The warm desert evening was bright with the full moon, and orange blossoms scented the air. Dad and Connor put up outdoor café lights, and they opened the wall of accordion windows in the living room so people could move freely between the house and the poolside area outside.

We were celebrating the Thunderbirds making the playoffs, and my clinical rotations ending. Word had gotten out I was leaving. A few players even bought me a plant, and their card read "Fine, you traitor. Leave then." Titus gave me a gift card to Five Guys Burgers. He'd written on the envelope "So you can get your own damn fries." I got a little teary-eyed after reading it, and Connor chuckled.

We ordered food from a local barbeque dive, and Abby and I prepped the drink bars before everyone came. I noticed Titus staring at Abby throughout the night.

Several other players had brought dates and significant others. It was illuminating to meet some of them.

I stood talking with Jackson out on the patio when Rudy walked over. "Hey Isa, are you gonna take Ben up on his job offer?"

"How'd you know he offered me a job?"

Jackson grinned. "Because he told us he did. And several players mentioned to him he'd be an idiot not to."

"That's so nice, and a little surprising."

Rudy squeezed my shoulder. "Not really."

"All this Wednesday bonding bullshit has been fun," Jackson added. "It's been a great season, even with the Coach Bailey drama."

Rudy nodded enthusiastically, and I poked his arm. "It's because you won that karaoke contest last week, isn't it? How come no one knew you could sing like that?"

He shrugged modestly. "I met Martina at The Cockpit a couple of months ago, and we hatched up our half-baked plan."

Jackson snickered. "You should have seen Wyatt's face when you started singing. And when Martina stepped in? Holy shit."

Rudy chuckled. "Yeah, that was pretty damn awesome."

Mikael walked over, and Jackson turned to him. "We're re-living karaoke night, and Wyatt getting owned."

Mikael grinned. "Aw, yes. How do you say it? Priceless, it was priceless." We all started laughing.

Three weeks later, Connor chartered another private jet to fly us to Seattle for my graduation. He also wanted to reserve an enormous suite at the Four Seasons in downtown Seattle.

I argued with him. "Connor, it's too much. Dad and I can stay with one of my friends. Or we can find an Airbnb, and we'll split it."

He sighed and hung his head for a moment. Then he looked up at me. "You and I need to talk. Come here." We were in his home office, and he swiveled his chair around and patted his lap.

When I raised an eyebrow at him, he smirked. "I promise, we'll just talk."

A few days ago after Elodie left for school, we'd had enthusiastic sex in here, starting on his desk, then in his chair, and then against the wall, before ending up back on his desk. We found out it was the perfect height.

"Come here," he demanded.

I walked over and sat on his lap, and he curled me into his chest.

He rested his cheek against the top of my head. "I have money. In fact, I have a lot of money. And it makes you uncomfortable."

I nestled my nose into the crook of his neck and sniffed him. He smelled so good. "Sometimes."

"There will be times I want to use that money to make our lives better or easier. Can you let me do that? And I promise I'll talk to you before I make any big purchases. Although I wouldn't consider this a big purchase."

"That's what makes me nervous, McCoy."

He squeezed me, then kissed the top of my head. "Your graduation is a huge fucking deal, and it's something that will never happen again. I want us to be together this weekend, and not have to worry about anything."

"Okay. I understand."

"Thank you. Elodie and I are looking forward to it, and I think it would be good for her to see. Consider it our graduation gift."

I also wanted us to stay together, and he had valid points. We were both learning to compromise.

Sighing, I hugged him. "Okay. And thank you. I was thinking about how much a suite at the Four Seasons is going to cost over graduation weekend, let alone chartering a jet. But I do want to show you where I went to school, and take Elodie to some of the places I love in Seattle."

That Friday morning, I officially graduated. When I looked out and saw my loved ones cheering me on, I got a little teary. It had rained the night before, but the day was sunny and green, and the air smelled like plants and wet earth.

My brother Liam had also flown in for my graduation.

He glared at Connor as he drew me in for a hug. "I can't believe you're graduating. Damn, I'm so proud of you." Liam looked over my shoulder. "Now introduce me to your cradle-robbing boyfriend."

"Behave yourself." I smacked his arm.

Elodie tilted her head and looked up at Connor. "Daddy, what's cradle-bobbing?"

Connor studied Liam. "Cradle-bobbing is when a man loves a woman and plans to marry her as soon as he can get her to say yes, then plans to have babies with her. And really enjoys practicing. Over and over again."

"Oh, hell," I groaned and slid my hand down my face. Thank God Dad had gone to the bathroom. Elodie looked thoroughly confused.

"Ouch, man. She's my sister," Liam complained.

"Did you get a boo-boo?" Elodie asked Liam. "Because guess what? Belly can make it better."

"Yeah. She does make things better, doesn't she?" He finally held out his hand to Connor. "I'm Liam, Isa's brother. I'd say it's nice to meet you, but I have serious doubts."

Connor smirked and shook his hand. "Noted. I'd have serious doubts too if I were you. But I love her and plan to keep her, so I hope we can get along."

We ate dinner that evening at my favorite seafood restaurant near the Peer. Elodie was fascinated by the octopus Liam had ordered.

"How can the octopus swim if you eat one of its legs?" she asked him, looking down at the grilled, seasoned tentacle on his plate.

Liam looked at me for help, and Connor laughed into his craft beer. Dad kindly explained that the octopus didn't need its leg anymore.

We showed Elodie the troll statue with the VW Beetle under the bridge, and rode the great Ferris wheel.

I also took her to the infamous chewed gum wall at Pike's Place.

"Why would people stick their chewed gum on the wall?" she asked in disgusted wonder.

I held up my hands. "I have no idea, Ellie. It's just one of those weird things."

Before Liam left on Sunday morning to take the train to the airport, Dad and I met him for coffee in the Four Seasons foyer.

"So. Connor McCoy," he began.

"Yeah. I'm not sure how it happened. But... yeah."

"It's been a roller coaster." Dad shook his head.

Liam studied me. "A man who bluntly tells a woman's brother he loves her and plans to keep her isn't messing around."

Smiling, I patted his hand. "You should have seen the look of horror on your face when he talked about practicing to have babies."

Dad groaned. "Lord, I'm glad I missed that."

"Like I said. He's not messing around," Liam said, grimacing.

"I love him."

"Okay then. I could probably start liking him. In about ten years." He checked his phone and sighed. "It's time for me to get going."

"Just wait until it happens to you. I already miss you so much. Where are you going to next?"

"D.C. today, then Amsterdam next week."

"Don't forget about us, okay? Come stay this Christmas. Connor's house is huge, and Dad has a spare bedroom."

He cocked his head. "Do you think you'll still be there in December? You're too good for him. You know that, right?"

Dad smiled and patted Liam's back. "She's too good for anyone. And the miracle is she doesn't know it. She'll still be there."

Liam stared at Dad. "Damn. You like the guy."

"Yeah, I do. He sacrificed the rest of his career for Elodie, and he loves Isa the same way. He bought her skateboard shoes and origami paper when she wouldn't let him give her a Mercedes. He loves her the way she needs to be loved."

On the flight home, I sat quietly next to Connor thinking about what my dad said to Liam. Dad and Elodie were asleep, so I slid over into Connor's lap and curled around him.

"Thank you for making this weekend so wonderful. And for not drop-kicking Liam."

He wrapped his arms around me. "I just kept reminding myself I couldn't kill your only sibling."

I palmed his cheek. "I need you to know something."

"Yeah? What's that?"

"I love you. I love your kindness and patience. Your generosity, even when it's hard for me to accept it. And your possessiveness. I also love how you adore Elodie and are willing to learn little girl hairstyles and watch princess movies with her. You're it for me, and I love you."

His hand spasmed on my thigh, and I heard him release a long breath. "Fuck, sweet girl. I love you too. And I'm glad you love my possessiveness because it doesn't seem to be going away."

I smiled up at him. "That's okay because neither does mine."

# *Epilogue*



*Four Years Later*

I parked my car in the oversized garage and got out. A couple of years ago, Connor had finally persuaded me to accept the Mercedes I'd first driven when Noah vandalized my car.

"These are the safety ratings on the Mercedes, and these are the ratings on your sedan." He'd leaned back and let me study the data.

"Huh. I might see your point."

"And you drive Elodie around sometimes. That means you have not just half, but my whole world in that little sedan. Work with me here, Bella."

So I agreed to take the car. He was a methodical, persuasive man when he really wanted something.

As I slammed the car door shut, I looked down at my finger and smiled at the beautiful platinum band there. He'd wanted to give me a gigantic diamond ring, but I reminded him I worked with kids every day.

"I could scratch the hell out of some poor, unsuspecting sick kid with that thing. It's too big. Work with me here, McCoy."

He mumbled something about fucktwit single dads, and then came up with a thick platinum band that had small round diamonds of varying sizes embedded in it. The ring looked like sparkling raindrops had been splashed across the surface, and I loved it.

Our lives were happy and quiet. Dad still lived in the little house on Connor's estate, and we walked back and forth several times a day. Especially Elodie.

Noah was in prison. He'd gotten out of jail, and been picked up for distribution of heroin a few months later in California. I often wondered if Connor and Zeke had anything to do with Noah's arrest. I was sad for Connor, but relieved Noah was out of our lives.

Mémé passed away last year, and Amelia still lived with her sister in Vancouver. Connor and Dad took Elodie to her funeral, but I didn't go.

Dad sighed when he told me about the service. "Mémé was well loved, but I think her family brought her more grief than joy. And Amelia didn't approach Elodie. She seemed heavily medicated. She may not have even recognized her."

My heart hurt for Elodie, but she seemed to take it all in stride. She was my daughter now, and nothing would ever change that.

She opened the garage door and stuck her head out. "Yay, you're home! Dad's trying to feed Lila, but she's not loving her bottle. Even Javy didn't have any luck."

Grinning, I headed inside. Connor and I got married just over two years after I graduated from PA school. I took the pediatric position in Palm Springs, and I also worked the home hockey games with Ben until our daughter, Lila, was born. I missed it sometimes.

Slinging my arm around Elodie's shoulder, we walked inside together. "He doesn't have the right equipment. And no amount of money can buy him milk-filled boobs."

"God, Mom! I don't need to hear about your milk-filled boobs. Javy's taking me to soccer practice in ten minutes." She kissed my cheek. "Love you."

Dad had been ecstatic when Lila was born. The first time he held her at the hospital, he'd turned to Connor and me with tears in his eyes. "Thank you for giving me two beautiful granddaughters." He bent down and kissed Lila's head. "I just wish their grandma could be here to see them." I'd cried right along with him.

Elodie ran off to get ready, and I walked into the living room where Connor was bouncing a fussy Lila.

He smirked. "I heard you. And I actually could buy milk-filled boobs. They're called wet nurses."

"Hand her over, McCoy." I sat down next to him, unbuttoned my shirt, and pulled out a very engorged breast.

Little Lila was gorgeous. She had Connor's thick, curly hair and my amber-colored eyes. She was a sweet baby, and she loved Connor to distraction. Unless she was hungry.

Connor watched me feed her. "Your breasts are something else. They make me want to tie you up and play with them until you beg me to fuck you."

I gasped, laughed, and then tried to cover Lila's ears. Connor still had a dirty mouth.

"You'll ruin her! Between you and the hockey team, her first words are going to be 'fuck' and maybe 'asshole.' And that's if we're lucky."

He smirked. "No, her first words were already 'da da' even though you keep denying it."

"Maybe, maybe not. I still think it was gas."

He wrapped his arm around me and watched her feed. When I needed to switch to the other side, he burped her for a minute then handed her back. After I fed her, he burped and bounced her again, and when she'd fallen asleep on his shoulder, he walked her into the converted nursery and laid her down for her nap.

When he came back, he leaned down and kissed me softly. "I love you. Thank you for giving me another wonderful daughter to love."

I smiled against his mouth. "I love you too. And thank you for giving me *two* beautiful daughters."

Just then, we heard Elodie yell goodbye and run out of the house. Connor pushed me down on the couch and crawled over me.

"You're welcome. Now let's practice making a third."

I laughed as I pulled his mouth down to mine.

# Afterword

Thank you for reading *Whiskey Wednesdays: Book 3 in the Palm Springs Poolside Series*. If you liked this novel (and even if you didn't) please leave a review on Amazon or Goodreads. Your feedback helps authors share their work and become better writers.

Visit my author page on Amazon at Amazon.com/author/jlbrannick

To my family and tribe–thank you for your support. We make a great team.

Thank you to my beta readers and editors, Shelby Nesbitt, Gennifer Ulman, Whitney Tanner, and Susan Keillor.

And to my cover designer at Smart Mouth Publishing LLC.

Follow me on social media and subscribe to my newsletter for the latest news, free giveaways, exclusive bonuses, and new releases!

https://jlbrannick.com/
https://linkfly.to/JLBrannick